“Are y

Genna’s voice sounded shaky. “I’ve been driving around, and didn’t want to go to your place unless you were there.”

“I’m sitting in my driveway,” Parker said. “Did something else happen?”

“Yes and no. Would you mind watching for me? I’m about five minutes away. I’ll only stop once I’m absolutely sure that I’m not being followed.”

“I will wait right here. Please stay on the line until I can see you.”

“I will. Right now, no one is following me. I’ve been on the lookout for a black SUV. I haven’t seen it since lunchtime.”

The fact that she had seen it again wasn’t lost on him. Though he wanted to press her for details, he knew it could wait until she was safe and sound with him and ready to talk.

“How was your tour?” she asked, her voice still shaky. Understanding her need to discuss something ordinary, he told her about the group.

“I’m almost at your place,” she said once he’d finished. “Thank you for talking.” She paused for a moment. “I really just needed to hear the sound of your voice.”

Dear Reader,

As you may know, the Coltons series are among my favorites to write. This one is set in the gorgeous state of Alaska, a place I've visited before (if only while on a cruise!). I adore second chance romances, and this one was a blast to write. Parker Colton and Genna MacDougal have a past that left Parker hurt. Genna has been dealing with her own demons and is leery of working with Parker due to her still-strong attraction to him. Throw in a serial killer, Genna's stalker, mutual passion and the capricious Alaskan weather, and what a story!

I hope you enjoy reading this book as much as I enjoyed writing it.

Karen Whiddon

COLTON ON GUARD

KAREN WHIDDON

Special thanks and acknowledgment are given to Karen Whiddon for her contribution to The Coltons of Alaska miniseries.

Recycling programs for this product may not exist in your area.

ISBN-13: 978-1-335-47163-5

Colton on Guard

Harlequin Enterprises ULC
22 Adelaide St. West, 41st Floor
Toronto, Ontario M5H 4E3, Canada
www.Harlequin.com

Printed in Lithuania

Karen Whiddon started weaving fanciful tales for her younger brothers at the age of eleven. Amid the gorgeous Catskill Mountains, then the majestic Rocky Mountains, she fueled her imagination with the natural beauty surrounding her. Karen now lives in north Texas, writes full-time and volunteers for a boxer dog rescue. She shares her life with her hero of a husband and four to five dogs, depending on if she is fostering. You can email Karen at kwhiddon1@aol.com. Fans can also check out her website, karenwhiddon.com.

Books by Karen Whiddon

Harlequin Romantic Suspense

The Coltons of Alaska

Colton on Guard

Texas Sheriff's Deadly Mission
Texas Rancher's Hidden Danger
Finding the Rancher's Son
The Spy Switch
Protected by the Texas Rancher
Secret Alaskan Hideaway
Saved by the Texas Cowboy
Missing in Texas
Murder at the Alaskan Lodge
Vanished in Texas
Alaskan Disappearance

The Coltons of Owl Creek

Colton Mountain Search

Visit the Author Profile page at Harlequin.com for more titles.

To all my faithful readers who enjoy the books
I write—thank you from the bottom of my heart.
Your emails make my day.

Chapter 1

"Yes, ma'am, I apologize that we left your son off the booking for this tour," Parker Colton told the red-faced, mean-eyed woman. "I'll get them added immediately, so all three of you can join the group leaving in ten minutes. I'll just need to collect the payment. Will it be cash or credit card?"

His perfectly reasonable question only appeared to infuriate her even more. "You know, you might be used to skating by on your good looks and charm," she ranted, "but that's not going to fly with me. You made a mistake and you need to fix it!"

As her voice rose and the other guests stared, Parker interrupted to tell her fine, they'd let her teenager go along without an extra charge. Since this appeared to be what she'd wanted and expected, she jerked her head in a nod and closed her mouth.

Then, as tour guide Hetty Amos got everyone rounded up and herded them outside, Parker sagged against the counter in relief. Hetty made sure to circle back around and clap Parker on the back. "It's okay, Pretty Boy," she said, grinning. "Even with those good looks and charm, you got everything handled."

Before Parker could come up with a response, Hetty

waved and sauntered outside to join her group. They were all going on a wildlife tour.

Watching them leave, Parker smiled ruefully and shook his head. As part owner of the family business Rough Terrain Adventures, or RTA for short, he usually handled taking tourists on tours. Hiking, climbing, four-wheeling and fishing. He wasn't usually the one working the front counter and handling bookings, which might explain how that awful woman's son had been inadvertently left off the reservation sheet.

Parker loved RTA and, most of the time, his life. At this very moment however, he'd have gladly traded places with anybody else. Running tours had always been the ideal occupation for someone who'd always preferred to spend every possible waking hour outdoors, no matter the weather. The beautiful mountain town of Shelby, Alaska, offered ample opportunities to enjoy nature. RTA specialized in allowing tourists to enjoy outstanding hiking trails, world-class fishing, unbeatable backcountry skiing, recreational cycling, kayaking, northern lights viewing, snowmobiling, and glacier cruises in stunning Prince William Sound.

No wonder Parker's job in the family business working as RTA guide and manager often felt like an extended vacation with pay. He got to take people on adventures, doing things he himself loved and enjoyed. Talk about fun. Never a dull moment. He couldn't have asked for a better, more enjoyable career.

Until now. His sister Lakin, who'd been basically the brains of RTA and kept everything running smoothly, had left them high and dry to renovate an old hotel with her longtime boyfriend. Parker had zero patience for juggling the various office tasks she'd previously taken care off. Reservations, phone calls, logging both accounts receivable and accounts payable were time-consuming and, frankly, he found them tedious and unpleasant. He'd rather be outside where he belonged.

Add in the fact that his father and his uncle had taken to constantly dropping by to check on things, and Parker thought he might lose his mind. Which is why he felt desperate enough to consider calling Genna MacDougal and asking if she wanted a job. She'd worked at RTA for the entire four years she'd been in high school. Part time during the school year and full time in the summers. She'd been Lakin's assistant the entire stretch and knew how to do everything Lakin did. Everything Parker and Spence and Hetty now took turns doing.

Genna with her light blond hair and luminous green eyes. Beautiful didn't even begin to describe her. She was, Parker thought, everything he'd ever wanted in a woman. And the fact that he knew he couldn't have her only served to make him want her more.

Despite the truth that facing her again made him wince, hearing she'd moved permanently back to Shelby had felt like an answer to a prayer. He needed help and he'd heard she needed work. It would be a win-win situation.

As long as they could both get past what had happened between them a little over a year ago. And as long as Parker could figure out a way to regard her as just another employee and not the woman of his dreams.

About to pick up the phone, he looked over when the bell above the door jingled. His cousin Spence, who also co-owned RTA and worked as a guide, strode in.

"I'm here to help," he said, his broad grin and sideways glance inviting Parker to share in the joke.

Except Parker wasn't in the mood for games. "Good,"

he said. “You can take over checking the online reservation system. I’m way behind on that.”

Though Spence’s smile never wavered, he did a double take. “Do you really think that’s the best idea?”

“We don’t have a choice,” Parker snapped. “Now that Lakin left, someone has to do it.”

Spence didn’t move. “I thought we were going to hire someone.”

“If I do, will you be able to train them?”

“Me?” Spence scoffed. “Call Lakin and make her do it. Or you could call Genna MacDougal? She worked here for four years. It’s been a while, but she probably knows how to run this place better than you or I do.”

Since none of his family was aware of Parker and Genna’s one-night stand, Parker shrugged. “I’m still thinking about it.”

“We need the help. Call her.”

“I don’t have her number,” Parker lied. Once upon a time, he would have given anything to have located a way to reach Genna, but he’d managed to lose her number because he hadn’t bothered to enter it into his phone. Now that Lakin had actually provided Parker her contact information, he hesitated to use it.

“I do,” Spence said, pulling out his phone. “Let me send it to you.”

Once he’d done so, he crossed his arms and waited. Parker made a show of opening the text and saving the contact.

“Well?” Spence finally said. “Are you going to reach out to her or not?”

Parker thought for a moment. Maybe he was making too big of a deal out of nothing. After all, an entire year had passed. They’d both been consenting adults and a good time had been had by all. No doubt Genna had moved on.

He met his cousin's gaze and slowly nodded. Then, taking a deep breath, he made the call.

When her cell phone rang, Genna MacDougal glanced at the screen and took a second look. Parker Colton. Almost a year too late. Funny, she'd saved his number and must have forgotten to erase it. She'd figured he'd long ago tossed hers.

Naturally, she debated not answering. But curiosity won out in the end. "Hello?"

"Hey, Genna." He sounded nervous. *Good.*

"What do you want, Parker?" she asked, not even bothering to try to sound nice. She had no idea of the etiquette when speaking with a man who'd ghosted her after a one-night stand, but she really didn't care. Parker had figuratively kicked her when she'd been down. That wasn't something she'd easily forget or forgive.

"I'd like to offer you a job," he said. "Temporary, but still… We need a new general manager at RTA and since you worked for us before—"

"Go to hell," she said, cutting him off. Then she ended the call. The sudden flare of anger she'd felt surprised her.

Hanging up on Parker should have felt good. Better than that, it should have felt great.

Except it didn't. Instead, a wave of remorse swept through her. One year ago, she'd been at her absolute lowest. When Parker had come up to her at the bar, he'd not only been the sexiest man she'd ever seen, but was physically the polar opposite of her ex-husband. Still stinging from Chad's betrayal, she'd acted solely on impulse when she'd gone home with Parker. And she couldn't even blame the passionate night they'd spent together on too much alcohol since she'd barely had two drinks.

Nope. She'd been raw and needy. Having the guy she'd crushed on back when she'd been in high school and home from college take an interest in her had been exactly the boost she'd needed. He'd been witty, charming, and oh so easy on the eyes. They'd shared one magical evening, laughing, dancing, and she'd given him her phone number. But then, just as she'd been about to leave, he'd pulled her into an embrace. His kiss had made her head spin.

Hand in hand, when he'd led her out to his truck, she'd gone home with him without hesitation. Even though she'd never, not even once, had a one-night stand. Until then.

It had been a magical night. Exactly what she'd needed to make her feel like a desirable woman again. Parker had given her just the right amount of passion combined with respect. Nearly reverence. They'd made love over and over again until they were both spent and she'd fallen asleep in his arms.

And when she'd woke in the morning, he'd been gone. He'd scrawled a note and left it on the nightstand. *I'll call.*

Except he never had. Part of her hadn't really expected him to. She'd left town without ever hearing from him again.

Until now. She couldn't believe the mofo had had the nerve to call and offer her a job. Even though she really needed one.

These days she was putting all her effort into getting her life together. With her messy divorce and dissolution of property behind her, she'd taken her parents up on their offer to house-sit here in Shelby, Alaska, while they tried living in a long-term rental in Hawaii. Though she had the funds to survive indefinitely, she wanted to keep as much money in her savings as possible. Therefore, she needed to get some sort of job.

She hated that Parker's offer actually tempted her.

Sure, working at Rough Terrain Adventures had been fun back in high school, but no way would she be able to spend her days side by side with Parker after what had happened. That kind of humiliation wasn't easy to forget, especially when she'd just been shattered by her cheating husband.

Nope. Some other kind of work would come along. It had to. She didn't want to blow through her savings, so she needed a source of income. Shelby might be on the small side, but she knew the right opportunity would open up in time.

Less than an hour after hanging up on Parker Colton, her doorbell rang. Frowning, since she wasn't expecting anyone, she opened the door to find her old friend, Lakin Colton, on her doorstep. Still a stunning beauty, Lakin wore her brown-black hair long and straight. Her brown eyes sparkled with friendliness.

"Genna!" Lakin exclaimed, pulling her in for a hug. "It's so good to see you again."

Smiling, Genna invited her in. Tall and athletic, Lakin dressed to hide her curves. She wore her long, dark hair straight.

"You haven't changed a bit," Genna said.

"Neither have you!"

They chatted for a while, Lakin full of enthusiasm for a hotel renovation project she was doing with her boyfriend Troy. It took a few minutes, but Lakin finally got to the reason for her surprise visit.

"I understand my brother called you to talk about coming to work at RTA," she said. "They've kind of been floundering since I left."

Genna stiffened. "He did," she replied. "I turned him down."

"But why?" Leaning forward, Lakin regarded her earnestly. "You know that business better than anyone outside of my family. We need you, you're looking for work. The pay is decent. So why on earth would you say no to what seems like the perfect fit?"

Not wanting to go into the sordid details, Genna shrugged. "I just don't want to," she said.

Naturally, Lakin shook her head. "That's not a good reason. Now, what are you not telling me?"

Before Genna could think up a nonresponse, her doorbell rang again. This time, Lakin and Parker's cousin Spence stood outside. "We need your help," he said, not bothering with pleasantries. "We can even bump up the salary, if that would help."

"Why do I feel like you Coltons are ganging up on me?" Genna asked, only half joking. "Surely you can find someone else?"

"You're already trained!" Lakin and Spence replied in unison. "And our family knows and trusts you."

The doorbell chimed yet again. "This is getting ridiculous," Genna muttered, going to answer. Sure enough, two more members of the Colton family had arrived. "Abby and Sasha," she said, stepping aside and gesturing them to enter. "Did you all plan this or is it a spontaneous gathering?"

Seeing Lakin and Spence there, the two new arrivals burst out laughing. "Definitely not planned," they said. "We all just really would appreciate you coming to run the office at RTA. You're perfect. We heard you'd turned the job down, so we stopped by to see if we could change your mind."

Now resigned, Genna crossed her arms. "The only person not here is Parker," she said, not bothering to hide her irritation. "Is there a reason for that?"

Spence shrugged. "I think he's a little upset that you hung up on him. What's up with that anyway?"

Though she felt her face heat, she refused to air her dirty laundry to Parker's family. Clearly, he hadn't told them anything about what had happened a year ago. Therefore, neither would she.

"Everyone, I'm very sorry, but I'm just not interested," Genna said. "I hate that you wasted your time coming over here, but me working at RTA just isn't going to happen."

Spence looked at Lakin, who nodded. "Do you happen to have a pen and paper I could use?" he asked.

Perplexed, she went into the kitchen, grabbed a pen and the pad she jotted her grocery list on and brought it out for Spence. "Here you go."

He jotted something down before handing the paper back. "We can pay you that," he said.

The number he'd written was far higher than she'd expected. "You must really want me to work for you," she said. "I'm not sure what to say."

"Just say yes!" Lakin exclaimed. "You know you want to."

Though Genna knew no such thing, she was also well aware she couldn't make that amount of money working anywhere else in Shelby.

"I'll think about it," she said, hoping this attempt at compromise would be enough.

Apparently, it wasn't. No one made a move to leave. Abby and Sasha exchanged a quick glance. "We're sorry,"

Abby said. "But we really need you to agree to take the job before we go."

"No pressure," Lakin added, clearly tongue in cheek.

Spence shook his head. "This is serious. At least, to our family. Rough Terrain Adventures is important to us. And to the town."

She almost took pity on them. Almost. She understood where they were coming from and, if not for the fact that she'd have to work alongside Parker, she would have accepted their offer the moment she'd seen the salary.

"I don't like being bullied," she finally said. "And the more you all try to pressure me, the less likely it is that I'll accept your offer. I need some time to think."

"How long?" Spence asked, appearing worried.

"I can let you know by morning."

Spence nodded, the others murmured their agreement, and they all trooped toward her front door. Only Lakin lingered. She waited until the others were gone before turning to face Genna. "There's something you're not saying. What is it?"

In years past, Genna might have blurted out the truth. Now, she simply shook her head. "I'm sorry, Lakin. I promise to decide quickly. I'll call Spence the second I know."

Expression crestfallen, Lakin nodded. "It's just that I feel so guilty. They're all acting as if me leaving is a death knell for our business. I'm finally doing what I've long dreamt of and, while I know they don't begrudge me that, apparently RTA is having difficulty functioning without me."

"I'm sorry." Genna gazed at her old friend. Lakin would be shocked if she knew the reason for her hesitation. Lakin clearly adored her brother and Genna refused to say or do anything to change that. "I'll let you know as soon as I decide."

Lakin nodded. "I'm sorry for the intrusion." Tugging on her long braid bashfully, she smiled. "I promise I'll still love you, no matter what you do."

"Right back atcha," Genna said. "Isn't it nearly the end of the season anyway? Snow will be starting soon."

"That's true and, yes, it does mean some of our adventures will be coming to an end until spring. But there are a lot of snow enthusiasts. We've added snowmobiling, ice fishing, ice-skating and snowshoeing to our ski trips."

Which ensured RTA didn't have to close down for winter. In other words, Genna would still have a job.

Once Lakin had also left her house, Genna locked the door behind her and then sank down onto her couch. This shouldn't be so difficult. She'd loved working at RTA back in the day and imagined she would still. She'd worked with Lakin and knew how things ran, so there wouldn't be a long learning curve. Not to mention the salary. Considering that she'd been out of the work force for a number of years and had a huge gap in her résumé as a result, she felt positive she couldn't make that amount elsewhere. And she definitely needed to find a job.

Those were the pros. And there was only one con. Parker.

It has been a year, she told herself. The man probably didn't even remember much about that night and, if he did, he obviously wasn't embarrassed about the way he'd ghosted her. Maybe she was making too big a deal out of nothing, getting worked up too much inside her own head.

Still, while she understood they were probably used to getting their own way, the fact that the Colton family had descended upon her en masse spoke to their own desperation. While she'd found them all showing up on her doorstep unbelievably pushy, she got where they were coming from. When you truly cared about something, you went all out.

The fact that she couldn't make a simple decision really bothered her. She needed to go ahead and accept the job offer. After all, since she'd be living in Shelby, she couldn't avoid Parker forever.

Instead of waiting until morning, she decided to drive over to RTA and let Parker know in person. His reaction to her would go a long way in helping her decide if they could manage to work together.

She grabbed her car keys and headed off before she could talk herself out of it.

As she approached the RTA building, a sprawling log cabin just outside the center of town, her heart rate accelerated.

Pulling into the drive, she parked. She took a moment while sitting in her car to eye the place. The large cabin with the metal roof looked welcoming, especially the numerous porch areas with railings. Someone had placed potted flowers around the spaces and this gave off a cheery, summery vibe.

As the number-one tour company in town, RTA was extremely popular. Their customers came from all walks of life. Tours included rafting and camping along mountain rivers, hiking the glaciers, helicopter skiing, seaplane trips to out-of-the way fishing spots, and other sorts of outdoor adventures. Right now, in peak tourist season, they were open seven days a week.

Like all the other tour companies, RTA tended to close down during the heaviest snow, December through February, though they had added a few snowmobile adventures to their already large catalog.

Each of RTA's ten or so employees was extensively trained in their own area and knowledgeable about whatever activity they were assigned. Prices were high, but reasonable, and they were usually booked out six to nine months in advance.

If she took the job, Genna would be in charge of coordinating all this. It sounded incredibly complicated and fast-paced, but since the guides—including Parker—spent most of their time out of the office on adventures with clients, she'd have a lot of alone time.

This knowledge reinforced her decision to accept the job. She remembered the reservation software, the way they used GPS to keep tabs on their guides and their guests. She had the organizational skills to manage all of it.

Now to face Parker and let him know she'd be coming to work on Monday.

Pushing the door open, a little bell on top announcing her arrival, she looked around at the apparently empty office. A man popped up from behind the counter. "Sorry, I was trying to fix the..." His words trailed off as he took in her presence.

To her dismay, Parker Colton looked even better than she remembered. If anything, his dark brown hair seemed shaggier, his blue eyes sexier, and his unshaven face gave him a rugged, bad-boy appearance. At six-two, he towered over her and his muscular body made the room seem smaller somehow. If she'd never seen him before, she suspected her knees would have gone weak. Even being prepared, the first sight of him felt like a punch in the stomach and she struggled to catch her breath.

"Genna," he said, his gaze searching her face. "It's good to see you."

"Is it?" Remembering she'd be working with him, she had to rein in her snark. "Uh, anyway. I just stopped by to tell you that I've decided to accept your job offer."

"You do?" Confusion flitted across his handsome features. "What changed your mind?"

"Spence, Lakin, Abby and Sasha. They all came to visit."

"And convinced you to work here?" He crossed his arms. "How?"

"The salary. It's too good to pass up. Even if I have to—"

"Work with me?" he finished for her. "It's okay, I get it."

Deciding it would be safer and more professional not to go down that road, she nodded. "I can start this coming Monday."

To her surprise, he groaned. "Monday? That's an entire week away. Is there any chance you could start right now?"

"Today?" Not sure how to react, she shifted her weight from one foot to the other. She hadn't dressed for work, though from what she remembered, RTA issued all employees several green work shirts emblazoned with the company logo.

"Yes. Today. You're already here, so why not?" He swallowed hard. "Please."

Was that a trace of panic she detected in his tone? She glanced at her watch, as if she actually had some place else she was supposed to be. "Fine," she finally said. "You might as well tell me up front. How bad is it?"

He smiled, his amazing blue eyes crinkling in the corners. Everything inside her went still for a few heartbeats before she remembered to breathe. Did this man have any idea of his effect on her? Somehow, she doubted it, because if he did, no doubt he'd use that to his advantage.

"Come take a look," he replied. "Lakin had everything pretty organized, but since she left and all the rest of us have been trying to alternate between being guides and keeping the place running, it's gotten way out of hand. How much do you remember from when you worked here before?"

"I'm sure it will all come back to me." The moment she walked behind the counter, Parker handed her a three-ring binder. "Lakin made notes about everything. We've all been referring to them constantly, but once you get into a routine, you'll probably have them all down pat in no time."

He reached under the counter and pulled out a cardboard box. "New work shirts are in here. Find your size and take as many as you need."

Standing this close to him, his scent brought back instant memories of that night she'd spent in his arms. The masculine combination of outdoorsy evergreens and something less tangible made her briefly close her eyes as she battled a sudden longing.

No, she told herself, straightening and making a show of rummaging through the box of green shirts. *No attraction, no love affairs, none of that.* She'd decided to focus on herself and figure out what she wanted from life. Parker Colton with his bedroom eyes and magnetic smile would be nothing more than a coworker from now on.

A couple of cars and a small tour bus pulled up out front. As people began exiting, milling about in the porch area, Parker smiled again, his relief evident. "There's my next tour group. I'll leave this in your very capable hands." After grabbing a clipboard with a checklist from the counter, he took off, the bell over the door tinkling merrily behind him.

Taking a deep breath, she grabbed a green RTA shirt out of the box and hurried off to the bathroom to change.

Chapter 2

Greeting the tour group, Parker began checking everyone in, using the list he'd printed out and attached to his clipboard. He'd never been happier to have a distraction than right this moment. When Genna MacDougal had walked through the door, he'd taken one look at her and his entire body had gone on full alert. Everything had come rushing back; the steamy sex they'd shared, her perfect body, and how sensual and uninhibited she'd been.

Since she'd made it clear she wanted to forget about that night, he'd have to figure out a way to do so. They needed someone to keep RTA running way more than he needed to rehash what had been a pretty spectacular night one year ago.

At least it had been to him. Obviously, Genna didn't feel the same. When her deep green eyes had met his, he'd seen no hint of the desire that had been coursing through him. Though not unfriendly, she'd been detached and professional. Exactly as any new employee might be.

He finished checking in the guests. In the future, Genna would be doing this task. Once he knew he had everyone, he gave his standard safety speech and then they all followed him toward one of the storage barns to collect their four-wheelers. This adventure consisted of a lot of off-road driving, which had always been one of his specialties. Just what he needed to take his mind off their new office manager.

Two hours later, as he led the group back to the RTA storage barn, he went through the motions of signing everyone out as they returned their four-wheelers. Once everything was done, he sent them all back inside to speak with Genna and check out. He had to clean the vehicles and make sure the gas tanks were full so they'd be ready for the next group. Which would be tomorrow. Since the end of season neared, everyone seemed determined to pack in as many adventures as possible. Which was great for business. Lakin had claimed she'd hated to leave while RTA was so busy, but since there rarely was a time when they were completely slow, this would be as good a time as any.

Even though winter had always been their quietest season. Most people tended to hunker down with family, choosing to take their vacations in better weather.

Except for the snowbirds and the native Alaskans. As soon as the first flakes of snow started to fly, they geared up for fun. Skiing, snowboarding, ice fishing, all of that. It might be cold, but these clients were too busy having fun to care.

RTA had been under a lot of pressure to add guided hunting to their expeditions, but so far, they'd resisted. There were a lot of hunting guides already operating in the area and in such an overcrowded field, the competition was fierce. Safety shortcuts were routinely taken and the Colton family wanted no part of a client getting hurt or, worse, killed.

Instead, they stuck to the tried-and-true winter activities. This decision had worked well for them so far. For

RTA employees, winter had become a time of rejuvenation and peace.

Parker always got restless this time of the year, though he wasn't sure why. Certain activities had begun to wind down though others had picked up. Aurora season was at a prime and RTA took advantage of that, leading numerous and popular late-night expeditions. October also brought in several guests to take fall sightseeing and wildlife tours, and since trout were abundant, Parker led a lot of successful fishing trips.

The change of seasons hovered on the horizon and the temperatures had begun to drop. The gray skies became more frequent, though there were often a few brilliantly gorgeous days full of sunshine. The scent of snow often swept in on the crisp north wind, though when moisture fell, it was rain. Nature seemed to be waiting, holding her breath.

Since Parker loved winter almost as much as summer, he waited impatiently for the first snow. He'd always loved the comforting ritual of building a fire in his woodstove and kicking back to watch the white flakes fall. If he felt lonely, which he did sometimes, he brushed it off. His job kept him busy and, for now, that had to be enough.

He moved on to the next four-wheeler. This one needed air in one of the tires, so he took care of that before topping off the gas tank.

Since this was mindless work, his thoughts returned to Genna. Once he'd learned she'd returned to Shelby, he'd never taken the time to seek her out and explain what had happened and why he'd never called her.

After the wild night they'd had, he'd had to get up at the crack of dawn to meet a 6:00 a.m. tour group and then realized when he'd gotten back that he'd lost her number.

RTA had been super busy that weekend, so by the time he'd found a minute to go look for her, Genna had already left town. And then he'd learned from Lakin that Genna was married. No wonder she'd said she wasn't looking for a relationship. She'd already had one. She'd been in town visiting her parents before returning home to her husband.

While he had no idea what kind of man her husband might be, she must have needed that single hot and passionate night as badly as he had, maybe even more. Though he'd found it difficult to think of her as the kind of woman who'd cheat on her husband, the passion that had blazed between them had revealed the truth.

Since he hadn't wanted any part of being the other man, he'd put Genna from his mind. Until she'd returned to Shelby. And even then, he'd managed to avoid her.

But then Lakin had revealed that she'd learned Genna had been going through a nasty divorce the last time she'd been in town. Which meant she *hadn't* been having an affair with Parker. She'd been dealing with a lot at the time of their hookup. His ghosting her had likely made her feel even worse.

The thought made him wince. No doubt about it, he owed her an apology. That way, they both could move on with their lives.

Once he'd finished up with the four-wheelers, he locked the shed and headed back toward the office. By the time he got there, most of the tour group had gone. Only one vehicle, a large, jacked-up truck, remained in the parking area.

Pulling open the front door, which sent the little bell tinkling, he saw the remaining guest leaning on the front counter, talking to Genna.

"Jeff Prentiss, right?" Parker said, letting himself in

behind the counter. The tall, broad-shouldered man had been a bit of a show-off on the trails, but at least he'd listened when Parker had given instructions.

"Right," Jeff replied. With all his attention fixed on Genna, he barely looked at Parker. "So, what do you say, Genna? Drinks tonight or tomorrow?"

Expression tight, Genna nonetheless managed a smile. "Thanks, but like I said, I'm not interested. Here at RTA, we appreciate your business. Now, if there's not anything else, you're all finished up and you can go."

Jeff didn't move. As if he thought by standing his ground, Genna would somehow change her mind.

Parker took a step forward, his hands balled into fists. "Is there something else you need?" he asked, allowing a hint of warning to enter his voice. "If not, I'll be happy to escort you to your vehicle."

Finally, Jeff turned his head to look at Parker. The open hostility in his ruddy face made Parker straighten. "I'd appreciate you giving us a little space," he said. "I'm still talking to Genna."

"No, we're all done," Genna countered. "As a matter of fact, I'm about to go back to my office and start getting caught up on things."

"But you haven't agreed to go out with me yet," Jeff said. "I can't leave until I know when we're meeting."

About to open his mouth to tell the guy off, Parker closed it when Genna shot Jeff a withering look. "First off, I'm not going out with you. Not tonight or tomorrow night. Not ever. I don't know how to make that any clearer."

She took a deep breath and then pointed to the exit. "Since you don't seem to understand how to take no for an answer, let me make things clear. You need to go. You're finished with your trip. If you want to book another, you can do that online. Have a nice day." With that, she spun around and disappeared into the back office.

For the space of a few heartbeats, Parker thought Jeff might be foolish enough to go after her. He got ready, just in case he needed to physically stop him.

"She needs to listen to me," Jeff muttered. "I know I can convince her."

"No, you can't, and no, she doesn't."

Jeff narrowed his gaze, focusing on Parker. "I just need five minutes." He made a move, like he intended to slip in behind the counter and head for the back office.

"I wouldn't if I were you," Parker said. "You need to leave. Right now."

"How about you and me settle this outside?"

"I'd be glad to." Though Jeff wasn't a small man, Parker had several inches and at least twenty pounds on him. Maybe a fight would be just the thing to help him get over his jumbled feelings.

Clearly, Jeff hadn't been expecting Parker to take him up on his offer.

"Let's go," Parker said, moving out from behind the counter to the door and holding it open. "I'm suddenly in the mood for a fight. My only rule is no weapons—no knife or gun or anything other than fists."

Jeff mumbled a curse and stalked past him. Parker followed him out. But instead of turning to make good on his threat, Jeff strode over to his lifted truck and left.

Since the next group wasn't due to arrive for an hour and Spence would be taking them river rafting, Parker locked the dead bolt. When he turned around, he saw Genna had come back out front.

Remaining behind the counter, she watched at Jeff drove off in his SUV. "I don't think he should be allowed to book again," she said once the vehicle had gone. "If you hadn't been here, I don't think I would have been safe." The slight quiver in her voice made his gut clench.

"I agree." Dragging his hand though his hair, Parker swallowed. "I'm sorry that you had to deal with that, especially on your first day."

Eyeing him, some of the tension left her face. "He sure was pushy," she said. "Thanks for getting him to leave."

Though he wondered if she had to deal with stuff like that often, he also knew it wasn't any of his business. "After the Fiancée Killer started murdering women, Lakin had a panic button installed near the computer," he told her. "Thankfully, guys like that are rare. But if you press that button, it sends out an alert to the police station and also to mine and Spence's phones."

"Good to know." Green eyes pensive, she shrugged. "I sure as heck didn't expect something like that to happen on my first day. And, yes, with four women dead, that serial killer has just about every single female in Shelby nervous."

"Justifiably so. Hetty is our only female tour guide, though she's also a pilot, and she's nervous, too. We've instituted a policy where no female, whether employee or guest, is ever left alone at night on the premises."

"Good." She glanced around. "I'm guessing that's not possible in the daytime."

"We try, but mostly it's not," he answered. "The good thing is, since we're super busy, there will nearly always be a guide either coming in or out, not to mention constant groups of guests."

"Good. I confess, I wasn't too worried until you brought up the Fiancée Killer."

"I'm sorry," he said. Deciding now would be as good

a time as any, he swallowed. "There's something else I need to apologize for."

"I doubt it." After this clear dismissal, she turned to head into her small office.

"Wait," he said then softened his voice. "Please."

She turned slowly. "What's up?"

Slightly nervous, he cleared his throat. "Back when we, uh, got together. A year ago. I said I'd call you, but didn't. I wanted to explain why."

"Oh, there's no need—" she began.

"But there is," he interrupted. "I lost your number. Then, when I went to ask my sister for it, she told me you were married. Since I didn't want any part of being the other person in an affair, I didn't even try to call you. It was only when you came back to town that Lakin realized she'd been wrong."

"I was going through a pretty nasty divorce," she said. "But it's been a year and you shouldn't even give that a second thought. I wasn't upset that I didn't hear from you. Not at all. You were exactly what I needed at the moment—a good time. Nothing more." She laughed. "Don't worry about it. I haven't."

Then she turned and disappeared inside her little office in back, leaving Parker staring after her, his ego bruised. No, more than bruised. Battered.

If she hadn't hung up on him when he'd first called to offer her the job, he might have believed her. He'd explained why he hadn't contacted her. That's all that should have mattered. What had he expected anyway?

Despite the fact that he hadn't ever stopped thinking about her, he knew he should figure out how to put her out of his mind.

Maybe working side by side with her, day after day,

would help. Though, when Spence had first come up with idea, Parker had felt it would be almost a kind of torture.

He'd have to get over that. And pronto. Because, like it or not, she worked for RTA now. And he wouldn't do anything to jeopardize that. The family business had to come first.

Alone in the small manager's office, Genna tried to focus on getting used to everything. Lakin had always been organized; so, mostly, Genna needed to familiarize herself with the system. The detailed notes in the binder would definitely help with that.

The reservations were all online, as were the schedule of the tours. As she scrolled through the upcoming groups, she saw that Parker's assessment had been right. RTA appeared to be booked solid. Most days had back-to-back tours.

Good for them. Might as well get as much done before the snow started falling.

Scrolling ahead to the month of December, she saw Lakin hadn't been kidding. While the types of outings had changed, each weekend was marked "Full." During the week, things slowed quite a bit, but Genna imagined the employees were glad to have a bit of a break from the nonstop bookings.

She remembered from working here before that the summer was the busiest season. Tourists flooded the area in good weather; families on vacation and work groups needing a bonding activity. Since school wasn't in session, RTA made sure to have child-friendly activities such as whale watching and wildlife tours.

She heard the bell tinkle over the door and realized

Parker must have unlocked it. The sound of voices told her the next bunch of clients must have arrived.

Putting down the binder, she hurried out to greet them.

By the end of the day, exhaustion had Genna dead on her feet. She'd met four of the ten RTA guides, not including Parker and Spence, whom she already knew. When Spence had arrived for his group and had walked into the building to see her working, he'd grabbed her up into a laughing bear hug. After twirling her around, he set her back on her sneakers. "You're here!" he exclaimed. "Thank you so much."

His enthusiastic greeting made her grin. "It's been busy. Luckily for me, Lakin made detailed notes. I remembered quite a bit from when I worked here, but she made it easy for me to look things up and double check to make sure I was doing everything correctly."

The front door opened then. A large group that appeared to be several families, including six teens, came inside. They were all talking at once, the teens roughhousing, and Genna simply waited at the front counter for them to choose one person to speak to her.

"You've got your hands full," she muttered to Spence.

He smiled. "Just the way I like things."

Once she'd checked the group in, she watched as Spence herded them off to a bus to ride out to where RTA docked their boats. Since the days were still long this time of year, RTA took full advantage of the sunlight. This group would be doing some fishing, which ought to be interesting with so many rowdy teens.

Taking a final glance at the schedule to make sure that was the last group, Genna dropped into a chair and sighed.

The bell above the front door tinkled again, making her look up. Parker strode in, glancing back over his shoulder and shaking his head. Once again, she caught herself melting at the sight of him.

"Spence should have a time with that group," he said, smiling.

Her stomach clenched.

Pretending that his smile didn't affect her, she nodded. "That's what I told him. He didn't seem to mind."

"He doesn't." Moving closer, he studied her. "Personally, I think he thrives on chaos. How was your first day?"

"Part day," she corrected, trying not to let her eyes roam over him. How any man could look so sexy while just standing there bemused her. "This job is definitely fast-paced. It's not for the faint of heart."

Her choice of words had his smile widening. "But do you think you'll enjoy it? Or at least find it tolerable?"

Not sure how to respond to that, she made busywork organizing a stack of brochures and settled on a noncommittal answer. "It's fine. I like it so far."

"I'm glad." He came a little closer, though he stayed on his side of the counter. "Listen, would you like to go have a drink with me after we shut this place down? My treat?"

As tempting as she found the idea, she knew she had to decline. Opening her mouth to tell him no, she lost the capacity for thought when his gaze met and held hers.

"Strictly as coworkers," he continued, possibly noticing her hesitation. "I thought I'd invite the rest of the gang, too, so you can get to know everyone a little better. I know you already know most of them, but you've been gone awhile and might want to get reacquainted."

Despite being tired, she appreciated the thought. "How about we do that, but maybe on Friday night instead? With this being my first day, I'm really tired."

Immediately, he nodded. “Friday sounds great. I’ll let everyone know. Maybe we can do dinner and drinks.”

“I’d like that,” she replied. Hopefully, she’d have grown accustomed to being around him by then and she wouldn’t feel that low-key electric buzz under her skin every time he got close.

Gathering her things, she waved goodbye and left.

Her parents called shortly after she arrived home. Though they’d both lived in Alaska their entire lives, they’d decided to make a major change. Shortly after Genna had asked to move back home once her divorce was finalized, they’d decided to move to Hawaii. “We’re not getting any younger,” her father had announced, grinning from ear to ear. Her mother had been giddy with excitement. Now that they were retired, they said it was time to live somewhere warm. They’d leased a modern condo near the beach and were loving the tropical weather.

They were thrilled when Genna told them about her new job.

“That’s wonderful, honey!” her mother exclaimed. “You loved working there before.”

“I did,” Genna agreed. “And I’m sure it’ll be the same this time. Right now, I’m just relearning how the operation is run.”

“The Colton family do a great job with RTA,” her father said. “They treat their employees right and they have a great reputation around Shelby. Heck, around all of Alaska, the Lower 48, and even into Canada. People come from all around to go on one of their adventure tours.”

“I see that.” Genna dropped onto the sofa, wishing she’d thought to pick up a bottle of wine.

“Any news on that serial killer?” her mom asked, not hiding her worry. “I hate that they haven’t caught him yet.”

"Me, too," Genna answered. "But the police and FBI are actively searching for him."

"But what about you? Are you being careful?"

"Yes. Me and every other woman in Shelby."

They chatted a few more minutes. Her parents told her how much they loved their rental house, the tropical weather and the Hawaiian culture. "I do miss the beautiful wildness of Alaska," her father admitted. "But not the cold."

After the call ended, Genna wandered around the house where she'd grown up. Since the move had been more of an experiment, her parents had taken very little with them. The furniture and artwork made Genna feel as if she'd stepped back into the past.

This had been comfortable at first. Now, she found it stifling. Since her parents had needed a house-sitter and she'd been looking for a place to stay, the situation worked. For now. Though, lately, Genna had found herself aching to paint a wall here or there, add some color, brighten the dark rooms up. With wood-paneled walls, wood floors and dark furniture, the house often felt somber and stifling. The exact opposite of the colorful life her parents were now living in Hawaii.

Though they'd told her she could use the master bedroom, that had felt weird. Instead, she slept in her old bedroom, which her parents had blessedly changed into a generic guest room. Here, she'd decorated to her own taste, bringing in items she'd salvaged from the home she'd once shared with her ex-husband.

The one thing she really wanted to do was to have an alarm system installed. Once, Shelby had been relatively crime free. But with this serial killer on the loose, and being a single woman, she felt the need to protect herself.

She knew she'd certainly sleep better at night once she had some kind of protection. She just hadn't gotten around to calling someone to come out and do it.

Genna had even considered getting a dog. Something big with a loud bark. But she wanted to adopt and didn't want a puppy. So far, she hadn't made time to make the trip into Valdez to check out the animal shelter.

Despite telling herself she wouldn't be in any danger from the Fiancée Killer, the truth was that no one had figured out what exactly his type might be. So far, four bodies had been found. Each of them had been clothed in a little black dress, a fake diamond on their ring finger. They'd been strangled before being partially buried with the head and left hand always visible. Thinking about this scenario kept Genna, and likely most of the women of Shelby, up at night.

As all women everywhere did, living in a larger city, she'd always stayed super aware of her surroundings, kept her keys in her hand when walking to her car, and if she thought even remotely that someone might be following her, she never went directly home.

That had all been in a larger city. Honestly, coming home to Shelby, she'd thought life would be different. The way she remembered it being. But the Fiancée Killer had changed all that.

Like everyone else in town, Genna hoped he or she would be caught soon. Sooner or later, a mistake would be made and it would be over. Until then, all she and everyone else could do was be careful.

The rest of her first week at RTA went by quickly. As she got used to the various aspects of her position, she started to relax. She expanded the customer satisfaction survey that Lakin had instituted and made sure to ask each guest about their experience. On the rare occasion that a problem arose, she made sure to take care of it with courtesy and kindness.

Though the tour guides were in and out, she got to know several of them. As Friday approached, she found herself looking forward to hanging out with them for a meal and a drink.

Except for Parker. Though on the surface he acted friendly, she could sense him going out of his way to avoid being alone with her for any longer than absolutely necessary. She understood, sort of. She guessed she must have bruised his ego when she'd told him she'd never given him a second thought after their torrid night together. A bold-faced lie to be sure, but she knew a man as hot as Parker would have had no shortage of females vying for his attention. To be honest, she'd been surprised that he'd even remembered their one-night stand.

As for Genna, she wondered if she'd ever be able to forget it.

Luckily, her job kept her too busy to dwell much on Parker. Tuesday and Wednesday had been a flurry of guests, meeting other guides, and making sure everything ran smoothly. Reservations were coming in for winter as well as for next spring. She had to update the software, make sure each tour group wasn't overbooked, and handle the schedule months in advance.

She loved every freaking second of it.

As she became accustomed to the routine, her confidence grew. She'd always loved customer service work, especially here. The guests were universally in a great mood, excited about their adventure to come. And since

RTA did exactly as they advertised, Genna had yet to have an unsatisfied customer.

Lakin's notes in the computer helped Genna identify repeat customers and some of the personal details enabled her to ask about their children or pets. Genna loved the way some of the guest's faces lit up when she mentioned their family.

All of the guides seemed friendly, too. With RTA so busy, often with back-to-back groups leaving for different adventures, she'd met most of them. Even if their interactions were necessarily brief, most mentioned how much they were looking forward to their planned dinner out on Friday.

Despite her full days, her entire body knew every single time Parker was near. She didn't understand it, but her nerve endings would prickle, her skin would flush, and despite trying not to, she was uber aware of his movements. If he happened to glance at her, she felt the heat of his gaze all the way to the soles of her feet.

Hopefully, that would be only temporary. She was bound to get used to being around him eventually.

At the end of every workday, even though the sun wouldn't fully set until almost seven, she appreciated how one of the male guides always hung around the place to make sure she wasn't alone. The last tours usually came in around six and once she'd finished processing everyone, it would be time to close for the day.

They'd had to figure out her schedule, because she couldn't work twelve-hour days every day of the week. Since she lived fairly close to the building, she volunteered to do split shifts, but in the end, she'd decided to base her daily schedule on what tours they had booked.

Their slowest days seemed to be Mondays and Thursdays, so she said those would be her days off.

Everyone seemed relieved and Parker and Spence promised to make sure her desk was covered when she wasn't there.

Teamwork, she thought. Always a good thing. Now she just needed to figure out how to think of Parker as just another coworker and she'd be all set.

Chapter 3

The next morning, which was Friday, Parker arrived at RTA shortly after sunrise. He'd slept well and grabbed breakfast and coffee on the way in to work. His first tour group would be a morning hike finishing up with some trout fishing, but they weren't due to arrive for another hour.

Even though they'd agreed that Genna would have Thursdays off, her new schedule wasn't set to start until the following week. Selfishly, Parker was glad. Though he didn't spend a lot of time inside the office, when he did, he found himself constantly wanting to be near her.

He didn't understand how she could have such a strong effect on him, especially after all this time. Since she'd clearly moved on and regarded him as just another co-worker, he wanted to do the same.

But he couldn't. And for good reason. Not only was she beautiful, but there was something about her. When she smiled, the woman freaking *glowed.*

The guests adored her. The other RTA guides did, too. No wonder Parker still struggled with a fierce rush of attraction every time they shared the same space.

He wondered how long it would take for him to get

past that. If he would *ever* be able to change the way he felt about her. He had to.

Tonight, they'd all be going out for an informal meal and a drink or two. He'd already told himself several times that he needed to keep his distance from her and to let the others all get to know her.

Even if he wanted to do exactly that more than he would have ever believed possible. In the few days that she'd worked for RTA, she'd been politely professional. Nothing more. Nothing less.

Once at the office, Parker made a pot of coffee and poured himself a second cup.

Genna walked in about thirty minutes later. "Good morning," she said, smiling. "You sure are here early. If I remember right, your group isn't scheduled to leave for another half an hour."

Though his heart leapt into his throat the instant her bright green gaze found his, he managed to smile back. "The weather is looking iffy," he said, pulling out his phone and opening the weather app. "See. Look at the radar."

Accepting his phone, she studied the screen before handing it back. "It's a few hours out," she said. "Hopefully, it will break up before it reaches us."

After pouring herself a cup of coffee, she flashed an impersonal smile and disappeared into her office.

Which left him alone in the front counter area, with nothing to do but wait for his group to arrive.

The tour went off as planned, and even though he made sure to be attentive and give his guests the best possible time, his thoughts kept returning to Genna. He didn't know what it was about her, but he'd thought about her more than he should have.

He had three more tours after this one. He'd better keep his attention focused where it needed to be.

When he returned with the morning group to headquarters, Genna had already left for lunch. Spence was filling in for her. He laughed when he noticed Parker looking around for her. "She'll be back, cuz."

"Who?" Parker asked, fooling no one. "I need to eat something before I go back out. I was hoping I could get Genna to bring me something."

"So call her." The phone rang just then and Spence went to answer it.

Pulling out his own phone, Parker scrolled through his contacts until he found Genna's number. Then, shaking his head, he decided he'd just go grab something to eat himself. He had another batch of clients due to arrive in an hour. Who knew? Maybe he'd even run into Genna when he was out.

After asking Spence if he wanted anything, Parker jumped into his truck and headed off. The closest fast-food place also happened to be his favorite. Pulling into the parking lot, he did a quick scan to see if he could spot Genna's car. Once he realized she must have gone somewhere else for lunch, he decided to go through the drive-through and take his burger back to eat at RTA.

He'd barely finished eating when he spotted Genna's little red car pulling up. His heart rate accelerated as he wadded up his wrapper and tossed it in the trash. He couldn't help but watch as she crossed the parking lot. With the sun in her gold hair and her jaunty walk, she embodied everything he found attractive in a woman.

As she breezed through the front door, Spence looked up from the computer and greeted her. "I'm glad you're back. It looks like my next group and Parker's are back-to-back."

"Great," she said, smiling at him. She barely even glanced at Parker. "I like being busy."

As if on cue, several SUVs pulled up.

"That's probably my group," Parker said, keeping his voice casual. "Let me know once you get them checked in, please."

"Will do," she chirped, still avoiding eye contact.

"Thanks." Stung, Parker went back into the storeroom, pretending he needed to get supplies.

Spence followed him. "What the hell was that?"

Not even bothering to pretend he didn't know what his cousin meant, Parker shrugged. "I'm not sure. She seemed fine when I left this morning."

"You didn't do something, did you?"

"No," Parker replied. "I did not."

"Is it like this every day between the two of you?" Spence crossed his arms.

"No. Maybe she just had a bad lunch. No idea." He glanced at his smartwatch. "I've got to go. I'm due to take my group out in ten minutes."

"Wait. Are we still all meeting up as a group tonight for dinner and drinks?" Spence asked.

"Yes." Parker didn't tell his cousin that he'd been looking forward to tonight all week. Maybe once Genna was out of the office, the two of them would be able to interact in a friendlier manner.

The instant Parker stepped into the main area, several of the guests greeted him. As regulars, they always made sure to book tours with him. All of the tour guides had their favorites and, honestly, seeing the familiar faces from years past just made the outing more enjoyable.

"Is everyone checked in?" Parker asked, directing his question to Genna.

Without looking up from her computer, she nodded. "Yes. You all are ready to go."

"Excellent." Looking around at all the guests' excited faces, he grinned. "Let's head out."

They all followed, talking at once.

The rest of the day went in similar fashion. He brought back one group, had a small break, during which he did his best to avoid Genna, and then his next batch arrived.

The overcast skies had threatened rain all day. Parker kept an eye on the clouds while taking his latest group four-wheeling up the mountain. When they reached their destination, a meadow with a small lake, the wind swirled the colorful leaves. Several of the guests dismounted, walking around and taking pictures.

When Parker pointed out the black bear on the other side of the water, cautioning guests to remain close, more people got out their phones to snap photos. This group had traveled from the Lower 48, where the sight of any kind of bear was uncommon. They all seemed thrilled.

The rain held off for the trip back down, too. Parker counted his blessings as they parked the four-wheelers in the storage barn and made their way back to headquarters. This time, instead of getting everything ready for the next trip, Parker followed the group into the building. He hung out in the waiting area while Genna checked the guests out one by one. All of the other employees, including Spence, had left for the day. With her broad smile and efficient process, she somehow managed to make each individual feel special. He marveled at the way each person reacted to her charm.

As the last guest said his goodbyes, thunder shook the

building, followed by a bright flash of lightning. Startled, Genna squeaked then flashed him a sheepish smile. "I hope he makes it to his car," she said as they both watched the guest break into a run.

As the man drove away, the sky opened up. Rain came down in sheets, the wind sending it sideways. More thunder, several rounds this time in succession, several lightning flashes and a loud boom.

"That sounded like an explosion," Genna said. Just then the power went out.

When she made another tiny squeak, Parker fought the urge to go to her and pull her into his arms. "It's going to be all right," he said instead. "Lightning struck somewhere close." He went to the front window and tried to see out. "As long as it didn't start a fire, we'll be okay. We can just hang out here until the storm passes."

She made a sound that might have passed for agreement.

Another crack of thunder and immediately a lightning flash illuminated the room, showing him she remained on the backside of the counter.

"That was close," he commented. The need to hold her, touch her, tell her he'd keep her safe, consumed him. Instead, he reminded himself that they were only coworkers, nothing more.

"I don't like this," she said, sounding disgruntled. "I checked the weather this morning before I came to work and it wasn't supposed to rain until later tonight."

Since RTA had a fireplace, he knew he could light a fire. They often did, especially in the winter when they needed to chase away the chill. If the day hadn't ended, he might have. He could imagine himself and Genna, sharing a glass of wine on the couch with a fire blazing in the background.

Clearly, he'd gone over the edge. Digging out his phone, he pulled up his weather app. "Judging by what I see on the radar, it's going to rain for a good while."

"Great, just great. I guess we'll need to cancel the get-together tonight."

The disappointment in her voice matched the way he felt. "I think we should. Let me send out a group text and let everyone know. We'll reschedule it for next Friday."

She nodded, waiting in silence while he sent out the text. Her phone pinged, too, since he'd included her in the group. She glanced at the message and sighed. "I've been looking forward to this all week."

"Me, too," he admitted, earning a startled glance from her. "Since it's still pouring out there, how about I drive you home?"

"I can drive myself," she said, though she didn't sound certain. "As long as the roads don't wash out."

Which she knew as well as he did, they would in this kind of storm. "My truck sits up higher than your car," he pointed out. "Also, if you were to run into any trouble on the way home, I'd hate for the wrong person to find you."

"Like the Fiancée Killer." Her loud sigh told him what she thought of that. "I doubt even he'd be out hunting for victims in this."

"You never know," he replied. "Please, let me take you home."

"What about my car?" she asked. "I don't like the idea of being stuck at the house without transportation."

"I can pick you up in the morning and bring you to work. You can get your car then."

Outside, the sound of the rain increased, becoming a

roar. Parker had always loved the sound of rain drumming on the metal roof of the RTA building. But right now, it sounded more threatening than soothing.

"At least we don't get tornadoes here," Genna commented. "I spent some time in Texas in the springtime and those tornado warnings are scary as heck."

He loved that she didn't swear. "You lived in Texas?" he asked. "I didn't know that."

"My ex-husband's family lives there," she said. "We were visiting them."

The mention of her ex only reminded him of the night they'd spent together. He swallowed hard, forcing away the stab of longing. To distract himself, he tried opening the front door.

The wind nearly blew it out of his hands. Struggling, he managed to pull it closed. Turning, he wiped the rain off his face with his sleeve. "I don't think we're going anywhere for a bit," he said, pulling out his phone and turning on the flashlight app. "We keep some camping lanterns in the storeroom just for this purpose," he said. "I'm going to go get them."

"Okay," she replied. "I know I saw a couple of three-wick candles on the bookshelf in my office. If I can find a lighter, I'll get those lit, too."

When he returned with the two battery-operated lanterns, he saw she'd gotten the candles burning. Between their flickering lights and what the lanterns provided, they could actually see each other. Definitely a step up, he thought. And kind of cozy, too.

Outside, the storm continued to rage, rain pounding the metal roof. "That's really loud," Genna commented.

"Yes, it is," he agreed. "Since we're going to be here awhile, I know we have a bottle of cabernet somewhere, from our last open house. Want to have a glass while we wait this out?"

When Genna didn't immediately respond, he glanced at her. Shadows danced across her face in the flickering candlelight, making her eyes seem huge in her delicate face. "I'd rather just go home," she finally said. Then, before he could comment, she strode over to the front door and opened it.

The rush of wind and rain nearly knocked her off her feet. Parker helped her push the door shut.

"I guess not," she muttered, using the bottom of her shirt to dry her face. "I thought maybe it might have died down a little since you tried to go out."

Instead of commenting, he went to the small kitchen area. She trailed along after him. He located a bottle of wine and two plastic cups. He had a corkscrew on his pocketknife, so he used that to open it. After pouring himself some, he took a sip. "It's not beer, but it'll do," he said. "Do you want some?"

She came closer. "Maybe just a little."

He poured her some and handed her the cup. To his surprise, she drank all of it in one swallow. "Okay," she said, a hint of a smile playing on her mouth, "we had wine. How about we try to get home?"

What could he do but smile back? "Let me close this wine up first."

"If you can do that, do you mind if I take it with me?" she asked.

That made him chuckle. "Sure. No problem." He located one of the wine stoppers that Lakin always kept lying around. "Here you go." He handed her the bottle.

"Thank you."

"It sounds like the rain is letting up," he said. This

time, when he opened the door to check, the wind and rain didn't beat him back. Though still pouring, the gusts had died down. "I think we can make it home now."

Plastic cup still in hand, she crossed over to peer out. "Good. As long as no trees are down, it looks drivable."

"In my truck, yes." He kept his voice firm. "Please, let me take you home."

"I just can't be without a vehicle, even if it's just overnight," she said. "How about you follow me instead? That way, you know I get home safely."

Though he'd rather they just went together in his truck, he nodded. While she blew out the candles, he returned the camping lanterns to the storeroom, using his phone flashlight to make his way back to the front.

Genna waited near the door. She'd donned a yellow rain slicker that she must have grabbed from storage. Since the thing was at least two sizes too big, she'd rolled the sleeves up. With the hood up, she looked achingly vulnerable, a fact that he knew she'd hate.

"Ready?" she asked. At his nod, she stepped out onto the front porch that, now that the wind had died down, provide ample shelter from the rain.

Once he'd locked the office up, they both eyed the rain. The damp cold seeped into his bones, making him long for snow.

"Follow me," she said before dashing out into the deluge.

He waited until she'd gotten into her car before running for his truck. Though he would have preferred to take her home, he had to respect her wishes. He only hoped she remembered how to drive in the mud.

Paved roads or not, this kind or rain brought flooding, which in turn coated some of the roads in mud. Parker had only seen this happen a few times in his lifetime, but he'd never forgotten the indignity of once as a teen having to call his cousin to tow him out when he'd gotten stuck.

As he followed Genna from the parking lot, he kept a tight grip on the steering wheel. He was able to turn his windshield wipers down a bit from high. More proof the rain was slowing.

Driving, he kept his attention on the road, despite the distraction of emotions whirling inside him.

When they turned onto Genna's street, he shook his hands out one by one. They'd actually started cramping. And when she pulled into her driveway, the last of the tension left his body. He exhaled, more relieved than he should have been.

Pulling up behind her, he kept his truck running. He'd wait unto she got inside before backing out and heading home.

Except, when she exited her car, instead of going in, she stopped halfway. And then she turned and moved toward his truck instead of the house.

She went around to the passenger side, opened the door and climbed in. Her stricken expression made him instinctively reach for her. "What is it? What's wrong?"

"My front door is wide open," she said, her voice shaken. "I know I locked it when I left for work this morning. What if whoever broke in is still inside the house?"

Heart pounding, Genna sucked in her breath. Inexplicably, her eyes filled with tears.

"I'm calling the police." He immediately dialed 9-1-1.

"But—" She gripped his arm.

Still giving information to Dispatch, he shook his head.

"A unit is on the way," he said. "You stay right here with me until they arrive."

Though she struggled to keep herself from shaking, she did as he asked. Her legs would likely be too weak to carry her anyway.

In less than five minutes, two squad cars pulled up, lights flashing. Parker grabbed his umbrella and got out in the steady rain, crossing over to her side. Before he could open her door, Genna joined him. She kept her rain hood up, even though he made sure to keep his umbrella over her, which she appreciated.

The policemen got out slowly, taking care to open their own umbrellas. Genna waited patiently, glad of the time to collect herself before explaining to the officer what she'd seen.

"I'm glad you didn't go inside," the one officer said once she'd finished. "Let us take a look and make sure it's safe."

Genna nodded. She stepped closer to Parker, aware he'd think it was to make better use of his umbrella. She would have given much to have the right to let him put his arm around her and pull her close. They both watched silently as the officers disappeared inside.

"Why my parents' place?" she asked, proud that she managed to keep her voice steady. "I mean they've owned this house for thirty years and never once had a break-in. Not just that, but there's very little of value inside. They aren't big on updating. The only thing new is the TV and those aren't even that expensive anymore."

"I don't know," he replied. "I'm sorry this happened to you."

He still didn't touch her. While she understood, she really wished this time he would make an exception. Just this once.

A few minutes later, both police officers emerged. "We did a thorough search. No one is inside and, quite honestly, nothing appears to be damaged or missing. Are you absolutely positive you didn't leave the door ajar and maybe the wind blew it open?"

"I'm sure," Genna responded. "And the front door looks damaged to me. Like someone kicked it in. Even from here, I can see that part of the frame is broken."

"High winds can also do that." The officer scratched his head. "It seems kind of odd that anyone would bother to kick your door in and then not touch anything."

She bristled, but decided it would be best not to respond.

"I take it you don't have any kind of burglar alarm?" the other officer asked, his expression kind.

"No," she replied. "I've been thinking about getting one ever since that serial killer started going after local women. Now I really wish I'd gotten one installed. I'll start making calls first thing in the morning."

The older of the two policemen nodded. "Now might definitely be a good time to do that." He handed Genna his card. "Call us if you need anything."

Accepting it, she thanked him.

She and Parker stood silently and watched them drive off.

"Do you want me to walk you inside?" Parker asked.

"Yes, please." Feeling extremely vulnerable, she clutched at his arm. When he covered her hand with his, her heart squeezed.

"Stay near to me," he said, tugging her a tiny bit closer. Then they stepped into the house.

"Wow," he commented. "It's very neat. I get why the police officers thought no one could have broken in."

"Yeah, I get it. It's also very dated. Since I'm housesitting for my parents, I've been afraid to change anything."

"Late nineties?" he asked. "Just to hazard a guess."

"Let me put it this way. This room looks exactly the way it did when they brought me home from the hospital for the first time. They've never bought anything new."

She pointed to the couch, covered with one of her mother's old comforters. "When things wear out, they simply cover them up. I guess they like the comfort of having everything stay the same and familiar. That's why their decision to move to Hawaii was such a big shock."

Reluctantly, she let go of him and began to inspect the place.

He followed her from the living room to the kitchen, then down the hallway to check on each of the three bedrooms. Everything appeared undisturbed, including the guest bedroom. "This is mine," Genna told him. "Notice the splashes of color?"

"I do."

"As far as I can tell, nothing was stolen." Perplexed and worried, Genna shook her head. "This is making me question why someone would go through all the trouble of breaking in."

"Since the policeman already asked you if you're sure you locked the door, I'm not going to repeat the question."

"I appreciate that," she said, meaning it. Despite feeling traumatized, when she looked at him, she still found herself battling an aching sort of longing.

If he realized this, he didn't show it.

"Well..." he said, swallowing hard and turning to go.

"I'll see you in the morning," he finished. "Make sure and lock up after me."

"Wait." Not wanting him to leave, she hurried over and touched his arm again. Still in her yellow rain slicker, she looked up at him, hoping he could somehow sense her fear. "I can't lock up. The door won't even close properly. Look." She showed him.

"Judging by the way the wood had splintered around where the lock had been, it does look like someone busted in the door," he said. "Wind wouldn't do that."

"I know." Exhaling, she fought to keep her voice steady. "There's not a chance I'm staying here alone with no way to keep an intruder out. What if they were to come back?"

His gaze found hers. "You have a point."

"I feel…violated," she said, breathing hard.

As if unable to help himself, he pulled her close and held her.

Offering comfort, nothing more, she told herself.

"I'm not going to let you be alone," he said, smoothing her hair away from her face. "Would you be willing to go back to my place with me? You can stay there tonight. We can work on getting your door repaired in the morning."

"Separate rooms?" she asked, her face still pressed against his chest.

"Of course," he promised. "I'd never try to take advantage of you, especially when you're down. If we ever get together again, you'll be the one to initiate it. Sound good?"

"Well, that will never happen," she said, her tone dry.

That made him chuckle.

Again that wild rush of attraction. Even now. Grappling with her mixed emotions, she attempted to summon up a smile, and thanked him. "I appreciate you offering to help me, more than you could ever know."

His glance met and held hers. "Does that mean you're coming with me?"

"Yes," she replied. "I just need to pack a few things. Give me a few minutes and I'll be right back."

"Okay," Parker replied. She could feel his gaze on her as she turned to go.

In her room, she tossed a change of clothes and some toiletries into a backpack. Despite everything, she found she actually liked the idea of spending nonworking time with him. On a friendly basis, of course. Maybe this would help her get over her constant awareness of him. She certainly hoped so.

When she returned to the living room with her backpack in hand, he turned and eyed her. "Listen, I should probably ask if you'd rather have me stay here with you rather than go to my place."

Her gut clenched. "That's even more kind of you, but no. It wouldn't be safe," she said, hoping he couldn't see her terror. The howl of the wind and the rain made it even worse.

"It sounds pretty nasty out there," he pointed out. "But if you're sure, let's go."

Chapter 4

Outside, the wind had picked up again, rattling the partly closed front door. Rain drummed in a steady fury. Just to make sure, Parker crossed to the window. The storm had definitely intensified once more. Rain came down in sheets. He couldn't even see his truck parked in the driveway.

Which meant the drive home might be tricky, to say the least. Again, he debated the possibility of simply staying put. If not for the thread of fear he'd heard just now in Genna's voice, he might have tried to convince her.

While he tried to figure out the best course of action, she joined him. "Wow," she said.

"See what I mean?"

"Yes." She turned to face him. "But, honestly, I'd much rather brave the weather than risk being here when the intruder comes back."

He noticed she said *when* rather than *if*.

"I can keep you safe." He meant every word.

"Maybe so, but even if you stayed here with me, I'd be jumping at every single sound. Best to just go somewhere else, at least until I can get the front door repaired and an alarm system installed."

Slowly, he nodded. "What about securing your belongings? We can try to put something to block anyone from coming in the front door."

"And leave through the garage." She looked around the room. "How about we just pile up a bunch of furniture against it. I know that wouldn't really stop someone determined to enter, but it might provide a bit of a deterrent."

"Good plan."

Once they'd moved everything in front of the front door, he stepped back. "That'll have to do."

"It's better than nothing."

They went out through the garage. Genna grabbed a spare opener from a hook on the wall. As soon as he used his remote to unlock his truck, they exchanged glances and ran for the vehicle.

Despite the short distance, they both got drenched. Or he did. Genna still wore her rain slicker with the hood up.

Inside his truck, they turned to look at each other. With one hand, he pushed his soaked hair away from his face. "I wish I had a raincoat like yours," he said.

Her smile made everything worth it. "You'd look good in yellow," she teased.

"Not as good as you," he replied, perfectly serious. He noticed she lowered the hood finally, fluffing her wavy blond hair with her fingers.

The mad urge to kiss her went through him. He froze, took a deep breath and waited until it passed. Then he started the truck and drove out of the parking area.

Headed back to his place, Parker focused on getting them there safely. He could not afford to be distracted by the beautiful woman sitting next to him. The wind-driven rain made it difficult to see, even with his windshield wipers on high.

They inched slowly forward, caution over speed. He

could feel Genna's tension, hear it in the quick shallow breaths she took. He didn't dare take his hands off the steering wheel or his attention from the road, so the only comfort he could offer was words. "It's going to be all right," he said.

They rounded a curve and slowed. Ahead, the road was washed out, water coursing over the pavement, making it impossible to tell the depth. *Turn around, don't drown* had been drummed into everyone's heads since childhood. Yet, every time they had a flash flood, there were always numerous individuals who ignored that warning and found themselves stuck in several feet of water. First responders were kept busy saving these people.

Parker didn't want to become one of them. Yet with an already tense Genna next to him, he didn't really have a choice.

He stopped the truck and shifted into Park, considering his options.

"Is there another way we can go?" Genna asked nervously. "Driving through all that water doesn't look safe."

"There is," he answered, finally able to look at her. "But not only is it about thirty minutes out of our way, there are several areas of that particular road that are likely to be washed out even worse. This is our best bet."

Slowly, she nodded. "I trust you," she said, catching and holding his gaze.

His heart squeezed. "Thanks," he managed to respond. "With this lift kit on my truck, it sits a bit higher than normal. I feel reasonably confident we can make it through."

Reasonably confident. He hoped she didn't ask the odds.

"Okay. Like I said, I know you'll keep us safe."

"I'm definitely about to try," he told her, shifting back into Drive.

One final quick glance at Genna, who'd gone back to gripping the door, and he gently pressed the accelerator, sending them moving toward the water.

Between the swift-moving current, the rain and wind, it took all of his strength to keep the truck on the road. *Slow and steady*, he reminded himself, using continuous pressure on the gas pedal.

Despite their slow speed, water plumed up, splashing the windows and making it even more difficult to see.

Still, they continued to plow forward. Foot by foot, with the water rising the farther they went.

They must have reached the middle, because just when he thought it might make it to his running boards, it began to recede. And then finally they came out onto the other side, eventually reaching dry road.

Once they had, he coasted to a stop for the moment and looked back. "That was easier than I expected," he quipped. "Though I don't want to have to do it again."

"Me neither." She gave a sigh of relief. "Hopefully, this storm will pass and the roads will clear up by morning."

"My house is just a few hundred yards past here," he said. "We'll be there in no time."

When they pulled up into his driveway, he used his automatic garage door opener and got ready to pull in. Since he had to park his truck at an angle due to the length, he only tended to use the garage in the cold months. But this downpour warranted the extra effort.

Genna sat up and watch with interest as he maneuvered his truck inside. He got it parked on the first try.

"Nice," she commented, smiling. "I'd hoped you'd figured out a way to get this huge truck inside your garage."

"I'm just lucky there's extra height in here. Otherwise, being able to fit the length of it wouldn't matter."

He got out, intending to make his way to her side to open her door. But by the time he got there, she'd already grabbed her backpack and jumped out.

"I really appreciate you letting me stay here," she said, her expression earnest. "I promise you won't even know I'm here."

Though he doubted that, he simply nodded. Pushing the button on the wall that closed the garage, he opened the door to the house. "Come on in," he said, gesturing at her to precede him.

Once inside, he flipped the wall switch so they could see. They were in his laundry room, just off the kitchen. "This way."

He led her past the kitchen, which opened up to the living room, and down the hallway. The second door on the left had been designated his guest bedroom. Though it rarely got used, he'd recently put fresh sheets on the bed because one of his old friends who'd moved away had been supposed to come back to Shelby for a week. The visit had been canceled at the last moment, but everything had been made ready for a guest.

"Serendipity," he said, telling her the story as he turned on the light. "This will be where you'll be sleeping."

She brushed past him on the way in, her body making brief contact with his. That small touch was enough to send desire blazing through him.

His swift intake of breath had her turning to look at him. When she met his gaze, she took an almost involuntary step closer. Then, as if she'd realized what she'd done, she moved away, placing her backpack on the bed with great care.

Of necessity, he moved to the doorway, not wanting her to see the physical proof of his sudden arousal. With effort, he found his voice. "Since we didn't have dinner, I'm going to look around the kitchen and see what I can rustle up for us to eat," he said.

Pretending not to notice his voice sounded like rusty nails, she nodded. "If you'll give me a few minutes to freshen up, I can come help you."

"Sounds good." Stiffly, he moved away. He also needed a few minutes of alone time, so he could get his body's reaction to her under control.

Mentally berating himself, he opened the refrigerator and began inspecting the contents. Since he cooked for himself most nights, he kept it pretty well stocked. A few minutes of perusing the dinner choices and he'd managed to return to normal.

"So, what are you thinking?" Genna asked from behind him. Then, without waiting for an answer, she continued. "I'm thinking you should let me make dinner. It'll be my way of thanking you for helping me out."

Since the idea of the two of them cooking side by side now felt too intimate, he nodded. "Okay. The fridge and freezer are stocked up, so is the pantry. The only thing I'm sick of eating is salmon."

This comment made her laugh. "Isn't everyone? Honestly, I've tried so many different recipes, trying to make it taste different."

"That's what happens when something is so plentiful," he said. "I heard people in Maine are like that about lobster."

"Not me. I can always go for a fresh lobster tail and butter." As she smiled up at him, this time his heart did a little flip-flop. "I'm thinking a steak, baked potatoes and maybe asparagus."

Impulsively, he hugged her, a move he instantly regretted. Releasing her as fast as he could, he stepped back. "That's my kind of meal. I even thawed a nice Porterhouse, intending to grill it tomorrow. It's big enough that it should feed both of us."

"Sounds perfect," she said, keeping her gaze averted. He found himself wondering if he should apologize for the quick hug, just in case. Good thing she didn't know how close he'd come to kissing her.

"Genna," he began. "I'm sorry if—"

"It's all good," she said, cutting him off. "Now, I'd better get busy doing my thing. I'll holler if I need you."

Dismissed, Parker did the only sensible thing. He retreated.

If it hadn't still been raining outside, he'd have gone for a walk. Getting outside always eased his tension. Instead, since he was confined to the house, he took an early shower and changed into comfy clothes.

When he emerged, the smell of steak broiling made his mouth water.

In the kitchen, Genna had set the table and had just removed two foil-wrapped baked potatoes from the oven. "You're just in time," she said, smiling.

Somehow, this made him feel worse. "Genna, I never want to make you feel uncomfortable."

His words wiped the smile from her face. "You're overthinking things. Please, sit down and let's have a nice meal. It's been a spectacularly bad day. I'm really not in the mood to make it any worse."

Damn, he liked her attitude. Quietly nodding, he asked her if there was anything he could do to help.

"Nope. Just sit and eat," she replied.

"Yes, ma'am." He sat.

She picked up their plates and carried them to the stove. When she returned and placed them on the table, they each had a perfectly cooked portion of steak, baked potato and asparagus.

"This looks way better than anything I could have made," he admitted.

"Thank you." She took a seat and gave him a mock stern look. "Dig in."

Genna wasn't sure if it was because of the handsome man sitting across from her, but the dinner they shared tasted better than anything she'd ever made.

Parker definitely appeared to like it. Making appreciative sounds as he ate, he cleaned his plate in record time. "That was amazing," he said, sitting back in his chair and watching her eat.

Once she'd finished, he grabbed both plates and carried them to the sink. "I'll wash up."

"Thanks." Suddenly exhausted, she didn't move. Instead, she covertly admired his backside while he washed off their plates and everything she'd used to cook.

When he finally finished and turned around, he studied her. "Did you want to watch some TV?"

Though she really wanted to crawl into bed, it was still early. "Sure," she said, rising and stretching. "I don't care what we watch. You choose."

They settled in the living room. She took the couch and he sank onto his recliner. Using the remote, he chose a crime drama. "I've watched a few episodes of this," she said. "It's pretty good."

Appearing lost in thought, he nodded.

Relaxing slightly, she grabbed a throw blanket from the end of the couch and used it to cover up.

She must have dozed off because the next thing she knew, Parker gently shook her. Confused, she sat up, blinking sleepily. The room had gone quiet, the television turned off.

"Did you want to sleep here?" he asked quietly, bending over her. "I wasn't sure if you'd rather I left you alone, or woke you so you could move to the bed."

Heaven help her. Maybe her defenses were in tatters due to her being only half awake. Without really thinking, she reached up, pulled his face down to hers, and kissed him.

Oh, what a kiss. It was everything she'd thought it would be, just as passionate and perfect as she remembered. Tongues tangled as they deepened it. Desire, which always seemed to be simmering inside her when he was around, blazed to life.

It would have been a simple thing to tug Parker to her, his full body on top of hers. Though fully clothed, shedding those would have been a simple thing.

Except she knew doing so would be a terrible mistake.

To his credit, Parker kept himself back. Only their mouths met, though he tangled one hand in her hair. If he wanted more, he made no move to take it. Instead, he continued to thoroughly kiss her, letting her make the next move. Which, despite how badly she wanted to, she couldn't take.

Finally, they broke apart, both breathing hard.

Talk about awkward. She didn't know where to look, what to do with her hands. Meanwhile, he waited, clearly giving her time and space to choose what she wanted to do next.

What she wanted had nothing to do with anything.

"I guess I ought to go to bed," she managed to say. "Thank you for waking me."

Instead of responding, he straightened and nodded. Moving stiffly away, he glanced back over his shoulder at her. "Please turn the lights out when you go."

A moment later, she heard the sound of his bedroom door closing. The slight click made her wince.

Well, she'd certainly made a mess of things.

Feeling an uncomfortable combination of both arousal and embarrassment, she briefly considered spending the rest of the night on the sofa. But aware she'd likely regret that decision in the morning, she pushed herself up and made her way toward the guest room. She shut off the lights as she left.

After a quick detour to the guest bathroom to brush her teeth, she returned to her little room and closed her own door. Quickly changing into her pajamas, she slid between the cool sheets and gave a sigh of relief.

When she opened her eyes again, it was morning. The instant she woke, sitting up in Parker's guest bed, she immediately realized she'd made a huge mistake.

She'd kissed him.

Moving on autopilot, she tried not to think. Today was another workday, and they'd be working side by side for large chunks of it. There couldn't be any lingering awkwardness between them. She had to clear this up. Somehow.

While she showered in the guest bathroom, she tried to think of what to say. Should she apologize? Explain that she'd been barely awake and…what? Acted on the constant, simmering desire he aroused in her? No, that wouldn't work. It sounded too much like an invitation to try again, or to take things even further.

She definitely didn't want to lead him on. Because, plain and simple, they were coworkers. Nothing more. Nor could they ever be. She wasn't willing to risk this blowing up in her face yet again. Especially since her livelihood would be affected.

After finishing, she shut off the water, toweled dry, and tried to clear her mind. She hadn't been able to come up with much and decided she'd simply apologize and leave it at that. Decision made, she ignored the butterflies in her stomach, dried her hair and got dressed. As a general rule, she didn't wear a lot of makeup, just mascara and lip gloss, which meant it didn't take her long to get ready.

Sadly, Genna didn't feel refreshed. She hadn't had much success sleeping. The kiss and the break-in had weighed heavily on her mind, making her toss and turn all night long. Every time she'd managed to drift off to sleep, booms of thunder had yanked her back into awareness. The storm had continued into early morning, finally moving on right before dawn.

Because thinking about the break-in terrified her and dwelling on the kiss made her want to cry, she wished she could get through the morning without thinking. At least until she got to work. Once at RTA, she could keep herself busy enough so she wouldn't have to dwell on anything. Except, she did need to have the front door repaired and call an alarm company and make an appointment to have a system installed.

But first, she had to face Parker. He'd been kind enough to offer her a place to stay, and then she'd kissed him. What if he'd taken that to mean she wanted more than just a kiss?

And what if she did? Too much to consider, especially since she'd always been a fan of weighing all her options.

She'd kissed him. Damned if she hadn't wanted to do a whole lot more.

Admitting that brought to mind visions of their night together. She relived every moment, wondering how it could be seared inside her brain. Their tangled bodies, the passionate kisses and the way he'd made her feel sexy, beautiful and whole again. Special. At least until he'd disappeared without a call or text.

In retrospect, that had turned out to be a good thing. She hadn't wanted to go straight from her disastrous marriage into another relationship. She'd needed to learn how to live on her own and rebuild her self-respect, especially after being betrayed not only by her husband but by a woman she'd considered her best friend.

Genna never wanted to feel that level of pain again. Yet when she'd gone slinking back home to her parents to lick her wounds, and she'd been ghosted after she'd indulged in one amazingly carnal night with the sexiest man she'd ever met, it had hurt nearly as much. Maybe because she'd been vulnerable.

Even though Parker had belatedly, one year later, offered up an excuse, the rejection still stung. Likely more than it should have. Maybe she needed to finally let it go.

Giving her hair one final swipe of the brush, she stared at herself in the mirror. Then she took a deep breath and opened her bedroom door. The scent of coffee brewing drifted down the hallway, making her mouth water. When she made it to the kitchen, Parker was standing at the stove, his back to her, stirring something.

Dang, he looked good. Flushing, she remembered she owed him an apology. Not yet though. She needed to be fully awake for that. Needing fortification, she made a beeline for the coffeepot.

"Morning," Parker said, turning to smile at her. "Mugs are in the cabinet to the left of the coffee maker. I have half-and-half in the fridge and sugar in the smallest of those canisters on the counter."

"Thanks," she replied, pretending that his smile hadn't knocked the breath from her. "Any reports on storm damage?"

"Not yet." He filled two bowls and carried them to the table. "Since we're opening RTA, we can fill everyone else in once we get there."

Slowly, she nodded. "What are you cooking?" she asked, feeling ridiculously tongue-tied.

If he noticed, he gave no sign. "I made some oatmeal with raisins."

Though she usually nursed a cup of coffee until fully awake, since she felt like she'd been up for hours, she appreciated the hot meal. "That's very kind of you," she said, grabbing a mug from the cupboard and filling it. Once she'd added her cream and sugar, she took a seat at the table and took a sip. He'd already placed a couple of spoons there, along with paper napkins.

The aroma of oatmeal, cinnamon, and raisins made her realize she was starving. No one had made her breakfast since her mother when she'd lived at home. The small kindness made her insides go all gooey. She decided maybe she'd wait on the apology, at least until after they'd eaten.

"Dig in," he said, dropping into the chair opposite hers.

Though she tried not to watch him through her lashes, she couldn't help herself. He ate quickly and efficiently, the way he did most everything—except make love.

Again, the thought made her entire body flush. She concentrated on finishing her breakfast, glad he couldn't hear her thoughts.

"Do you think the roads have cleared?" she asked, wondering if she should offer to help with the dishes. Since doing so felt too intimate, she stayed put while he carried their bowls and utensils to the sink and rinsed them before placing them in the dishwasher.

"Yes," he replied, turning back to face her. "Despite the early morning clouds, it looks like the sun is trying to come out."

His phone rang before she could comment. She sipped her coffee, watching as his expression changed. The grim sound of his one-word responses sent a shiver up her spine.

"Thanks for letting me know, Eli," he said. "Please keep me posted if you learn anything else."

"What's going on?" she asked. She knew his brother Eli was a state trooper.

"Another body was found. This time on a remote hiking trail outside of town. Young woman, same scenario as the other four. Black dress, and cause of death appears to be strangulation."

Genna swallowed. "That's awful. They haven't even identified the fourth victim and now there's another. Even more reason to worry me and all the other women in Shelby."

"They need to catch the bastard." A muscle worked in Parker's jaw. "I know Eli is frustrated. I'm sure everyone working the case is."

Just then, a ray of sunlight broke through the clouds and beamed through the sliding-glass door. Parker turned, walked to the door and opened it. He stepped out onto his back porch, leaving the door open.

Unsure whether or not to follow, Genna pushed to her feet. After getting a second cup of coffee, she ventured outside, walking on the balls of her feet. She wanted to be ready to turn and go back in at the first sign that he might want to be alone.

Leaning on the railing, he drank his coffee and eyed the forest. "This used to feel like the safest town on earth," he said. "At least, growing up here. We used to ride our bikes and explore the woods from sunup to sundown. No one worried we might be abducted."

She walked up to stand next to him. "All the bonfires we had near the river in high school. My parents always knew I'd make it home safe."

"Yeah." He glanced at her. The dark shadows in his eyes made her heart ache. "Now everyone has to worry. Lakin has promised to never go anywhere alone. Would you mind doing the same?"

Though touched, she had to shake her head. "That's not possible," she replied. "I live by myself. I have to buy groceries and go shopping. There's no way I can live my life if I have to constantly look for someone to accompany me everywhere."

He acknowledged the truth of her statement with a dip of his chin. "Okay, but don't take any solitary hikes until this killer is caught."

"Now that, I can do," she murmured, cupping her mug with both hands. In the distance, an eagle circled, hunting. "I've never been much of a hiker." She didn't tell him that she'd gone once as a teenager with a boy she'd thought she'd liked from school and had nearly been raped. She'd been able to talk her way out of danger and had made it home unscathed, but the experience had made her understand how dangerous the wilderness could be. Not solely from wild animals, either.

"Really? It's one of my favorite activities when I'm not working."

"Isn't that one of the things you do when you *are* working?" she asked, her tone dry. "I know you take out a lot of hiking expeditions."

"True." He shrugged. "I enjoy being outdoors. There are too many fun activities, no matter the season."

She eyed him briefly. For a second, she considered asking him if he'd ever enjoyed sitting in front of a blazing fire in a warm and cozy living room, watching the snow fall outside. But then she realized it wasn't anything she needed to know. Better to think of Parker as someone completely incompatible.

Chapter 5

Parker took a deep breath. With beautiful Genna standing beside him, raw longing nearly took him out at the knees. How easy to imagine what they could be, if she'd just allow him in.

She'd kissed him. And the kiss had rocked him to the core. For one moment, one shining moment, he'd believed she'd wanted him as much as he did her.

At least she hadn't apologized.

Putting his attention back where it belonged—on the discovery of yet another likely victim of the Fiancée Killer, he took a deep, shaky breath. That woman, whoever she was, had been someone's daughter, sister, friend. To have her life snuffed out in such a horrible way was gut-wrenching.

"I hate that another woman lost her life at that serial killer's hands," Genna said, her voice somber. "I sure hope they figure out who he is and soon."

"Me, too. I think everyone does," he replied.

Taking another sip of her coffee, she looked up at him. "We'd better head for the office," she said. "I need to get the place opened up and ready for the first group. It's going to be a busy Saturday."

He glanced at his watch, saw she was right, and turned

to walk back inside. "I can go whenever. How long do you need?"

"I'm ready now."

Surprised, he nodded. "Let me grab my keys and we'll go."

She followed him into the kitchen, setting her mug down next to his in the sink. The simple act made his heart squeeze. *Ridiculous*, he chided himself, snatching his truck keys off the counter.

"Let's go."

As they drove toward headquarters with the sun shining, it was hard to believe the road had ever been under water. Everything—the trees, the grass, even the pavement—glistened.

Next to him in the passenger seat, Genna fidgeted.

"Are you okay?" he finally asked her.

"Yes," she replied. "No. Not really. Listen, we need to talk about what happened last night."

"No, we don't. Don't worry. Everything is all right."

She sighed loudly. "But it's not. You were kind enough to let me stay in your home. You fed me, too. And while I deeply, deeply appreciate that, I'm afraid I might have given you the wrong impression when I—"

"Nope," he interrupted. "No wrong impressions were made. You were asleep. You acted without thinking. If anything, I took advantage of you by kissing you back."

"Oh, please." He could almost hear her rolling her eyes. "Would you at least let me finish? I owe you an apol—"

"No." He stopped the truck, glad no one else was out and about on this road so early. "Don't you dare apologize to me. At least let me hang on to what shreds of dignity I have left."

Eyes huge, she stared at him. "I don't get it. I'm confused. What do you mean?"

As their gazes locked, again that pull of attraction passed between them. At least for him. He found it difficult to believe this could be one-sided.

"I wanted that kiss as much as you did," he elaborated. "Probably even more. If you'd have invited me into your bed, I would have gone without hesitation. To put it mildly."

Heaven help him, his blunt words not only made her swallow hard, but he swore he saw a flare of desire in her green eyes. She swayed toward him, making him realize she wasn't as immune to their connection as she pretended to be.

Now was not the time. For both their sakes, he knew he had to be strong. Turning to face the road, he shifted into Drive and continued on. Genna sat silent beside him.

They reached headquarters without incident. Everything appeared to have returned to normal and, aside from standing water in some of the ditches, he couldn't tell that there had been any flooding.

As soon as he parked, Genna had the passenger door open and was out. He followed at a more leisurely pace while she used her key to unlock the front door. Once inside, she turned on all the lights and booted up both front-counter computers before going into the back.

"Would you mind getting the coffee started?" she called out, her voice professional as she continued on her way to her office. "I need to check the schedule, but I'm pretty sure we have a tour group arriving in under an hour."

"We do," he answered. "It's my group."

"Hiking?" She turned and grinned at him.

"Not this time. Four-wheeling. Demand is high this time of the year to head up the mountain and see the fall foliage."

"Got it." And she disappeared into her office, leaving him staring after her. This wanting, this craving, made him restless. Uncomfortable in his skin. He didn't have any idea how to cure it or to make it go away. To be honest, he wasn't even sure if he wanted to.

After turning on the coffee maker, he wandered back outside to make sure no trees had been felled by the storm.

Spence arrived just as Parker returned from making sure the path up the mountain hadn't been blocked. As far as he could tell, it had looked clear.

"I'm worried about the river," Spence said after they exchanged greetings. "I'm supposed to take a small tour group out fishing. But after that storm, I'm concerned."

"I hear you. You might end up river-rafting instead," Parker quipped, only half joking.

"Exactly." Spence checked his wrist. "I'm going to drive down there. Want to go with me and check it out?"

"I wish I could, but my group will be here in fifteen minutes," Parker answered.

Spence responded with a wave and strode off to his truck.

The rest of the day passed in a blur. As always, Parker enjoyed the hell out of the four-wheeling expedition. He'd always liked mud and, after all the rain, there was plenty of that to go around.

Lots of laughs, cheers, especially when they had to tow one of the four-wheelers out of the mud. Sunburned, mud-splattered and happy, the group finally returned to RTA headquarters where Parker turned them over to Genna. She raised a brow at their appearance, but didn't comment.

Instead of taking himself off for a shower, Parker stood near the door and watched Genna interact with the customers. Her friendly smile clearly charmed them. Several of the guys flirted with her, which caused a muscle to twitch in Parker's jaw.

As they finished checking out, one by one they left. Several high-fived Parker on the way out. One guy gave him a fist bump and a few just waved.

Finally, they were all gone, leaving Parker alone with Genna.

"You should see yourself," she said, still smiling. "Every single one of your group looks like they took a mud bath."

"We kind of did," he admitted, grinning back at her. "It was a blast."

He could have stood there for eternity and allowed himself to get lost in Genna's gaze.

Instead, the door opened behind him and Spence walked in. The instant he caught sight of Parker, he burst out laughing. "Damn, I wish I'd had that trip instead of mine. Though with the river as high as it is, I might get a little bit wet."

"Do you think it's safe?" Parker asked.

"As far as I can tell, yes. We'll turn back if we encounter anything concerning."

Spence's group started straggling in and Genna busied herself with checking them in. Hetty Amos, their pilot and guide, arrived, laughed at Parker, and signed on to the other computer. Parker asked her quietly if she would be around awhile since Spence would be taking his group out and Parker wanted to run home, shower and change.

"Sure," she replied. "I know the rule. No females are to be alone. I got you. Go get yourself cleaned up. I'll be here for the next couple of hours."

Relieved, he thanked her, waved at Genna, and headed out.

Once home, he shed his muddy clothes and jumped into the shower. An image flashed into his mind of Genna, naked in the shower with him, water sluicing off her perfect, glistening body. Forcefully, he shoved the thought, and the instant bolt of heat it brought, away.

After drying off, he dressed in clean clothes and wandered into the kitchen in search of something to eat. He made a sandwich and ate it alone at the kitchen table. While he did, he realized his house felt…empty. In the brief time Genna had been there, her vibrant presence had filled the space with something he hadn't even realized had been missing.

He really had it bad. Grimacing at his own foolishness, he finished his meal, washing it down with a big glass of water. When had he become so lame, sitting around mooning over a woman who alternated between wanting no part of him and pulling him down for a kiss?

That kiss. Heat had instantly consumed him, taking him right back to the night they'd spent together. They'd feasted on each other, laughed and made love and slept before making love again. Parker had never lacked feminine attention, but what he and Genna had shared had been on an entirely new level.

Then last night, alone in his bed after she'd kissed him, achingly aware of her asleep in the room down the hall, he'd burned with wanting her.

Now he couldn't stop thinking of things he wanted to do to her, with her. Most of them carnal.

But some of them, surprisingly, were not. He dreamt of sharing things with her. A sunrise at the top of the mountain, a quiet moment in a double kayak out in the middle of a serene lake. Dinner and drinks, holding her close as they swayed to the music of the band.

In short, he wanted more. In fact, he realized all of it sounded an awful lot like a relationship. Something he'd avoided like the plague the last several years.

He had his reasons, most of them centered around how badly he'd been hurt when he fell for Genna the last time. Also, he told himself that he liked his freedom far too much to give any of it up for another person. Now, he had begun to understand that maybe he simply hadn't met the right one.

Shaking his head, he pushed such foolish thoughts away. Genna had made it crystal-clear that she had no desire to pursue any kind of romantic anything with him. Except, then why had she kissed him?

Unsure what to take away from all of that, he decided it would be better not to dwell on it at all. Otherwise, her simple kiss might give him false hope. Which could be painful. He'd never been the type to moon over a woman and he didn't plan to start now.

Yet he couldn't seem to stop yearning for her.

The way he saw it, he had two choices. He could work hard to force himself to see her only as a friend—unlikely. Or he could try his best to get her to open herself up to the possibility of a fresh start between them.

Because right now, he had to believe they were meant to be together.

Once Genna finished checking in the latest group of excited tourists, Spence loaded them up and drove them away. Needing to avoid how the quiet office made her worried thoughts resurface, she made small talk with Hetty. Both Shelby natives, they were close in age. Genna didn't know her well, being a couple of years older than Hetty and they hadn't hung out together in high school. She did know Lakin was dating Hetty's youngest brother Troy.

The fact that Hetty had become a pilot fascinated Genna and she told the other woman so.

"You'll have to come up with me some time," Hetty said, smiling. "It's beautiful, so peaceful and serene. I do my best thinking when I'm high above the ground."

"I'd love that." Genna checked the time. "But right now I've got to make a few personal calls. I need to call a door repair place and an alarm installation company."

"What happened?"

Genna told her about the break-in, though she omitted the fact that she'd spent the night at Parker's.

"I've got a guy," Hetty said, "both for the door and the alarm. Let me give you their names and numbers."

Grateful, Genna thanked her. Hetty scribbled down the information on a slip of paper and handed it to her.

"Does Parker know about this?" Hetty asked, her expression serious.

Genna slowly nodded. "He does. He said something about repairing my door himself, but I'd rather just hire someone."

"If they can get out today, I get it. But if they can't, let Spence and Parker see what they can do. As I'm sure you're aware, it's not safe."

"I know. And thanks for the idea. I'll definitely talk to one of them if I don't have any luck," Genna replied, meaning it. Especially since it was unlikely she'd find anyone who could come out and do the repair today. Maybe if she'd had time to call earlier in the morning. She'd have to try and see.

To her surprise, both the door company and the alarm place sounded eager to have her business, especially when she told them Hetty had referred her. They each promised to be out between five and eight that same evening.

After agreeing, she hung up and marveled at her luck. Then she told Hetty she'd need to leave a little early to meet the workers.

"I'm just glad it worked out," Hetty said. "And don't worry, I can cover the front desk for the rest of the night."

"I appreciate that. But we've got to make sure you're not here all alone."

Drumming her fingers on the counter, Genna thought for a moment. "Hopefully, Parker or Spence or one of the other guides can stay here with you once I leave."

"I'm sure we'll find someone." Hetty didn't seem concerned. But then she looked up at Genna and frowned. "What about you? Is anyone else going to be there at your place when you meet up with the door and alarm companies?"

Surprised, Genna shook her head. "I live alone," she explained. "I'm sure it'll be fine. I don't know if both companies will be there at the same time, but I'm just relieved I can get someone out tonight. Once I get all of that done, I should be able to sleep safely in my own house."

Hetty shook her head. "Girl, you are missing the point. What if one of those workmen aren't on the up-and-up?"

Dumbfounded, Genna stared. "But you referred both companies to me. Are you saying they aren't reputable?"

"That's not what I'm saying at all. Don't you watch

any true crime TV? What if the Fiancée Killer took out one of the legitimate workers and traded places, just so he could get to you?"

"Seriously?"

"Yes." Hetty nodded. "Heck, even serial killers have jobs. You never know what that guy does when he's not going around murdering women. You have to be prepared for any possibility, even if it seems unlikely."

The front desk phone rang just then, saving Genna from replying. After she dealt with the caller, she turned to see that Hetty had gotten on her phone, too.

Though she thought Hetty's scenario disturbing, once uttered, it took root inside Genna's mind. Suddenly she found herself nervous, unsure if she should go through with her plans for that evening.

Except, she really needed to have her front door repaired. And an alarm system wasn't something she was willing to put off any longer.

Parker's truck pulled in. She watched through the front window as he got out and strode up to the front porch. She needed to check the schedule, but she thought he had one more trip that afternoon. He'd be taking a group of hikers up to look for wildlife and fall foliage.

Which meant he'd likely finish before she had to leave.

Maybe she'd ask him to go meet the workmen with her.

Entering the room, Parker greeted her and Hetty with a broad smile. "It's a beautiful day," he said. "Hard to believe it was storming so badly yesterday."

Genna nodded. Hetty ended her phone call and frowned. "Genna's leaving a little early. She's having two different workmen at her place tonight. With everything that's been going on, I don't think she should be alone with them. Don't you agree?"

He swung his blue-eyed gaze to Genna. “Definitely,” he replied. “Genna, would it be all right with you if I come over and help? Just in case?”

She liked that he’d asked her instead of just insisting. “That’d be great, but we also need to make sure Hetty isn’t alone here after I leave.”

“Spence will be back by then,” Hetty noted, dismissing her concern with an elegant wave of her hand. “He’ll stay.”

Two vehicles pulled up and parked. “I think your next group is starting to arrive,” Genna said.

“I’m ready.” Parker rubbed his hands together. “It’s a small group this time. There are only six. Once you get them checked in, we’ll take off. It’s a two-hour hike with a break at the top of the mountain. When I get back, after they’re all processed, we’ll head out. I’ll follow you to your place.”

The front door opened before she could respond. Six people filed through the door, all talking at once. She checked them in one by one, enjoying their obvious excitement.

Finally, they were ready to go. Parker gave them a brief talk, made sure everyone had what they needed in their backpacks, and led them out the door.

Genna watched him leave, unable to look away until he and his group disappeared from sight.

“So that’s how it is?” Hetty teased, grinning. “The sparks flying between the two of you just about set this place on fire.”

Though Genna felt her face heat, she managed to play it off. “You definitely have a huge imagination,” she replied, trying to keep her voice level.

“Whatever.” Hetty shrugged. “Not any of my business.”

The rest of the afternoon passed swiftly. Spence and his bunch returned with plenty of fish. They were a group of happy customers. As Genna checked them out in the system, several volunteered that they planned to write glowing reviews.

"We appreciate that," Genna said, smiling. Even Hetty looked up from scrolling her phone and grinned with approval.

Nonchalant, Spence strolled around to the back counter. "I aim to please," he announced with a cheerful wink.

After they'd all left, Genna filled Spence in on her situation.

He nodded with approval when she told him Parker would be following her to her house. "Good," he said. "And I'll stay here and help Hetty close the office. Right now, no female in Shelby needs to be around strange men when she's alone."

"That's what I said," Hetty chimed in.

"Then I'm glad Genna listened." Spence's cell phone rang and he stepped outside onto the front porch to take the call.

Since she'd be leaving early, Genna got busy filing all her electronic paperwork and setting everything up for whoever would be opening tomorrow. She had the day off; something she was actually looking forward to.

The last part of the afternoon seemed unusually quiet. She answered a few phone calls inquiring about tours, directed them all to the website, and checked a few times to see if there'd been any new reservations.

Hetty had gone outside to talk to Spence. Genna could see the two of them sitting in the oversized wooden chairs enjoying the sunshine. They made a cute couple. The love they shared was palpable.

This job, this place, and these people, felt like family, she realized. This sense of belonging, of camaraderie, was exactly what she needed at this stage of her life. Even if she had some definitely different kinds of thoughts about Parker.

Eventually, Parker and his group wandered back in. Some of them were red-faced and perspiring, other seemed out of breath, but they all appeared happy. She began the checkout process, asking each one about their experience. Without exception, the guests raved about the wildlife and the colorful autumn foliage, glad they'd taken the hike and gotten the exercise.

After they'd all cleared out, she looked up to see Parker and Spence deep in conversation. Hetty had answered the phone and, from the sounds of it, had signed the caller up for one of the winter snowmobile tours.

Heart full, Genna began gathering up her belongings, getting ready to leave. When she straightened, backpack over her shoulder, she noticed Parker watching her. The heat in his gaze made her knees weak.

"Are you about ready to go?" he asked.

"I am." She nodded, looking away. "How about you?"

"Ready when you are."

After waving goodbye to Spence and Hetty, Genna headed outside with Parker right behind her. She got into her car and started it. Driving away, the sight of Parker's large pickup truck in her rearview mirror comforted her.

As she pulled up into her own driveway, hitting the button to open her garage door, she wondered if their strategy to block the front door had worked. If not, she realized the possibility existed that an intruder might still be inside.

After turning off her engine, she waited for Parker to

get out of his truck. Catching sight of her expression, he lightly squeezed her shoulder. "Do you want me to go first?" he asked.

"Yes, please."

Staying close to him as he stepped inside, she fought the urge to reach for his hand. Instead, she focused on switching on the lights.

In the living room, the furniture they'd carefully piled against the front door appeared to be undisturbed. Relieved, she exhaled.

"It doesn't look like anyone tried to force their way in," Parker said. "Let's get all this moved so your door guy can work on this."

Once they'd done that, she offered him a soft drink or an iced tea. He asked for water instead.

Right after she'd brought him a glass, her doorbell rang. Since the front door wouldn't close all the way, she was glad they hadn't knocked.

"I'm with Shelby Alarm Service," the young, bearded man announced. "I understand I'm here to do an installation."

"Come in," she said, suddenly glad Parker had insisted on keeping her company. "I'm sure they told you already, but I signed up for the full package. Window and door sensors and motion sensors. With monitoring."

He consulted his clipboard. "Yes, ma'am. That's what I show on my work order."

"Perfect." She stepped back. "Then I'll let you get to it. I'm expecting someone else to repair my front door."

That contractor arrived a few minutes later. He took one look at the splintered frame and damaged door and shook his head. "You're going to need to replace all of this," he said. "It's not repairable."

Hearing him, she glanced at Parker for confirmation.

"I don't know about that," Parker said. "Can you show me why you can't just replace the frame?"

Genna went to check on the alarm guy while the other two men discussed the front door.

She found him installing sensors on all her windows. "When your system is armed, if anyone tried to open a window, or a door for that matter, it will alert."

"Just here?" she asked. "Or at the monitoring center, too?"

"Both. Once it alerts, if you don't deactivate it, we will call you and ask for your password. If you don't answer or give an incorrect response, we contact the police."

Which was exactly what she wanted.

"I heard another body was found," the man said, not looking up from his work. "I bet we get a ton of installation calls now. It's not possible to be too safe."

"I agree." That said, she left him alone to work and went back to check on the front door.

Parker smiled when he saw her. "Looks like you're getting a new everything," he said. "He's putting in a reinforced steel door instead of a wooden one."

"Perfect," she told him. Then, because she imagined installers would much prefer to do their work without the homeowner standing over their shoulders, she took herself off to the kitchen.

To her surprise, Parker followed her. "When all this is done, how about we go out and grab dinner together?" he asked.

Surprised, she looked up at him. When she saw the heat in his eyes, she sucked in her breath. "As friends?" Her answer came out a bit shakier than she would have liked.

"Sure. Why not?" But the hint of mischief in his smile said otherwise.

She almost turned him down. Almost. But the part of her that had made her kiss him had her deciding to go. After all, she could either spend the rest of her life attempting to ignore the attraction between them and keep things on a friendly level, or she could go along with the flow. Judging by the way her luck with men and relationships went, it wouldn't take much to make Parker realize they'd be better off as simply coworkers. Possibly even friends. But nothing more.

"Sure," she answered, looking down so he couldn't see the conflicted emotions in her expression. "As long as it's not too late."

She opened the refrigerator and grabbed the leftover bottle of wine they'd shared during the storm. "Do you want a glass?" she asked. "I'm about to pour myself one and go sit out on the back porch. You're welcome to join me."

Since her yard was enclosed by a six-foot-tall cedar fence, she figured she'd be safe enough alone for a few minutes. Even if she wasn't, this was her home. She refused to spend every waking moment inside her house quaking in fear.

"I'll be out there in a few," he said, evidently reaching the same conclusion. "After I check on both contractors to see how much longer they've got."

"Let me know," she replied, pouring a generous glass. "And help yourself if you want wine."

Taking a small sip, she made her way outside. Already, she'd begun to reconsider agreeing to go out to eat with him. But then again, doing so seemed like the least she could do after all he'd done to help her.

She shook her head. She'd never been in the habit of lying to herself and didn't intend to start now. If she ever intended to regard Parker as nothing more than a friend, she had to get whatever this was out of her system. Starting tonight.

Chapter 6

When Genna agreed to have dinner with him, Parker felt like he'd won the lottery. He couldn't help but be glad she'd looked away, because he didn't want her to realize how stoked he was.

Actually, he hadn't really thought she'd say yes.

But since she had, he didn't want to take a chance he'd inadvertently give her any reason to change her mind.

The front door guy was nearly finished. He'd removed the splintered door frame and installed a new one. "It'll need to be painted," he told Parker. "She can also paint the new door. It's white. Most people like some color."

Since Parker had no idea what Genna would like, he simply nodded.

"It's a shame another body was found," the guy said, continuing to work. "I hate the way this serial killer has everyone in town on edge."

"Me, too." Parker replied. "And they haven't been able to identify that fourth body yet. Now there's been a fifth."

"Yeah, it's awful." Finishing with the bottom hinge, the worker started on the middle one. "I should be done in just a few minutes. Then I just have to write up the invoice."

Parker wondered how Genna would react if he simply

paid for the door. Not well, he suspected. "I'll go get her when you're done," he said.

Then he went to see how the alarm installation was going.

"I'm just about done with the window sensors," the installer said as soon as he saw Parker. "Obviously, I can't do the front door until it's in place. But I can work on getting the control box set up."

"How long will that take?" Though Parker didn't want to seem impatient, he couldn't wait to take Genna out to dinner. Even though neither had called it a date, just spending time with her in a nonwork setting sounded amazing. They could get to know each other, without pressure.

"Maybe thirty minutes."

Satisfied with the answer, Parker left to check on Genna outside. He found her kicked back in a wicker chair, feet up on an ottoman, sipping on a glass of wine.

The sky had barely started to darken, the setting sun coloring the western horizon in vivid shades of pink and orange. He walked to the porch railing and looked out over Genna's large, fenced backyard. A raised bed for vegetable took up one corner and strategically planted evergreens gave the space a balanced ambience.

"I've been thinking about getting a dog," Genna said. "Partly for companionship, but also as an added layer of protection. A dog would alert me if someone was skulking around outside."

Surprised, he turned to look at her. "Have you ever owned a dog before?"

"Growing up, we had Binx. My dad got him from the city animal shelter in Fairbanks. No one knew for sure what combination of breeds he was, but he was big and lovable. He lived to be nearly fifteen." She sighed. "We all missed him so much. My mom said she never wanted to feel that kind of pain again, so they didn't get another dog."

"What about you?" he asked, genuinely curious. "Once you moved out on your own, you never thought about it?"

"I did. But you know how it is. I never had the time, didn't want the responsibility. I wasn't ready."

"And now you think you are?"

She nodded. "Yes. Now, I think I am." Taking another sip of wine, she eyed him. "What about you? Do you have any pets?"

"Not currently. I lost my boy Trooper to cancer this past winter. He was my buddy. He and I went everywhere together. Hiking, fishing, four-wheeling—he loved it all. He was the unofficial RTA dog." He didn't even try to keep the sorrow from his voice. "That's his photo in the lobby. I miss him more than I can say."

"I'm sorry," she said, her gentle tone matching the compassion in her gaze. "I have an idea. I'm off tomorrow and have been thinking about driving over to Valdez to check out the dogs in the shelter. Would you like to go with me?"

Though he knew he had two tours booked the next day, he nodded. He would move the tours. "I would," he said, taking care to sound as casual as possible. "When were you thinking of going?"

Her smile lit up not only her face but sent a bolt of raw desire through him. "We can work around your schedule. It's only about a half-hour drive there, so just let me know when you're available."

Mouth dry, he managed to nod. Right then the front door installer came looking for Genna.

"All done," he said, handing her an invoice. "We take credit cards, Venmo or Zelle, however you want to pay."

She sat up, looking over the paper before nodding. "Let me get my wallet." Pushing to her feet, she headed inside, the installer right behind her.

Parker went, too. While Genna paid with one of her credit cards, he went to check on the alarm guy's progress.

"Almost done," the man said cheerfully as soon as Parker appeared. "I just need to run a quick test." He looked around. "But I'll need the homeowner here. We've got to set up her password."

Genna and the door installer appeared, just in time for her to hear the last comment. "I'll be right there," she said. "I need to check out my new front door."

Parker decided to go with her.

"You can paint this any color you like," he told her, noting the way she eyed the white door. Her former door had been emerald green.

"Good. I'm thinking red." She made a show of inspecting it. "Looks good. Thank you so much for coming out quickly."

"No problem." The man turned to go, but at the last moment appeared to remember something. "Extra keys," he said, pulling them from his pocket. "Here you go."

Accepting them, she watched as he got into his truck and drove away. Then, closing the door behind her, she returned to the hallway where the alarm control panel had been mounted on the wall.

When she chose her password, she made sure no one, including Parker, stood too close. Instead of feeling hurt, he wanted to clap. He liked that she took precautions to protect herself, even as he hoped she knew she had nothing to fear from him.

After a demonstration that involved having the alarm go off and the monitoring company calling, the installer declared he had finished. Genna paid him, too, and showed him to the door.

Finally, they were alone.

"Expensive day," Genna drawled, placing the invoice on the counter with the other. "But at least I'll have peace of mind."

Parker waited in the living room while she went to get ready to go out to eat. When she returned, she had changed out of her RTA shirt into a bright green T-shirt. The color matched her eyes.

She looked stunning.

"Where do you want to eat?" Parker asked, hoping she hadn't noticed his reaction. More than anything, he wanted to keep things casual. He sensed anything else would only frighten her away.

"I don't care," Genna responded. "Surprise me."

Briefly, he considered asking her what she liked and disliked, but decided not to. He didn't want to get in to one of those long discussions where one person suggests something, the other one vetoes it, and nothing is ever decided.

"You're sure you want me to choose," he asked, just to clarify.

"Yes. I'm too tired to even think about it. I just want to eat and relax. I'm sure you know where the best places to eat are. I'm down for whatever."

"Then let's go." He pulled out his keys. "I'll drive."

"Perfect."

He decided on sushi. A new place had opened up downtown and he hadn't tried it yet, though he'd heard good things. If for some reason, Genna didn't like sushi, there were several other items on the menu for her to eat.

As he drove, with the radio on KVAC, playing country music, he enjoyed the way Genna didn't feel the need to fill the silence with chatter. But as they pulled into the restaurant's parking lot, he glanced at her and realized she'd fallen soundly asleep.

When she'd said she felt tired, she hadn't been exaggerating.

Hating to wake her, he wasn't sure what to do. Should he drive around awhile, hoping she woke on her own? Or park and see if the simple lack of motion might do the trick?

His stomach rumbled, reminding him that he needed to eat. He decided to go ahead and park. Hopefully, she'd wake up.

Once he'd pulled into a slot and turned off the engine, Genna stirred. Not awake. Not yet anyway. She sighed, still sleeping, and then slowly opened her eyes. When her drowsy gaze found him, he sucked in his breath. A different kind of hunger filled him. He knew better than to act on it, so instead he allowed himself sit and watch her while she slowly came awake. "What happened?" she asked, stretching. Then, clearly realizing they were in his truck, she smiled sheepishly. "I'm guessing I fell asleep."

Before he could answer, she yawned, covering her mouth. "Sorry."

He found her so endearing that he ached. "No need to apologize. Do you want to go in and eat or would you rather I take you home so you can sleep?"

For the first time, she appeared to realize where they were.

"Sushi?" she asked, her voice incredulous. "You like sushi?"

"Yes. Do you?"

The brilliant smile spreading across her face made him think that she did. "I love it, actually. And I've been dying to try this place. I've seen good things about it online."

Just then, his stomach growled, loudly enough to make her laugh. "I can see you're hungry. I think I'm finally alert enough to go inside and eat."

Successfully fighting the urge to lean over and kiss her, he hopped out of the truck instead. Going around to her side, he managed to get the passenger door open before she did. When he offered his hand, she took it, sliding her fingers into his and allowing him to help her down.

When she didn't immediately pull away, he decided to go with it. They walked into the restaurant, hand in hand.

Inside, the place seemed fairly crowded. Busy, but not packed. They were immediately showed to a booth near one of the floor-to-ceiling windows and given menus.

Though he hated to let go of her, Parker helped her take a seat. He then slid across from her in the booth. Opening his menu, he began reading. When he glanced at her and she smiled, he felt the power of that smile all the into his bones.

"How about we try several different rolls and share them?" he asked. "That way we can sample a variety of things."

She nodded, appearing to like the idea. "That's fine with me as long as we split the bill half and half," she answered. "Sushi is expensive, after all."

He suspected she didn't want him to think this evening was an actual date. Which, as far as he was concerned, it definitely was.

"Sure," he said without hesitation. "I was thinking it was your turn to treat, but we can split it if that's what you want."

It took a moment for her to realize he was joking, though he'd made sure to keep his tone light. He saw the moment she got it. Her mouth tightened and she frowned.

"You know what?" she said, her voice firm. "I think I'll let you treat this time. I haven't gotten my first paycheck yet, so your kindness would be greatly appreciated."

He couldn't help but laugh. "That's what I wanted to do all along."

"You played me," she told him, wagging her finger at him but apparently unable to keep from smiling. "But that's okay. I'll get it next time."

"I'll hold you to that." Still smiling, he leaned back. "I'm just glad you agree there will be a next time."

Genna didn't respond. Instead, she glanced up at him through her lashes and smiled.

He decided to take that as a yes.

Sitting across from Parker Colton at one of the newest and trendiest restaurants in town, Genna felt rejuvenated. Whether from her brief nap or simply due to his presence, she wasn't sure. Either way, she felt more alive in this moment than she had since the kiss. And there it was again. *The Kiss*. An action she should have regretted but instead wanted to repeat. And more.

Parker wanted more, too. She could tell from the heat in his gaze when he looked at her, the way she caught him studying her when he thought she wouldn't notice. She had no idea what to make of the chemistry between them, but she could no longer deny it existed.

Part of her wanted to see where it led. But she loved her job. She really hadn't thought she'd find something she enjoyed that paid so well. And if she and Parker developed a relationship and it went south, then she'd lose her job.

The question she needed to answer was if she wanted him enough to risk that.

Which is why she hadn't responded when he'd hinted that he wanted a "next time."

The waitress arrived to take their order. Shaking her head, Genna gestured toward Parker, letting him order what rolls they'd share. She'd never have been able to decide anyway. All of them sounded amazing.

Taking another small sip of her wine, she studied the handsome man across from her. With his tousled mane of sun-streaked hair and bright blue eyes, he drew more than his fair share of glances from women walking by.

He looked both comfortable in his skin and at one with the outdoors. The kind of man who knew how to be gentle yet would place himself between her and a pack of hungry wolves and fight them off with his bare hands.

And in bed… A flash of heat shot through her entire body. Despite how much time had passed since they'd shared a bed and their bodies, she didn't think she'd ever forget how his lovemaking had made her feel.

Blinking, she realized Parker had tilted his head and was regarding her with a quizzical expression. "Are you all right?" he asked. "You look like you went very far away just now."

Since she definitely couldn't tell him what she'd been thinking, she simply shrugged.

The first of the sushi rolls arrived. One entrée had been arranged into an elaborate tower of sushi. "That looks too beautiful to eat," she said.

He grinned. "Not for me." To prove his point, he plucked one off the tower and plopped it into his mouth. Rolling his eyes, he made sounds of appreciation as he chewed.

What could she do but laugh and then try it herself?

They ate and talked and ate some more. She finished her wine and switched to hot tea. When all the platters of sushi had arrived, she'd figured there wouldn't be any possible way they'd eat it all. Turns out, she was wrong.

Replete, they passed up the waitress's offering of saki. When the check came, Parker paid. "Are you ready to go?" he asked.

So full, she could barely move, Genna nodded. She figured she'd waddle out to his truck and hope she didn't fall asleep on the way home.

"I feel like we kind of gorged ourselves on sushi," she mused.

Her comment made him grin. "I love watching you eat."

Unsure how to take his comment, she cocked her head. "What do you mean?"

Leaning in, he lowered his voice. "It's sexy as hell."

A jolt of pure lust lanced through her. To hide it, she looked down, fiddled with her napkin and her empty wineglass.

He held out his arm and she took it.

The simple act of being close to him kept her heart racing, though she hoped he couldn't tell. As they walked to his truck, her thoughts were a jumbled mess. Should she invite him in? Suggest a nightcap? Or maybe instead of taking her home, should she see if he might want to go someplace for a drink?

In the end, she decided to let him take her home. Then, depending on whether or not he acted reluctant to leave, she'd play it by ear.

When they pulled up into her driveway, he shifted into Park and killed the engine. "I'll walk you up to your front door," he said, his tone leaving no room for disagreement. "I want to make sure your new alarm system is working before I head home."

Hiding her disappointment, she slowly nodded. "Thanks. I appreciate that."

Using her key, she unlocked the front door. Immediately, her alarm began beeping. She hurried over to the keypad and keyed in her code to stop it. Turning, she eyed Parker standing near the threshold, as if reluctant to enter.

What the heck. She decided she might as well go for it. "Do you want to have a drink before you go?"

His easy smile once again kindled that spark low in her belly. "Normally, I'd love to. But I know you're exhausted. How about I take a rain check on that drink? I'll see you tomorrow when we drive out to Valdez."

"Sounds good." Despite it being anything but, she kept her tone light. Walking him out, she stood in the doorway and watched as he got into his truck.

His taillights had just vanished from view when her phone rang. Her mother. She stepped back inside, closed and locked the door before answering. "Hi, Mom."

"Why didn't you call and tell me about the break-in?" her mother demanded. "I had to hear it from Gladys. I called her a few minutes ago to catch up and she told me."

Proving once again how efficiently gossip spread in a small town.

"Honestly, I haven't had time," Genna said. "I had to work, and then schedule an appointment to get the front door repaired. The good news—that's done. I also had an alarm system installed."

For once, her mother was speechless. "You what?" she finally asked. Then, before Genna could answer, she turned and told Genna's father. "I'm putting the phone on speaker, dear," she said.

"Ok, Mom. Hi, Dad."

"I think you should close up the house and come stay with us in Hawaii," her father said, his gruff voice tinged with concern.

Surprised, Genna wasn't sure how to respond.

"I do, too," her mother said. "It's not safe for you there. I understand a fifth body was discovered."

Though Genna had always wanted to see Hawaii, leaving Shelby now would feel too much like fleeing. Which is exactly what she'd done when she'd left Anchorage as soon as her divorce had been finalized. Plus, she loved her job. Finally, she had to admit the thought of never seeing Parker again made her stomach hurt.

"I feel relatively safe," Genna said. And then she explained all the measures RTA had taken to ensure their female employees were never at risk.

"That's great, honey," her mom replied. "But someone broke into the house. You live there alone. How do you know that this Fiancée Killer isn't targeting you?"

The notion sent a shiver up Genna's spine. "I don't," she admitted. "But if it makes you feel better, I'm driving out to Valdez to visit the animal shelter. I've been wanting a dog for a while."

"A dog?" Both her parents spoke at once, sounding dismayed. They'd never been the kind of people to have pets.

"Yes. I'd like to adopt a large dog in need of a good home. Not only will he and I keep each other company, but he'll also be an added deterrent if anyone tries to break in here again."

"That does make sense," her mom said slowly. "Just don't let it on the furniture."

"Of course not," Genna lied. "Anyway, it was great to hear from you both. I promise to keep you posted."

"And check in more," her father said, his voice stern. "Your mother and I worry."

"I know you do. And I love you for it," Genna replied. "But please, try to understand. I'm just now finding my feet after the divorce. I don't want to go somewhere else and start all over yet again."

"Well, if you change your mind, you're always welcome here." Her mom sounded a bit teary.

"I will." Ending the call, Genna swallowed past the lump in her throat.

The rest of the night, Genna found herself jumping at every little sound. She set the alarm as soon as darkness fell, well before bedtime. Turning the TV on despite the fact that she felt too restless to sit down and watch anything, she found herself constantly picking up her phone. Hoping Parker would text or, even better, call.

Even though they were riding into Valdez together tomorrow, tonight she really needed to hear his voice. Quickly scrolling to his contact info, she pressed the button to call him.

When he answered on the second ring, her heart lurched. "Hey," she managed, feeling like a fool.

"Hey, yourself," he replied. How he managed to make two simple words sound so sexy, she had no idea.

"I just wanted to firm up our plans for tomorrow," she managed to say.

"I figured." His easy response went a long way toward settling her nerves. "What time does the shelter open?"

"Eleven," she replied. "They're open until four thirty."

"I'll see you at ten thirty," he said. "Sleep well."

She told him the same and then ended the call.

As she got ready for bed, to her relief, she realized she felt drowsy. Crawling in between the sheets, she switched off her lamp and hoped to fall asleep quickly.

A sound woke her, dragging her out of a deep slumber in the darkest part of the night. Sitting upright, she listened. Nothing. Then, reminding herself that she had an alarm system now, she put her head back on the pillow and tried to go back to sleep.

Just as she'd started to drift off, the loud shriek of her alarm had her jumping up. She started to turn on the light, but realized that if someone had actually broken into her house, that might make it easier for them to locate her.

Sixty seconds seemed to take forever. She thumbed down the volume on her phone, so when the monitoring company called, the intruder wouldn't hear. She wasn't sure if she should answer or not since she wanted them to call the police.

Halfway through her waiting, her mind still slightly groggy from sleep, she realized she should call 9-1-1. She did that and told the dispatcher in a quiet voice that she thought someone was inside her house.

A loud clatter from the living room made her freeze. "There's definitely someone here," she murmured. "They haven't turned on any lights so far. I'm hiding in my bedroom in the dark."

"Can you get out?" the dispatcher asked. "As in, leave now?"

Since to do that she'd have to go through the living room, she answered no. "Just send someone right away. I'm worried it might be the Fiancée Killer."

"We have officers on the way," the dispatcher said. "Please stay on the line until they arrive."

Another sound, louder and closer, nearly made Genna

drop the phone. Juggling it to keep it from hitting the floor, she accidentally hit the button to end the call. Aware they'd call back, she struggled not to hyperventilate. Now, she actually found herself regretting not taking her parents up on their offer to go to Hawaii.

Parker. She sent him a quick text, figuring he was probably asleep.

Someone is in the house. Alarm went off and I can hear them. Called 911. Police are on the way.

Not expecting a reply, she set the phone down on the carpet. As expected, the police dispatcher called back, but Genna didn't answer. Instead, she let the call go to voicemail.

Sirens sounded, still distant, but clearly getting closer. Though she wondered why they didn't try to be stealthier, she was grateful for the prompt response. Every breath, every heartbeat, the way she tensed at every sound, and how impossible it was to keep herself from trembling, spoke to her absolute terror.

Flashing lights reflecting on the wall announced the police car's arrival. Another loud crash from downstairs and then she heard the police rapping hard on her front door.

Should she risk leaving her hiding place to let them in? Since, otherwise, she knew they'd likely damage her brand-new front door, she decided to take the chance.

As she sprinted from her bedroom down the hallway to the front of the house, she prayed no one would reach out from the shadows and grab her.

Flicking on the light, she opened the front door. Two uniformed officers stood on her front porch, and as she stepped aside so they could enter, another squad car pulled up, lights flashing.

As she quickly explained the situation, the second officers joined the first two. Asking her to stay put, they told her they'd conduct a thorough search of her house.

"Genna?" Parker sprinted up the front steps and swept her into his arms. "Are you all right?"

Clinging to him, she nodded. "Now I am. They're searching my house. The alarm went off right after I heard a loud sound. It must have been someone breaking in."

"And they had no idea you'd installed an alarm."

Despite him holding her, she couldn't stop trembling. "Why?" she asked, not really expecting an answer. "Why is someone doing this to me?"

"I don't know." Pressing a kiss against her temple, he smoothed the hair away from her face.

A sound made her back out of Parker's arms.

Two of the police officers had returned. "Looks like the intruder busted in your back door. And, likely, that's how they left. It's sitting wide open."

Not another broken door.

"Can you tell us if anything is missing?" the second officer asked. "Would you mind just taking a quick look around?"

At first, she couldn't seem to make herself move. But then Parker took her hand and squeezed her fingers. "Come on," he said. "You can do this."

Slowly, she nodded. "You're right," she replied. "I can."

With him by her side, she walked through her parents' house. Once again, everything appeared undisturbed. "I don't think anything is missing," she said. "Which means the intruder..."

She couldn't finish the sentence.

"We'll need you to sign this, ma'am," the first officer said. "We'll file a report once you do. My suggestion to you is to install a stronger lock on that back door. A dead bolt, like the one you have up front. But for now, it should be secure enough."

"Thank you." She took his tablet and signed, deciding not to mention that "secure enough" had done nothing to keep the intruder out. "I'll get that done first thing in the morning."

Parker squeezed her fingers again. "I'll do it for you."

Grateful, she thanked him.

Together, they watched the police officers leave.

No way did she want Parker to go and leave her there alone. In fact, she didn't know that she could ever spend another night alone in this house again.

Chapter 7

Glancing at Genna, standing ramrod-straight and clearly struggling to hold it together, Parker clamped his jaw shut. He hated nothing worse than seeing a strong, capable woman like her reduced to fighting back tears.

When she raised her gaze to meet his, he saw the shattered emotions and terror in her eyes. Immediately, he pulled her close, noting how fragile her slender body felt. Trembling, she clung to him.

"I can't," she muttered, against his chest. "I just can't."

Unsure what she meant, he made a sympathetic sound and continued to rub her back. He'd offer her comfort until she let him know she didn't need it any longer.

And, despite the heat simmering in his blood as he held her close, he refused to take advantage of her distress. Not in any way, shape, or form.

When she pulled out of his arms, he quickly released her. Stepping back, he jammed his hands into his pockets so he wouldn't touch her. "Are you going to be okay?" he asked gently.

"No." She swallowed hard. "I'm not. In fact, I have a huge favor to ask. Would you mind if I stay at your house again?"

"Of course, I don't mind," he replied. "You're welcome to stay as long as you need."

"Thank you." Glancing around as if she expected someone to step out from the shadows, she met his eyes. "Until the police figure out who is trying to break into my house and why, I'm going to take you up on it."

Though his first reaction—joy—made him want to grin, he knew that was the last thing she needed right now. Instead, he gave her a grave nod. "Why don't you go get packed? Take as much as you need, but remember, we can always come back and get more clothes if you need them."

"Thank you." She didn't bother to hide her relief. "Give me a few minutes. Go ahead and help yourself to a drink or snack or whatever you want."

That said, she hurried out of the room.

When she returned a few minutes later, she not only had her usual backpack, but pulled a medium-sized duffel bag with wheels. "I think I got everything," she said. Her tremulous smile tugged at his heart.

"Let me help you." He grabbed her duffel, which she released without protest. Outside, he waited while she used her remote to set the alarm before locking the front door.

He waited while she got into her vehicle and started it, then jumped into his. She followed him to his place. He drove in silence, matching the quiet darkness of the middle of the night. The streets were mostly deserted, the stoplights flashing red.

When they arrived at his place, she got out of her car slowly, almost as if she were sore and hurting. Parking, he grabbed her duffel while she shouldered her backpack, and he led the way into his house.

Inside, he walked down the hall to the guest bedroom.

"I washed the sheets and remade the bed," he told her, turning on the light.

"Thanks." She took a step past him into the room. Looking around, she exhaled. "You know, someday, if you want, I can help you with a little interior decorating," she said, looking around the impersonal setup.

He chuckled. "You don't like hotel room chic?"

"It's okay," she said, her voice cautious. "I'm sorry, I'm being rude. You've been kind enough to let me stay here and then I critique your décor."

His chest squeezed. He couldn't help but notice the way her hands still trembled as she set her backpack on the bed.

"It's fine," he replied. "I admit, I hired a designer to do some of the house, but only focused on the areas where I spent a lot of time. Until you, no one has used this guest room, so there hasn't been much of a need to spruce it up."

Nodding, she covered her mouth to mask a yawn. He took that as his cue to go. "Get some rest," he said. "We'll sleep in since we're off. We can head up to Valdez once we're up."

She didn't even try to disguise her exhaustion or her relief. "Thank you," she murmured. "I'll see you in the morning."

When he stepped into the hall, she closed the door behind him. He stood out there in the hall for a minute, realizing how lucky she'd been. If not for her new alarm, the outcome could have been a lot worse.

The only reason her earlier text had pulled him from sleep had been that his smartwatch had vibrated. Late-night texts were rare and usually only brought bad news. Which meant, of course, that he'd sat up, turned on his lamp, and read it.

Pure adrenaline had jolted through him the instant he'd seen her words. Without conscious thought, he'd pulled on some clothes, grabbed his truck keys and sped to her house. He'd known better than to call to ask her to clarify. She'd said someone was in her house. He hadn't wanted to take a chance of giving away her hiding place.

He got undressed, slid into his bed and turned off the lights. She was safe and that's all that mattered. Except, he couldn't stop thinking of her, alone and frightened, trying to sleep in the room down the hall.

Finally, he somehow managed to drift off to sleep.

A tortured scream woke him. *Genna!* Leaping out of bed, jumped into the jeans he'd tossed on the floor and sprinted down the hall to the guest room.

He found her sitting up in bed with the light on, wide-eyed, her arms wrapped around herself. Even from the doorway, he could see how violently she was shaking.

"I'm sorry," she stammered. "With everything that's been happening, I think this triggered some past trauma."

Aching to comfort her, he moved closer and sat carefully on the edge of the bed. When she reached for him, he froze.

"I'm giving your words back to you," she whispered. "If anything happens between us, I'll have to initiate it. Well, I am. Now." She pulled his face down for a kiss. "Make love to me," she murmured. "Make love to me now. I need to feel alive."

Though it crossed his mind that he might be dreaming, the press of her sweet and perfect body against his set him aflame. When she pressed her lips against his, he kissed her back with reckless abandon.

The savage intensity of her response brought instant, nearly violent arousal.

Still kissing her, he struggled to maintain control. First, he managed to grab his wallet, fumbling to retrieve the condom. Once he'd put that on, he looked up to find her watching, passion clouding her gaze.

Climbing back into her bed, he slid his hands under her T-shirt, across her silken belly, down the curve of her hip, to find her ready for him.

One touch and she clenched against his finger, her entire body shuddering. Aware he needed to slow things down, he helped her to pull her T-shirt over her head and then stepped back to remove his boxers.

Pupils huge and dark, she looked on as he undressed. He liked that she'd left the light on so he could watch her. Crawling back into her bed, he covered her body with his. Flesh against flesh, he pressed his rigid arousal into her thigh and slanted his mouth over hers.

Wild, untamed, when their mouths met, they devoured each other. "Inside me," she rasped, guiding him to her. "I need you inside me."

She was ready for him. As her body sheathed his, he lost the last shredded remnants of his remaining self-control. Passion pounded with each thrust. Her eager response matched his in savage intensity.

They were one in that moment. Joined in more than just their bodies, he felt that zing of connection between their souls.

Certain that she felt it, too, he managed to hold back his release until she shuddered, her body clenching around his.

Only then did he let himself go. When he did, pure and explosive pleasure rocked his world, the intensity unlike anything he'd ever felt.

Except once before, with her. Only with her. As he

gave himself to her, surrendering, an amazing feeling of completeness washed over him.

Sated, they clung to each other while their rapid heartbeats slowed and the sheen of perspiration cooled and dried from their skin. She curled into him, a perfect fit, making him realize there would be no coming back from this. His life would never be the same again. He could only hope she felt the same way.

How could she not? Both physically and mentally, they'd stumbled across something rare and special, a once-in-a-lifetime chance at love.

He fell asleep with a smile on his face, Genna beside him in the bed.

The next morning when he woke, he slipped from the bed, leaving her asleep and still tangled up in the sheets. He turned once and looked back at her, his heart full.

They made a good couple. She might not realize it yet, but he had a sneaky suspicion that if they could manage to work things out, a long and happy road lay ahead for them.

Whether or not they discussed this now or later, he decided he wouldn't press her. Instead, he'd follow her lead.

After a quick shower, Parker headed to the kitchen to make coffee. Then he started breakfast, figuring he'd make something basic and hopefully she'd like it. Bacon, eggs and toast. Plus orange juice, if she wanted it.

Whistling while he worked, he realized he could get used to this. Though he knew she intended her stay to be temporary, just until whoever had been breaking into her house was caught, he couldn't help but hope she'd be there a while. Even though he fully intended to put the pressure on the Shelby police force to make sure they caught the guy. No one, especially not a woman he cared for, should be made to feel unsafe in their own home.

* * *

Pleasantly sore, Genna opened her eyes and reached for Parker, only to find his side of the bed empty. As she sat up, she realized she smelled bacon and coffee, two of her absolute favorite morning things in the entire world.

Locating her discarded T-shirt, she pulled it over her head. She grabbed a change of clothes from her duffel and went down the hallway to the bathroom to shower.

Standing under the hot spray, she wondered how she should act around Parker now that they'd made love. Could they go back to the casual friendship they'd begun to enjoy? Did she even want to?

And what about her job? If the two of them started some kind of relationship, would her employment status suffer if it didn't work out? While she hated to be pessimistic about their chances, she also had to be realistic. Her husband, the man who'd pledged "'til death do us part," had cheated on her with a woman she'd considered her best friend.

Not only that, but things had been rocky between her and Chad for a while before they'd ended. Which was an understatement. No way did she want to go through anything like that ever again.

She decided to be upfront and let Parker know she wasn't in the market for any kind of relationship. Though she wasn't fond of the term, if they could make a friends-with-benefits situation work, she'd be open to that. But nothing more.

Decision made, her nerves settled. She dressed, combed through her wet hair and headed to the kitchen to see what he'd rustled up for breakfast.

The moment she entered, he turned and smiled. She

felt the power of that smile all the way to the soles of her feet. For a split second, her resolve wavered.

"Good morning," he said. "Did you sleep well?"

Heaven help her, but she blushed. "I did," she replied, her voice surprisingly steady. "How about you?"

"Fine." His intent gaze seemed to peer into her soul. Her stomach turned over and her knees turned to mush.

"I still can't have a relationship," she blurted. "I'm just not ready."

"I understand," he said. Since she'd expected him to argue, she wasn't sure how to react.

"My marriage was pretty awful," she finally admitted, turning her back to him while she grabbed a cup of coffee. Bracing herself for a bunch of questions, she carried her drink to the table and took a seat, all without looking at him.

Finally, when he didn't probe, she raised her head. "I'm sorry."

"Don't be."

She had no idea how to respond, so she didn't.

"Do you want to talk about it?" he asked, his gaze steady.

To her surprise, she realized she did. "I met Chad in college," she said, sitting back and taking a sip of her coffee. "At first, he was everything I wanted in a partner. He was attentive, considerate, and he seemed to anticipate my every need."

She sighed and took another drink. "Later, I learned that's something narcissists do. It's called love bombing. I didn't know that then, though."

"How long were you married?" he asked, his voice as gentle as his expression.

"Seven years." She didn't even have to think about it.

"Once I had that ring on my finger, he changed. Or maybe he just allowed his true self to show."

Thinking of all his rules, his little punishments if she failed to follow them, and his escalating temper, along with all the insults and snide comments designed to put her down, she felt ashamed.

Something of her thoughts must have showed on her face.

"It's okay." Reaching out, he covered her hand with his. "You don't have to talk about it if you don't want to."

Eyeing the quietly handsome man across from her, she realized that she did. "He had anger issues," she said, waving her hand as if those simple words didn't convey a wealth of trauma.

Parker's jaw tightened. "Verbal or physical?"

"Both. I survived. But what matters is that I became a shadow of myself. Where once I'd been happy and outgoing, I withdrew inside." Her self-conscious laugh hid so many emotions; none of which she felt ready to reveal. "You wouldn't have recognized me. I was a docile, quiet person. Head down, withering away into a shell without any heart or soul."

Hand still on top of hers, he squeezed. "I'm glad you got out."

Those words had her lifting her chin. "I am, too. I suspect if I hadn't, I wouldn't be here on this earth any longer."

He swallowed hard. "I'm sorry you went through that."

"I am, too, but I'm not proud that I stayed so long. Looking back, it's unbelievable that it took him having an affair with my best friend to make me leave. All the abuse, the way he treated me, and it took his cheating to finally gave me the courage to leave."

Hearing herself say it out loud, she had to shake her head. "Actually, I didn't have the energy to leave. I learned in therapy that depression can do that."

Getting up the courage to meet his gaze, when he only nodded instead of commenting, she felt grateful.

"Anyway, long story short…" She gave a wry smile. "That's why I'm not in the market for a relationship right now. Maybe not ever. I think I might be too damaged."

Bracing herself, she waited for Parker to explain that he wasn't that guy and would never treat her like that. If he did, that'd mean he completely missed the point.

Instead, he simply nodded again. "That's understandable. Thank you for trusting me enough to share that with me."

Dumbfounded, Genna got up to make another cup of coffee, certain words would fail her.

"Do you still want to drive up to Valdez and check out the animal shelter?" he asked.

She waited until she'd finished fixing her coffee before she turned. "I don't know. Maybe getting a dog right now isn't the best idea, since I'm your temporary houseguest."

"I think you should still consider it," he said. "But, of course, that's completely up to you."

Sipping her second cup of coffee, she thought about it for a moment. "We can go look," she finally conceded. "But I doubt I'll bring one home. The timing is wrong."

Though he shrugged, something in his gaze told her he believed she'd go, take one look at some poor dog in need, and fall instantly in love with it. The old Genna definitely would have done such a thing. The woman she used to be, who'd believed in happy endings and rainbows, trusted her heart and acted on impulse, believing everything would work out in the end.

Not anymore. Now she knew better.

"What about you?" she challenged. "You said you'd been wanting to get a dog. Maybe this is your chance."

He grinned. "Could be, you never know. Let me get these dishes cleaned up and we'll head out."

"I'll get them," she offered. "You cooked, I can clean."

Though he appeared uncertain, he finally gave in.

It only took her a few minutes to rinse everything and put the dishes in the dishwasher. When she finished, she dried her hands off on a towel and turned to find him eyeing her. The intensity in his gaze sent a bolt of desire through her.

"Ready to go?" he asked, a slight smile curving his mouth as if he knew her thoughts.

"Sure. I'm driving." She already had her keys in her hand. "Since I invited you to go with me."

He nodded. "Sounds good. Lead the way."

Once they were settled in her car, she glanced at him in the passenger seat, unaccountably nervous. The drive would be a straightforward one, with a lot of beautiful scenery in between the two towns. There were two ways to get there. The quickest route was inland, but she preferred the meandering road that went by the water. She waited until they'd turned off Parker's street before asking him which route he'd like to take.

"That's up to you," he answered immediately. "You're driving. I'm good with whatever way you choose."

Since she was in a bit of a hurry, she chose the more direct route.

The City of Valdez Animal Shelter sat on a picturesque road with jagged mountain peaks behind it. The smallish wooden building had been painted blue, she guessed in an effort to make it look more cheerful. A white-lettered sign hung over the double glass doors, advertising pet food and supplies. Only one other car sat in the parking lot.

"Did you check online to see what kind of dogs they have available?" Parker asked once they'd pulled up to the building and parked.

"I meant to, but with everything that happened, I forgot," she admitted. "Since I'm not ready to adopt today, I guess that doesn't matter. We'll just go inside and take a look around."

"Okay, but before we do, what kind of dog are you looking for?"

She shrugged. "I don't know. Something big and intimidating, but secretly gentle and kind. In my situation, I need the kind of dog that would make an intruder think twice before breaking in to my house."

"That makes sense." He got out of the car. "Let's go see what they have."

The busy shelter worker hurried up front when they entered. "Are you looking for a lost pet?" she asked, tucking a wayward strand of gray hair behind her ear. "If so, I'm going to need you to fill out some paperwork."

Genna found her voice. "No. Actually, we came to take a look at the dogs available for adoption."

This made the woman beam. "Perfect. Just go through that door. All the dogs in those kennels are available. Just holler if you need any help." That said, she hurried off.

"Let's do this." Parker held out his hand. Without thinking, Genna took it. Together they went through the door.

They stepped onto a concrete walkway dividing two long rows of metal kennels. Immediately, all the dogs started barking. There was a smell that no amount of cleaning could erase, which made Genna sigh. Most of the cages were occupied, and dogs of all sizes, breeds and colors had rushed to the front, begging for attention.

Still clutching Parker's hand, she stood frozen, unable to make herself move forward.

"Are you all right?" he asked, looking down at her.

"I think so." Wide-eyed, she took a deep breath. "I don't know what's wrong with me."

"It's okay to feel bad for the dogs," he said, his voice gentle. "And just because you don't plan on adopting one today, doesn't mean you can't visit with them while you're here. I'm sure they enjoy the attention."

Though she nodded, she still couldn't make her feet move. Only Parker's gentle tug on her hand had her taking steps forward.

There were a few large dogs, though most of them seemed to be medium-sized. Some barked furiously as she approached, others leapt onto the metal mesh, desperate to be noticed. As she moved down the row of cages, she saw black dogs and brown ones, white-and-tan and multicolored. Most had short hair and short snouts, though she noticed one or two with long fur.

Releasing her hand, Parker stopped in front of more than one cage, visiting with its occupant. While he was having a conversation with a huge black dog, she spotted something in the corner of the kennel at the very end of the row.

She hurried down to get a better look. Inside, she saw a small dog cowering in the corner. She couldn't tell if it was a male or a female. Its long white fur looked dirty, tangled and matted. When she approached, it didn't get up to greet her or even acknowledge her presence in any way. Head down, the poor animal appeared defeated, without hope. Something about that reminded Genna of the way she'd felt after her divorce.

Telling herself that this small creature was the opposite of what she needed and that she'd decided she wouldn't be adopting a dog today, she turned away. Further down the aisle, Parker had stopped to converse with a shaggy brown dog of unknown age.

Just then, the shelter worker appeared. "Find anything you like?" she asked, smiling. "We have something for everyone."

Once again, Genna glanced back at the forlorn little dog. Almost as if the words were being pulled out of her, she heard herself asking "What about that one? What's his or her story?"

"That's June Bug," the woman answered, her smile widening. "She's a staff favorite. We all love her. She's a poodle/sheltie mix, spayed, and around five years old. Her owner died and the family didn't want her, so they brought her here."

Hearing her name, the little dog lifted her head. Her sad eyes momentarily brightened.

"Most people come in here wanting a large dog," the worker continued. "It being Alaska and all that. Sadly, she's become used to being overlooked."

"That's a shame." Still, Genna hesitated. She, too, had thought she preferred a big dog. Mainly for protection. Yet somehow she felt an overwhelming need to help this girl.

"Would you like to meet her?"

Genna nodded, at first still a little unsure, and then absolutely certain. "I would," she replied. "Please."

Down at the end of the aisle, Parker continued his dialogue with one of the other dogs. If he had any idea what

Genna was considering, he gave no sign. Either that, or she figured he was giving her space.

The worker unlocked the kennel. Though June Bug raised her head, she didn't move from her spot in the corner.

"You can go on in," the woman said, waving her hand. "Spend some time with her, get to know each other. Just go ahead and call me if you need me."

With that, the worker moved off.

Slowly, Genna opened the door to the kennel. Though June Bug stayed in her spot, she kept her stare fixed on Genna.

About a foot away, Genna stopped and dropped down to her haunches. "Hey there, pretty girl. How'd you like to get busted out of here today?"

Gaze locked on Genna, June Bug wagged her tail.

"But you're going to have to get up first," Genna continued, keeping her voice soft. "Will you please come over here and let me pet you."

To her disbelief, the little dog got to her feet and hesitantly came over. She sniffed Genna, her tail still wagging.

Deciding to take a chance, Genna gently picked June Bug up, holding her close while crooning to her. "It's going to be all right, I promise."

June Bug tilted her head and then, as if she understood Genna's words, she licked her on the cheek.

That sealed the deal. "You're my dog now," Genna said. Still holding the little dog, Genna got to her feet and stepped out of the kennel.

"What do you have there?" Parker asked, still hanging out with the dog at the end of the row. "Is that a puppy?"

He sounded so horrified she had to laugh. "No, she's

around five years old. Her owner died and the family didn't want her. Isn't she precious?"

"She is," he admitted, moving closer so he could get a better look. "But I thought you were wanting a dog for protection."

"I was." Trying not to be defensive, she gazed down at June Bug. "But this one needs me. And I need her."

Studying her face, Parker nodded. "You fell in love."

Surprised, she held his gaze. Instead of condemnation or mockery, she saw only understanding. "I fell in love," she repeated.

"Then she's coming home with us," he said. "Let's go fill out the paperwork. What's her name?"

He chuckled when she told him. "That suits her."

At the front desk, the shelter worker beamed when she realized Genna intended to adopt little June Bug. Once Genna signed the forms and paid the fee, she received some papers showing June Bug's vaccination history.

"Do you have dog food and treats? A collar and leash?" the worker asked. "We sell all of that here to make things easier."

Since Genna had never owned a dog before, she asked for recommendations. Once all the necessities had been purchased, she put June Bug's new collar on her before carrying her out to her car. Parker trailed behind, carrying the shopping bags.

"Are you going to let her walk?" he asked once they reached the parking lot. "Maybe she needs to go before she gets in the car."

"Good point." Walking to a grassy area at the edge of the pavement, she clipped the brand-new leash to June Bug's collar and gently set her down. "Go potty," she said.

Tail wagging, the little dog pranced over and took care

of her business. When she was done, Genna praised her and picked her up again. “Would you mind driving?” she asked Parker. “That way I can hold her.”

“Sure.” He smiled and held out his hand for the keys. “Let’s take her home.”

Chapter 8

Glad he had to keep his gaze mostly on the road, Parker couldn't resist occasionally glancing over at Genna, crooning sweet nothings to her new pet. The little dog appeared to be eating it up, tail constantly wagging, eyes bright and alert. If he didn't know better, Parker would have sworn June Bug was smiling.

At first glance, the dog wasn't much to look at. Scruffy and in need of a bath, she looked more like a gremlin-type creature than a pet. But despite her lack of conventional cuteness, the tiny animal had a sweet vulnerability to her. Parker felt certain she'd blossom with a little love and TLC. And he knew Genna would be just the person to give that to her.

As he drove, with the beautiful woman radiating happiness sitting in the seat next to him, he realized he'd never been happier. Sure, he loved his job and the house he'd renovated until it completely suited him. But he'd never realized that something had been missing, the difference between simply living a good life and living one that actually felt complete.

Damn. Hell of a revelation to have about a woman who'd made it clear she wasn't looking for anything serious.

When they finally turned onto his street, he realized

he'd been so lost in his thoughts that he had very little memory of most of the drive home. Once or twice, Genna had caught him looking over at her and her tremulous smile had made it difficult to breathe.

"What was your life like living in Anchorage," he asked, partly to pass the time but also because he genuinely wanted to know.

She grimaced. "Do you mean while Chad and I were married? Or after?"

"After," he replied. Since he couldn't bear the thought of her married to another man, especially one who had abused her, he wanted to hear how she'd rebuilt her life.

"I rented an apartment," she said. "It was new and modern and close to the center of town. It didn't take long to realize Chad and my former best friend Ann intended to make my life hell."

"Why?" This made no sense to him. "You gave him his divorce. Your so-called friend got what she wanted, your former husband. I don't understand why they'd feel the need to bother you."

When she spoke, her voice sounded level and matter-of-fact. "I can talk about this now," she said. "Because the time I spent in therapy helped me deal with it and dispel any lingering darkness. Chad lied to Ann. He told her I wanted to win him back, that I still considered him mine."

She sighed, glancing down at her sleeping dog before looking back at him. "Ann believed him to the point that she started harassing me. This gave Chad a kick, so he encouraged it. He even called me several times to gloat. Getting away from them was my only recourse, especially when Ann broke into my apartment and destroyed most of my belongings."

"Then you came back home," he said.

"Yes. I came home. Evidently, this made Ann realize I truly wasn't after my ex, because neither of them has attempted to contact me again."

"Did you change your phone number?" he asked.

"No. But I did block both of them. If they'd gone on to get disposable phones or something, then I would have changed my number. But as it turned out, I didn't have to."

If he hadn't been driving, Parker would have kissed her. She'd been through so much. And yet she'd managed to continue making a new life for herself and grow stronger.

"To be honest," Genna continued. "When I saw the broken door to my house, my first thought was Ann. But then I realized she would have had to drive all this way, or fly, and find a place to stay overnight, just to harass me—when I've made it as clear as I can that I have no interest in getting Chad back. It doesn't make sense."

He agreed and said so. "But then we have to figure out who actually did try to break into your place. Twice."

Stroking her little dog's fur, she nodded. "It's like choosing the best of two evils. I have to say I'd rather deal with Ann than the Fiancée Killer."

This made him chuckle. He decided not to tell her what he'd like to do to the man to whom she'd once been married. Like it hadn't been enough to cheat on Genna with a woman she'd considered her best friend, but then to taunt and badger her after she'd given him the divorce he'd wanted?

He managed to bring his anger under control after focusing on driving and taking several deep breaths. Genna didn't need to know how her words had gutted him.

As he pulled up into his driveway, he realized little June Bug had fallen asleep. Genna gazed down at the dog, her eyes shining with love.

"Isn't she just perfect?" she asked, clearly not really expecting an answer.

Nodding, he went around and opened her door, ready to help her out. Instead, she waved him off, moving carefully so as not to disturb June Bug.

He grabbed the bags with the food, bowls, toys and the fluffy round dog bed she'd purchased and hurried ahead of her to unlock the front door.

"Thank you," Genna murmured. As she moved past him, the little dog raised her head and looked around with interest. "I want to give her a spa day first thing."

A little mystified, he locked up behind them before asking her what she meant.

"You know, a bath, brushing her down, making her look beautiful. I bought some scented dog shampoo. Would you mind bringing it to me?" Without waiting for an answer, she headed into the bathroom. A moment later, he heard the sound of her filling the tub, all the while keeping up a steady conversation with June Bug.

He unpacked the supplies, located the bottle of coconut and passion fruit dog shampoo, and took it to the bathroom. She thanked him and he retreated, thinking of all the other dogs he'd seen in the shelter. They'd been all kinds, big and small, young and old. The one thing they'd all had in common was their desperate need for attention. Many still had remnants of hope shining in their eyes, though others appeared to have long ago given up.

In one way or another, people had failed them. They all needed homes.

Parker had been drawn to an elderly Lab mix in the very last run. Silver decorated the dog's black muzzle and when Parker had opened the run to go inside, the dog had been slightly unsteady on his feet, no doubt from lack of exercise. He'd still wagged his tail though, the entire time he sniffed Parker from head to toe.

Reading the kennel card been posted on the outside of the cage, Parker saw that his name was Revis and he was eleven years old. His owners had surrendered him because they'd no longer had time to devote to a dog they'd had since he'd been a puppy. While Parker felt sure that each of the other dogs had their own sad stories, for the life of him, he'd never understand how people could treat a canine family member that way. Never.

By the time Genna emerged with her clean and completely transformed pup, Parker had reached his decision.

"I'm going back to the animal shelter," he told her, glancing at his watch. "Since they're open until four, I have time."

"Why?" she asked, clearly not understanding. "What did we forget?"

"My dog," he replied, smiling. "He's an older black Lab whose owners no longer had time for him."

Genna's eyes widened. Both she and her new pet looked at him. Then she slowly nodded. "Go get him. June Bug and I can't wait to meet him."

Truck keys in hand, he dipped his chin. "I'll be back."

The drive seemed to take longer when he made it alone. Either that, or time stretched out because he was in a rush to get back to the shelter.

Halfway there, his phone rang. "Hey, Lakin. How are you?"

His sister chuckled. "I've never been better. What about you? How is Genna working out?"

He took a few minutes to tell her all about the multiple break-ins at Genna's place. "We still don't know who it is or why they're targeting her. She even had an alarm system installed, which helped alert the police."

"Wow." Lakin exhaled. "I wouldn't feel safe being in the house."

"She doesn't. That's why she's staying at my place."

"Say what?" Lakin sounded incredulous. "Whose idea was that?"

He felt slightly defensive, but had no idea why. "Mine. It's all aboveboard. She's using the guest room."

"The one that looks like a cheap hotel room?" Lakin asked, laughing.

He decided to ignore the dig. "Look, I'm just about to Valdez. I'm going to have to let you go."

"Valdez? Why are you doing there?"

Since he and his sister had very few secrets, he told her. "I'm adopting a dog."

And then, while she sputtered and demanded more details, he told her he'd pulled into the shelter parking lot and ended the call.

The same shelter worker sat at the front desk when he entered. Her brows rose. "I'm surprised to see you so soon," she said. "Is everything all right with little June Bug?"

"Yes, she's living the life. I'm not here about her. I came for Revis."

The woman's entire face lit up. "Seriously? He's the best dog."

Parker nodded. He thought of Genna's little pup. "I do need to know if Revis gets along with other dogs."

"He *loves* other dogs," the woman said. "Revis loves everything and everyone. He's one of the friendliest dogs I've ever seen. He couldn't be more perfect. People keep overlooking him because he's black and because he's older."

"Because he's black?"

"Yes. It's well known in rescue, though we're not exactly sure why. Some people associate the color with evil, like black cats and bad luck. Often it's because they're difficult to photograph. Either way, people pass black animals up."

"Not this time," Parker replied. "I want to adopt him."

"You've just made my day. First little June Bug, who also is good with other dogs, and now Revis." Glowing, she went to her computer and printed off the paperwork. "I just need your signature. His adoption fee is reduced since he's a senior."

After signing and paying the fee, he purchased a collar and leash, as well as a large bag of senior kibble and a raised feeder with two bigger bowls. "Let me take these out to my truck and then I'll go back and get him," he said.

When he returned, the worker had fetched Revis herself. The big, black dog sat at her side, alert and watching the door, his long tail sweeping the floor.

"There he is," Parker said, feeling a rush of happiness. The instant he spoke, Revis climbed to his feet, his regal calmness at odds with the furious tail wagging.

"Let's put your new collar on you," he said, scratching Revis under the chin. Once he'd done that and attached the matching leash, the shelter worker removed the slip lead.

"Looks like you're all set to go," she said, still beaming. Then she crouched down and kissed the top of Revis's graying head. "Have a great rest of your life, sweet boy."

After Parker drove off, Genna sat down on the couch, still holding June Bug. Gazing down at her scruffy little dog, she had a brief moment of panic. What had she been thinking? She'd wanted to get a big, loud dog for protection. Instead, she'd let her heart overrule her common sense.

Just then June Bug raised her head and licked Genna's chin, her large brown eyes luminous. And Genna knew she'd done the right thing. She and this scruffy little dog belonged together, no matter what.

Next to her on the sofa, with her head on Genna's leg, June Bug fell asleep. All of her previous tension appeared to have vanished from her small body. She felt, Genna realized, secure.

Then, curled up with her dog sleeping beside her, Genna allowed herself to doze off, too.

The sound of Parker opening the front door had her sitting up, rubbing her eyes. June Bug lifted her head and yawned, but apart from that, she barely stirred.

"Here we are," Parker said, grinning. "Revis, meet Genna and June Bug."

A stately black Lab with ancient eyes and silver sprinkled on his muzzle, walked at Parker's side. "I checked to make sure he likes other dogs," Parker said. "The lady at the shelter said he does. She also mentioned June Bug does, too."

The sound of the larger dog's toenails clicking on the wood floor finally got June Bug's attention. She sat up, her gaze locked on Revis, who was easily ten times her size. She whimpered, though judging by her alert posture, the sound was not from fear.

Immediately, spotting June Bug, the giant dog let out a low woof. Tail wagging, he took a few steps closer until he and the tiny dog were nose to nose. Parker kept him leashed, just in case, though Genna didn't fool herself by thinking he could do much if Revis decided to eat the smaller pup.

But both dog's tails were wagging and they genuinely seemed excited to meet one another. After a moment or two of sniffing, June Bug climbed back on top of Genna and fell back asleep. Revis sighed and laid down on the floor, his gaze fixed on the other dog.

"I think he's in love," Parker commented, smiling.

"Maybe so," Genna replied. "But who could blame him?" She grinned, petting June Bug's head. "If this first meet is anything to go by, I think they'll be getting along just fine."

"I agree." Parker sounded relieved. It dawned on her that he'd been really concerned that the two dogs wouldn't like each other. Since she and June Bug were simply guests in his home, if that turned out to be the case, she'd simply have no choice but to try to return to her own house. Even though the idea terrified her. Luckily, she didn't think that would be happening.

"My sister is probably going to be calling you," Parker said, his gaze alternating between the two dogs and her. "She seemed a little surprised to learn that you're staying here."

Genna couldn't help but laugh, imagining Lakin's reaction, especially after practically having to beg Genna to even consider working with Parker. "I bet she was," she said. "But I also have a feeling she understands. There's not a single woman in town who wouldn't get why I don't want to stay alone in my house when someone keeps trying to break in. And there also happens to be a serial killer lurking around town."

He nodded. "I agree. But that doesn't mean she doesn't

want to tease you. She would have with me, but I told her I had to go and hung up."

"If I don't hear from her, I'll give her a call tomorrow," Genna said.

They had sandwiches for dinner. Genna ate on the couch with a very interested June Bug watching her every move. Revis stayed close to Parker, who'd announced his plans to keep the bigger dog in his room at night. She wondered if he'd be allowing Revis to sleep with him in his bed, like she planned to allow June Bug.

Either way, having two dogs would help make sure one wound up in the other's room at night. Though Genna supposed this was a good thing, she couldn't help but feel a twinge of regret. But when she went to bed, having her little dog curled up by her helped.

The next day, though Parker had to go in to RTA since he'd been scheduled for a couple of tours, Genna had the day off. Two days in a row, which made her feel both decadent and guilty. She couldn't help but worry about how things would run while she wasn't there. Even though it had only been a short time since she'd started working there, she'd implemented a system. Everything ran like clockwork. Both the guests and all the other employees seemed happy.

As for Genna, she couldn't imagine a better job. Or better coworkers. If not for the break-ins at her house, she'd have to say her life felt pretty damn perfect.

Since she had the day to herself, she decided to stop by her house to make sure it was still secure. Since she'd activated the alarm system, she knew she'd get a notification if anyone set it off, but she'd feel better seeing everything with her own eyes.

Then she figured she'd go into town, maybe have lunch

at one of the places with outdoor seating. Usually that meant dogs were allowed. And since she intended to take her new pet with her, finding that kind of place to eat would be necessary.

Getting up from the kitchen table, she carried her coffee mug and cereal bowl to the sink. June Bug immediately trotted after her. Everywhere Genna went, the little dog went, too. Genna had taken to calling her JB for short.

Which was why she totally understood Parker's decision to take Revis into work with him today. While the aging Lab might not be able to take part in some of the more strenuous hikes, she'd bet he'd be fine lounging around the office.

Once she'd cleaned up her dishes, Genna went to her bedroom and emptied out her largest tote bag. One of the benefits of June Bug being so small meant she'd be able to carry her around with her.

"This tote should do nicely," she said out loud. June Bug immediately began wagging her tail. With the bag on the bed, Genna picked up her little dog and set her in it. JB sniffed around and then sat. When she did that, she wasn't visible at all.

"Perfect," Genna said. "Are you ready to go downtown with me?"

Grabbing the backpack she used instead of a purse, she slung it over one shoulder and picked up the tote and her dog. When she looked inside, she saw JB had fallen asleep. Obviously, she just might have the most perfect dog in the universe. With a sappy grin, she headed toward the door.

Driving to her parents' house, she couldn't shake a feeling of dread. At first, she assumed it had to do with returning to the place where an intruder had so recently been. But as she drove, she caught herself constantly checking the rearview mirror and she realized she couldn't shake the feeling that someone might be following her.

The closer she got to Shelby, the more unsettled she became. The two-lane road changed to a four-lane and some of the vehicles behind her passed her.

Nothing looked really out of place. But still… She decided to take a random right turn and circle back around just to see if anyone followed her.

No one did. Breathing a sigh of relief, she turned onto her parents' street. Pulling into the driveway, she sat in her locked car with the motor running. In the bright sunlight, the house looked welcoming and undisturbed. She got out, keeping her keys in hand, and picked up the tote with her sleeping dog. Then she took a deep breath and headed for the house. As she stepped up onto the porch, she turned and did a second check of the street. She didn't see anything suspicious; no unusual vehicles parked by the curb, nothing.

It all must have been her imagination. Though she felt slightly foolish, she couldn't deny she also felt immensely relieved.

Inside the house, she turned off the alarm and sighed. Since it was still set, that meant no one had been inside since she'd left.

Still, she walked around to check. Everything looked the same as it had when she'd left it. The busted back door that they'd jammed closed appeared undisturbed, though she figured another swift kick from outside would send it crashing open. Pulling out her phone, she put in a call to the door repair company she'd used earlier, but had to leave a voicemail. Whenever she was able to get the door replaced, she planned to have them reinforce it with multiple dead bolts if necessary. Between that, and the redone front door, along with her new alarm system, she knew she should be able to feel secure in the house where she'd been raised.

And she could leave Parker's place so he could go on about his life.

The thought made her feel sad. Shaking her head at her own conflicted emotions, she checked on JB, who somehow was still sleeping, and then let herself out through the garage.

Again she checked the street and, again, saw nothing out of the ordinary. She got into her car and after securing JB and her tote in the front passenger seat, she backed from her driveway and headed into town. Only then did she notice a black SUV pull away from the curb as if following her.

Chapter 9

To Parker's surprise and relief, Revis fit right in with the crew at RTA. Everyone loved the older dog and with all the people petting and loving on him, it seemed his tail never stopped wagging.

"We have a mascot," Parker proclaimed. He couldn't seem to stop smiling. Between having Genna staying at his place in such close proximity and his new family member, he felt happier than he had in a long time.

Spence went home and came back with a large, well-worn dog bed, which he placed it in a corner behind the front counter. As soon as Revis saw it, he claimed it as his own. Curled up with his head on his large paws, he kept an eye on everything. At least, when he wasn't dozing.

"The office dog," Spence said, grinning. "Great idea."

"Thanks."

"But I thought Genna was getting a dog," Spence continued, checking the computer to see who would be in his next group. "How'd you end up with one instead?"

"Long story," Parker replied, really not wanting to go into it at the moment. "Since your tour is about to start arriving, I'll save it for another time."

Reluctantly, Spence nodded. "I'll hold you to that. What about you? When's your next outing?"

"Not for a couple hours. I had one scheduled earlier, but they all canceled. It was a family outing. Turns out they've all come down with strep throat."

"Ouch." Spence grabbed his own throat. "Which means I'm guessing you're planning to hold the fort down here then?"

"Yeah, for now. Hetty is due in soon. She's taking out a small group this afternoon. I should be back before she has to leave. And you can fill in also. Between the three of us, we should be able to keep this place covered."

"Four of us," Spence corrected. "You can't forget Revis."

"As if I could." Parker's phone rang. Seeing Genna's name on the caller ID made his heart skip a beat. Answering, he barely got out a quick hello before she started talking.

"Someone is following me," she said, an edge of panic in her voice. "I stopped by my house to check things out, and when I left, this black SUV pulled away from the curb. I've been driving around downtown taking random turns and it's sticking with me. I don't know what to do."

"Are you close to the police station?" he asked. Though his heart rate accelerated, he tried to sound calm.

"No, I'm on the other side of town. But I can get there. It will take me about twenty minutes though. I'm just worried whoever this is might ram my car or try to force me off the road. I have June Bug with me."

Was she crying? Jaw tight, he battled the intense need to defend her, to help her, and hold her close.

"Keep driving." He took a deep breath, not wanting to let her know how alarming he found this situation. "How far are you from here?"

"From RTA? Maybe ten minutes."

"Then come here." Decision made, he asked her to

stay on the phone while he went back to the gun safe and retrieved his pistol.

"What's going on?" Spence asked. With Genna still on the phone, Parker filled him in. Once he had, Spence cursed under his breath before he also went to the gun safe and armed himself. "We've got you, Genna," he said, loud enough for her to hear.

"How far out are you now?" Parker asked.

"Five minutes. And the car is still with me. They're not even trying to hide it now."

The slight tremor in her voice had him clenching his jaw. "Spence and I will be outside waiting for you. Pull up right in front of the building. And stay on the phone."

"I will," she promised.

Tense and trying like hell not to be, Parker jogged down the steps from the covered porch and waited for her at the edge of the parking lot. He wanted to be able to see her car the moment she turned into the driveway.

Right by his cousin's side, Spence's grim expression told Parker that he'd do whatever he had to, to help. If Genna's stalker was foolish enough to follow her there, they'd make sure he never followed Genna again.

"There," Parker said, pointing at Genna's red car, just about at the driveway. And like she said, a black SUV followed right on her bumper.

When she turned, the SUV slowed but then kept driving on past.

As Genna pulled up and parked, Parker rushed over to open her door. When he did, she made no move to get out. Instead, she sat frozen, gazing up at him, her expression a mixture of relief and terror.

"Come here," he said, his voice rough. He held out his

hand. When she made no move to take it, he reached in and hauled her out of the car and into his arms.

"You're trembling," he said, smoothing her hair away from her face. "Are you okay?"

"No," she admitted, clutching on to him as if she might fall. "Do you think that was the same person who broke into my house? What if it was the Fiancée Killer?"

"That's highly unlikely," Spence interjected, startling Parker, who'd managed to forget all about his cousin. "It's not his normal method of operation. If you have a stalker, it's someone else."

The instant Spence spoke, Genna stiffened. She made as if to pull out of Parker's arms, but he tightened his hold. "You're still too shaky on your feet," he murmured.

She reared back, glaring at him, but made no other attempt to move away.

"Well, well, well," Spence drawled, grinning. "Is there something you two want to share with me?"

This comment did it. Genna stepped out of Parker's embrace and shook her head. "Your cousin is just being kind to a friend," she said, her tone daring either man to contradict her. "And I appreciate it greatly."

Just then, the tote back on her front seat moved. A furry little head poked itself out and then barked. "JB!" Genna cried. "I hope you're all right." She reached into the tote and scooped the tiny dog out.

Spence's brows rose. "What the heck is that?" he asked.

"Meet June Bug," Parker replied. "Genna's new dog."

"JB for short," she said, kissing her pet on the top of her head. "Isn't she adorable?"

When Spence didn't immediately respond, Parker elbowed him.

"She's something else," Spence finally said. "Um,

Parker, don't forget you brought that beast of a dog into work with you today. He looks like he could eat this one for lunch if he wanted to."

Genna shook her head. "They're already friends. Revis really seems to like JB and vice versa."

"They've met?" Spence glanced from one to the other. "I thought you just got the dog yesterday," he said, eyeing Parker.

Parker figured he might as well tell him. If he didn't, he knew Lakin would. "Genna's staying with me for a few days," he said. "She and I went into Valdez, which is where the dogs came from. The shelter had them both listed as dog friendly, and so far that seems to be the case."

Though Spence's eyes widened, he simply nodded and refrained from commenting. Parker figured for sure he'd be peppered with questions later, when Genna wasn't there.

"Let's get you inside so you can sit down," Parker suggested, taking Genna's arm. "Spence's group should be arriving soon, so unless you want to be put to work, maybe you should hide out in the break room."

Genna perked up at the mention of work. "I suppose I could do some—"

"No." Parker cut her short. "You're off today. No working. I'll check Spence's group in. Hetty will be here soon and she'll cover the office when I take my people out."

Smiling slightly, Genna nodded. "Parker, when is your expedition? I'm hoping maybe you can go with me into town at some point. As strange as it sounds, I'm a bit weirded out of going anywhere alone."

Just as Parker opened his mouth to reply, three vehicles pulled into the parking lot in rapid succession.

"Looks like my bunch has started to arrive," Spence

said, rubbing his hands together in anticipation. "Time to get this show on the road."

As soon as they got inside, Genna went behind the counter and directly toward the break room. Revis lifted his head when he saw her, tail swishing. As she passed, he got up and followed her.

Positioning himself behind the computer, Parker began the process of logging their guests in. Spence watched from the lobby, eyeing his cousin and clearly bursting at the seams with questions, but unable to ask them. Which Parker considered a good thing.

Once he had everyone checked in, Parker turned the small group over to Spence. As his cousin walked everyone outside, Parker breathed a sigh of relief. Then he headed back to the break room to check on Genna.

When he entered, she looked up from her phone and smiled. The smile didn't reach her green eyes. Her little dog sat in a chair right next to her, and Revis had curled up at her feet.

Relieved, Parker jammed his hands into his pockets so he wouldn't hug her. "You look like you feel better now," he commented, pulling out a chair and taking a seat.

"I do." She put her phone down and regarded him gravely. "I've almost convinced myself that I was imagining everything."

He wanted to tell her that he didn't think so, but also didn't want to get her worked up again. So, in the end, he simply nodded.

"As a matter of fact, I'm going to go ahead with my plan to head into town." Getting to her feet, she picked up JB, who appeared to really enjoy being carried. Revis got up, too, tail wagging, clearly ready for an adventure.

Conflicted, Parker wavered. He couldn't expect her

to sit around and wait for him to take out his tour and return, especially on her day off. "The black SUV did go on past," he said, thinking out loud. "So, hopefully, you should be safe."

Something in his tone must have revealed his concern because her eyes widened.

"It'll be fine," she said. He wasn't sure whether she was trying to convince herself or him. "I can't let this person, whoever they are, make me stop living my life. As long as I stick to town and more populated areas, I should be fine."

He knew then that she was thinking of the Two Bears River Trail, where the most recent victim had been found.

"I just won't go hiking," she said, confirming his suspicion. "It's not like I hike anyway, so I should be safe."

Though he wished he could cancel his next tour and go with her, he couldn't. Nor could he realistically ask her to wait.

The front door opened. He jumped to his feet and looked out. "Hetty's here," he told Genna.

"You bet I am." Hetty sauntered into the break room. "Hey, Genna. What are you doing here? I thought you were off today."

"I am," Genna replied. "I just stopped in to say hi."

Hetty narrowed her eyes and glanced at Parker. He simply smiled, not wanting to say anything if Genna didn't want to elaborate. He'd fill Hetty in later. Since they all looked after each other, he felt strongly everyone needed to be aware of anything weird going on.

"Are we still planning to have that get-together?" Hetty asked. "I know when it got canceled due to weather, you talked about rescheduling."

"Maybe soon," Genna replied. "Honestly, I've got so much going on right now. But even though I've met everybody by now, I definitely want to do it. I just don't know when."

Hetty frowned at first then shrugged. "I get it," she said. "Have a nice rest of your day off."

"I plan to," Genna chirped.

If Hetty noticed her overly upbeat tone, she didn't show it.

"Let me walk you out," Parker said.

"No, that's okay." Waving him away, Genna headed for the door. "I'll talk to you later."

Slowly, he nodded. "Stay safe."

Watching her walk away, he ached. He didn't know what he would do if anything happened to her.

Once the door closed behind Genna, Hetty touched his arm. "How long have you been in love with her?" she asked. "And more importantly, does she return your feelings or are you on your own?"

Genna kept up a brave front, strolling outside as if she didn't have a care in the word. She maintained her brave front until she reached her car and climbed inside. Promptly locking the doors, she made sure JB's tote was secured with the seat belt before starting the ignition.

Then, because she had a feeling Parker and Hetty might be watching her out the front window, she forced herself to put the shifter in Reverse and backed up enough to turn the car around.

Though leaving was the absolute last thing she wanted to do, she squared her shoulders, lifted her chin and drove away.

She'd barely reached the first streetlight on the outskirts of Shelby when little JB poked her head out of the tote and whined. Chagrined, Genna realized she'd forgotten to let her pet outside to relieve herself.

Though tempted to pull over and take care of that right now, her location felt too isolated. For all she knew, she'd get out of the car and that black SUV would come racing around the corner. Might be foolish, but she didn't want to take any chances. JB would have to wait until they were actually in town. The restaurant Genna had in mind for lunch had an actual dog park out back. There'd be people and other dogs around, and she didn't think her stalker would dare make a move under those circumstances.

At least, she hoped not.

By the time she got to the restaurant, the usual lunch crowd had begun to thin. She parked, grabbed the tote and went directly to the dog area out back. Once JB had taken care of her business, Genna decided to walk her over to the patio area. The little dog made an immediate beeline for one of the strategically placed water bowls, which also had Genna realizing she'd forgotten to make sure her dog had water.

"I'm sorry," Genna said, scratching JB's neck. "I promise I'll get better at this dog mom stuff."

"I bet you're excellent," a masculine voice said. Startled, Genna looked up to find one of the wait staff smiling at her. "Can I show you to a table?" he asked.

"Thanks, Ty," she replied, reading his nametag. "I appreciate that. June Bug and I would like to sit out here on the patio. It's such a beautiful day."

"It is," he said, leading her to a small table in one corner near the railing. "Will this work for you?"

"It will." Sitting in the chair he pulled out, she accepted the menu he offered. When he also handed her a smaller pet menu, she laughed out loud. On it were things like bone stew and mac and kibble.

Since she didn't want to mess up JB's digestion any more than she had to, she didn't order anything for her dog. For herself, she chose a strawberry, fresh greens and chicken salad, with light dressing on the side.

While she waited for her food, she people watched. The pace in Shelby felt different than it had in Anchorage. Maybe because the town was popular with tourists, it had a more relaxed, accepting vibe. Growing up, she'd never realized this, and it had taken living in the hustle and bustle of a larger city to make her appreciate her hometown.

Her food came. She took a moment to admire the beauty of the salad, which looked so fresh and colorful, before she dug in. It tasted as good as it looked.

While she ate, JB lifted her head once or twice, but didn't try to beg for anything. The little dog just seemed happy to be there, out in the fresh air with her new owner, the sun on her fur.

"You're such a good dog," Genna said, resisting the urge to slip her a tiny piece of chicken. JB gazed up at her and wagged her tail.

After finishing her salad, Genna pushed away her plate and exhaled. It had been a nice lunch. With the sun on her skin and a light breeze keeping her cool, she'd been finally able to relax and enjoy the beautiful weather.

The muted conversations going on at other tables merged with birdsong and light traffic in the street nearby. From her seat, she could not only see the snowcapped mountains in the distance, but the beautiful cloudless sky. People strolled the sidewalk out front, and customers entered and exited the restaurant. She watched food being served and tables being cleaned. Her server checked on her, asking if she'd like anything else, before removing her plate.

Just because she felt like she deserved it, Genna asked to see a dessert menu. Ty immediately brought it, telling her he'd be back after giving her time to decide.

JB had stretched out on the cool pavement under the table and watched people with interest, though she never barked.

"Such a good dog," Genna murmured. She thought Revis, despite his much larger size, might also be great to take out in public.

Maybe because they'd come from the same shelter and had been adopted on the same day, Revis and June Bug would always be linked in Genna's mind. Remembering the unabashed joy Parker took in his new dog made her insides go all soft and squishy. A special dog for a special man.

She couldn't help but miss Parker. He would have enjoyed this place, she thought. She'd even spent far too much time guessing what he might have gotten to eat.

Clearly, she, who wanted to steer clear of any romantic entanglements, had it bad. She'd be seeing the man that evening, for Pete's sake. She was staying at his house. Seeing him every day at work. And now she couldn't even enjoy a solitary lunch without missing him?

To be fair, he'd been the first person she called any time she'd been scared. And he'd showed up every single time she'd needed him. Like today, when she'd thought that black SUV had been following her.

Now that some time had passed, she'd halfway convinced herself that she'd imagined it. After all, the SUV had driven on once she'd turned into the RTA drive. If it had been some random stalker, they would have continued on with her, maybe boxing her in with their vehicle so she couldn't escape.

Even thinking this made her shudder.

"Have you decided?" Ty asked.

Since she'd barely even glanced at the menu, she asked him what he recommended.

"The chocolate lava cake," he immediately answered. "It's to die for."

"Then I'll have that," she decided, passing him back the menu.

"And would you like a dog biscuit for your June Bug?" he asked. "On the house."

Beaming at him, she nodded. "Thank you, I would." She had to give him points for even remembering JB's name.

When her dessert arrived, along with a baked bone for JB, she almost clapped. "That's stunning," she said, admiring the cake. She even went so far as to pull out her phone and take a picture of it before picking up her fork to dig in.

She'd just taken her first bite, briefly closing her eyes to savor the blast of chocolate sweetness, when the sound of tires screeching had her turning toward the road. She was dimly conscious of other diners around her doing the same.

Two cars had nearly collided, only narrowly missing hitting each other because one had slammed on their brakes.

It wasn't this that made Genna freeze though. When she realized one of the vehicles involved was the same, black SUV, she nearly dropped her fork.

"Is something wrong?" Ty materialized at her elbow,

his concerned gaze taking in her no-doubt pale expression and barely eaten dessert. "Is the cake not to your liking?"

Though her appetite had now completely deserted her, she managed to reassure him that the cake was, in fact, wonderful. "I'm just full," she lied.

"I'll get you a to-go box," he said. A moment later, he returned with one. "Here you go."

She thanked him and nodded, glad he hadn't brought the check. She wasn't about to tell him there was no way she'd be leaving while that black vehicle was anywhere in the vicinity.

Instead, she continued to watch, waiting for the driver of the SUV to emerge. She had her phone out, camera at the ready, intending to take as many photos of him or her as possible. While she waited, she got several pics of the SUV itself, though she didn't have a good view of the license plate.

But while the driver of the other car immediately got out to look for any damage, no one got out of the black vehicle. Instead, it reversed, swerved around the intersection, and sped off.

Hands shaking, Genna's first impulse was to call Parker. But she figured he'd be heading out with his tour group about now and she didn't want to bother him.

The other driver had noticed her watching and waved. "Did you see that?" he asked, walking over to the wrought iron that bordered the restaurant's patio area. "I didn't even think to get his license number."

She nodded, explaining she hadn't been able to get it, either.

"Luckily, there's no damage to my car," the man said. With a friendly nod, he walked away.

Though she no longer had any appetite for her dessert, Genna forced herself to take a few more bites, eating slowly, trying to get her heart rate to slow. She didn't understand why this person had decided to single her out, but this all needed to stop.

Now, the thought of leaving the restaurant terrified her.

Petting JB, she stared at the mostly uneaten cake, making no move to put it into the to-go box. Ty materialized and offered to take care of that for her.

Once he had, he smiled and left the check, telling her, "No hurry." Good thing, because she had no intention of moving just then. She honestly wasn't sure she'd be able to walk.

But eventually, she had to get up and vacate the table. It wouldn't be fair to the restaurant or to her server for her to sit there so long after she'd finished her meal.

First, she clipped the leash to JB's collar and walked her over to the grassy, shaded, fenced area that had been designated for dogs. Once JB had gone potty, Genna picked her up and carried her out to her car, continually scanning the parking area for any sign of the black SUV.

As soon as she got inside, she locked the doors and started the ignition. Slowly backing from her space, she drove slowly around the lot before exiting to the street.

A few blocks down she saw a large pet store. Since she could bring JB inside, this seemed like a safe place to pass a little more time. She needed to stock up on a few more dog supplies anyway.

June Bug appeared to enjoy riding in the shopping cart. Genna grabbed several more toys, another fluffy dog bed, this one for the office, and the perfect, pink harness. She wheeled up and down every aisle, including the fish and reptile area, hating that she had to constantly check over her shoulder. It didn't help that she had no idea what her stalker looked like, so she simply avoided everyone, male or female.

When it came time to check out, she tried to make small talk with the cashier, acting as though her heart wasn't racing. Once she'd paid for her items, she left the cart in the front of the store and loaded JB up in the tote bag. Taking a deep breath, she paused just outside the entrance and once again searched for any sign of the black SUV. She hated being so jumpy and on edge. And angry, she realized as she loaded the bags and her dog into her car. It was not only frightening, but infuriating to be made to feel like a target. There had to be a safe way to put an end to this.

Right now though, she just needed to avoid the stalker. No way did she intend to confront him alone.

She took another quick scan of the parking lot before getting into the driver's seat. Once inside, after immediately locking the doors and starting the ignition, she tried to figure out where to go next.

Her first thought—RTA headquarters—she immediately discarded. It looked bad enough that she'd already put in an appearance there on her day off. Yet she couldn't go to her house and she didn't want to take a chance on driving to Parker's while he wasn't there in case someone followed.

As she drove slowly down Main Street, her anger subsided and she realized she wanted to cry. Since she didn't consider herself a weepy kind of person, this only increased her irritation. Swiping at her eyes, she tried to blink the tears away while she decided where to go and what to do.

Chapter 10

As usual, Parker thoroughly enjoyed taking his eager group on the hike. Not only did he love the physical exertion, but it was fun watching the tourists' reactions to the beautiful foliage and the occasional wildlife sightings.

But he couldn't stop worrying about Genna. With two house break-ins and now a vehicle following her, the threat seemed urgent. Even if she had no idea who might be doing this or why, with a serial killer terrorizing young women, she couldn't afford to take risks with her safety.

The thought of something happening to her made his blood run cold. And Hetty, ever perceptive, had asked him how long he'd been in love with Genna.

He'd managed to blow the question off, acting incredulous that she'd even suggest such a thing. In reality, he knew he'd been fooling no one. If Hetty thought she knew, it wouldn't be long until everyone at RTA would be talking.

For himself, he knew he could live with gossip. With a business like theirs, run by family and employees who'd been there so long they were like family, it seemed there was always some rumor going around.

Parker and Spence tried to ignore them. Lakin had always delighted in them, claiming she found the talk hilarious.

But Parker didn't know how Genna would handle the rumors. She'd just started working for RTA and while she'd made everyone's acquaintance, she'd likely still feel like an outsider. With everything else she had going on, he wanted work to be a safe haven.

Returning after the hike to headquarters, he let Spence handle the checkout. He went back to the break room to grab a bottled water.

He wondered how Genna's afternoon in town had gone. Hopefully, there'd been no more incidents with someone following her. Pulling out his phone, he saw no missed calls or texts, so he had to assume everything had been okay.

Once the last guest had trundled off, Parker made his way out front. "I'm going to head home," he said. "You all set here?"

"Sure." Spence grinned. "Is Genna waiting for you to get home?"

Parker should have been surprised that Hetty had already spread the news, but he wasn't. Spence and Hetty were super close. "It's not like that, and you know it," he said, shaking his head at his cousin. "She's staying in the guest bedroom after someone has tried to break into her house twice."

At his words, Spence's teasing expression vanished. "And now she's had someone following her." He clapped Parker on the back. "Sorry, man. I just wanted to give you a hard time. You know I'm all in to do whatever you need to help catch this guy."

"I appreciate that." Barely able to contain his need to rush home, Parker said his goodbye. He called Revis and, after his dog jumped up into the back seat, got in his truck and headed home.

As he pulled up in front of his driveway, disappointment mixed with worry as he realized Genna wasn't there. With the truck still running, he got out his phone and called her. She answered on the second ring.

"Are you home yet?" she asked, her voice shaky. "I've been driving around with JB, and didn't want to go to your place unless you were there."

"I'm sitting in my driveway," he said. "Did something else happen?"

"Yes and no." She sighed. "Would you mind watching for me? I'm about five minutes away. I'll only stop once I'm absolutely sure that I'm not being followed."

"Revis and I will wait right here," he promised. "Please stay on the line until I can see you."

"I will. Right now, no one is following me. I've been on the lookout for a black SUV. I haven't seen it since lunchtime."

The fact that she had seen it again wasn't lost on him. Though he wanted to press her for details, he knew it could wait until she was safe and sound with him and ready to talk.

"How was your tour?" she asked, her voice still shaky. Understanding her need to discuss something ordinary, he told her about the group. They'd been repeat visitors, two families who lived next door to each other somewhere in California.

"I'm almost at your place," she said once he'd finished. "Thank you for talking." She paused for a moment. "I really just needed to hear the sound of your voice."

Stunned, he told himself what she really meant was the sound a friendly voice. Anyone would do.

While he waited, he opened the door so Revis could hop out, which he did, tail wagging and panting happily. For an older dog, Revis moved well. Parker ruffled his fur, telling him they were watching for Genna and June Bug. Revis's ears perked up, almost as if he understood every word.

Finally, Parker spotted Genna's car making its way down the road. Both he and Revis watched, waiting while she pulled into the driveway and parked.

She got out slowly, waving. Crossing around to the other side, she let June Bug out before reaching into the back seat and retrieving several shopping bags.

"Do you want some help?" he asked, ready to take some of the bags from her.

"No, thanks. I'm good."

He noticed she'd left something in the back seat and asked her if she wanted him to grab that. She told him no, it was JB's bed for the office and she'd leave it there until she went back to work

Genna and her tiny pet led the way into the house, Revis a few steps behind and Parker bringing up the rear. He couldn't help but reflect on how domestic all of this felt. Or would have, if not for Genna having a stalker.

Once inside, Genna carried her purchases to her room, both dogs following right behind her. She closed her door, JB and Revis still with her.

A sharp, staccato set of knocks on the front door, followed by multiple presses of the doorbell, told Parker that his brother Eli had come to visit.

Which could be a good thing or bad.

Opening the door, Parker motioned Eli in. At least his brother wasn't in his law enforcement uniform, which meant this call likely wasn't on official business.

"Evening," Eli said, his eyes scanning the room. "Where's your new dog? I've heard all about him and can't wait to meet him."

"He's around here somewhere," Parker replied, keeping his tone casual. He figured Eli had also come to check out the current living situation, since the gossip about him and Genna had no doubt made the rounds of the family.

"Oh. I want to meet him," Eli said.

Since Revis had gone with Genna, Parker wasn't about to go get him. "Do you want a beer?" Parker offered.

"Sure." Eli dropped onto the couch. "They finally were able to figure out the identity of the second victim. It was a woman named Allison Harris."

Parker got their beers, opened them and handed one to his brother. "I can't believe that guy still hasn't been caught."

"He will be." Accepting the bottle, Eli spoke with confidence. "Sooner or later, he's going to make a mistake. And we'll get him."

Genna appeared, evidently hearing voices, Revis and JB hot on her heels. Parker introduced Genna, and then each of the two dogs. They stayed close to Genna, both of them regarding Eli with thoughtful expressions.

"You're with law enforcement, if I remember right," Genna said, her expression hopeful. "Are you here to tell us that the Fiancée Killer has been arrested and will be brought to justice?"

"I wish." Eli shifted in his seat. "But I hear you've been having some trouble yourself. Your house was broken into?"

She nodded. "And now someone seems to be following me. It was a black SUV. Mercedes, I think. I wasn't able to get the license plate."

"Following you?" Eli asked, frowning. "For how long?"

Genna sighed. "Just today. They almost caused an accident at an intersection in front of the restaurant where I was eating lunch out on the patio."

"And you don't have any idea who it might be?"

"No," Genna replied. "I don't have any clue who or why."

Though Parker had hesitated to mention it before, he thought now might be a good time. "Didn't you say your ex-husband's new girlfriend was harassing you before you left Anchorage?"

"Ann?" Slowly, she nodded. "But that was back in Anchorage. There's no way she'd drive six to seven hours just to stalk me."

Sipping his beer, Eli appeared thoughtful but he didn't comment.

"Maybe not," Parker allowed. "But still, it wouldn't hurt to have Eli look into them."

Genna looked from one man to the other. "I'm sure Eli has enough to deal with, working on the serial killer case. I don't want to be a bother."

"You're not," Eli assured her. "If you'll just write down your ex-husband's name and address, as well as his girlfriend's, I can check them out."

"We'd appreciate that," Parker interjected when it appeared Genna might protest. "Just a few minutes of your time would go a long way to helping Genna feel safe."

Genna met his gaze, her expression troubled.

"Please," Parker said. "It can't hurt."

"Okay, I'll write their info down," Genna finally said. "But I'm telling you, it's not them. First up, they were cyber bullying me before as well as calling and texting. They're not now. Even though I've blocked both their numbers, they'd buy disposable phones just so they could reach me. All of that has stopped."

"Interesting." Eli shrugged. "Maybe they decided to torment you in person this time."

"They did that before, too. It accomplished nothing. And I'm here in Shelby now. They have jobs and lives in Anchorage. While it's a beautiful drive from there to here, it's also long. I honestly think Ann celebrated when she succeeded in running me out of the area. Now Chad is all hers. She has no reason to follow me here and torment me."

"Maybe not," Eli answered. "But you never know with some of these kinds of people. They can become so wrapped up in vengeance or whatever it is that they're trying to accomplish, all logic flies out the window. Let me check into them."

"As long as they aren't made aware, I'm fine with it," Genna said. "I don't want to do anything to bring me to their attention and potentially start things up again."

"They'll have no idea," Eli promised.

With a curt nod, Genna turned and disappeared into her bedroom. To Parker's surprise, both dogs remained where they were, their attention fixed firmly on Eli, though they turned their heads as Genna walked by. When she reappeared, she handed Eli a folded piece of notebook paper. "Here you go. I've included their home addresses and cell phone numbers, as well as places of employment."

If her thoroughness surprised Eli, he didn't show it. He tucked the paper in his pocket and thanked her before turning back to Parker and asking a question about RTA.

Taking a seat on one end of the couch, Genna listened. She made no move to join in the conversation, which would have concerned Parker if not for her relaxed demeanor. She'd had one hell of a day. More than anything, he wished he could sit down next to her, put his arm around her and pull her close. But then he could only imagine his brother's reaction of he did. More fuel for the family gossip.

This made him think of their sister. "Have you talked to Lakin lately?" he asked. "How's that hotel renovation project going?"

Eli smiled. "She says she's having a blast. Living the dream, in her own words."

"Good for her." Parker glanced again at Genna before turning his attention back to Eli. "I've been meaning to go by and take a look at the place. See what they've done so far."

Eli chuckled. "Good luck with that. She told me she doesn't need me looking over her shoulder."

"Maybe Genna should go," Parker said, smiling. "What do you think, Genna? You and Lakin were old friends back in the day."

Though she smiled back, she chose not to answer the second question. Instead, she made a noncommittal comment, saying she just might have to pay Lakin's hotel a visit. Parker couldn't tell if she meant it or not. He hoped she did, because as far as he could tell, Genna kept to her own company. It might be good for her to have a friend. Of course, that would be totally up to her.

Eli changed the subject again, telling them a little about the ongoing investigation. What information he could give them was limited, he said, but he promised he and his colleagues were all hard at work on it.

Genna excused herself, heading into the kitchen to get something. Eli took the opportunity to give Parker a look, one brow raised. "Is there something we—meaning the family—need to know?" he asked.

There were several responses Parker could have given. Luckily, he didn't have to give any of them because Genna returned, carrying a glass of wine.

"Why the serious expressions?" Genna asked, looking from one man to the other. She figured they'd been discussing her and her situation, and she couldn't blame them.

For whatever reason, giving Eli information on her ex-husband and ex-best friend had made Genna feel conflicted. Almost as if by doing so, she was dragging her old life into her new. Which she most definitely didn't want to do.

Had she somehow managed to make them think less of her? Surely not, since Parker already knew her story and she and Eli had only just met.

No doubt her moment of self-doubt was all in her head. They'd definitely gone right back to their conversation, a few seconds after a pause that might or might not have been awkward.

Watching as Parker and Eli talked, the way they spoke so affectionately about their sister, made her relax. Instead of feeling like an outsider, she felt…accepted. She also appreciated that Eli didn't make a fuss over her staying with Parker. Instead, he treated her presence as if it wasn't a big deal, which she appreciated, since it really wasn't.

Eli finished his beer and got to his feet. "I'd better go," he said. "I'll keep you both posted if there are any new developments on the Fiancée Killer."

"I hope you get a good lead soon," Parker said, walking him to the door.

"You and everyone else in Shelby," Eli replied.

Once the door had closed behind Eli, Parker returned. "How are you feeling?" he asked, settling next to her on the couch.

She shrugged. "Okay, I guess."

Parker took a deep breath. "I guess I should warn you. My family likes to gossip. I'm sure they'll be talking about you staying here with me."

"Why?" she asked. "Surely, once they find out the reason I'm here, they'll understand."

He shifted in the seat, clearly uncomfortable. "Yeah, they'll definitely get it. But that's not going to stop them from giving me hell. They all want to make this more than it is."

While she could have pretended not to understand, she did. Slowly, she got to her feet, scooping up JB. "I'm sorry that my being here is such an inconvenience. Give me a few minutes to get packed and I'll go stay in my own home."

"That's not what I meant," he protested.

Ignoring him, she carried her dog into her room. Revis lifted his head as they passed, but made no move to follow. As she set JB down on top of the bed and reached into her closet for her duffel bag, she realized she was crying. Tears streamed down her face. Furiously wiping them away with the back of her hand, she wondered what the hell was wrong with her. Usually, she considered herself even-keeled.

"Genna, please. I don't want you to leave. I really don't." Parker stood in her doorway, clearly keeping his distance.

She couldn't blame him. She was a hot mess right now. Keeping her face averted so he wouldn't see, she tried to pretend she was fine. "It's all good..." she began. To her absolute horror, her voice broke. "There's just been a lot lately."

"It's me," he said, gently pulling her into his arms. "Not you. That was my awkward attempt to let you know that my family will be giving both of us a hard time, even though it's completely unwarranted."

Though she held herself stiffly, she didn't pull out of his embrace. He smelled good, a combination of mint and outdoors. And the Parker she'd come to know would never be so callous. Clearly, she might possibly have misunderstood.

"Why?" she asked, finally lifting her face to his. "Why would it bother you so much if your family teases us?"

"You're crying!" Gently, he smoothed her hair back, using his finger to awkwardly wipe away her tears. "Genna, I never meant to hurt you. I just wasn't sure how to handle it. Obviously, I handled it wrong."

She didn't get a chance to respond, because he covered her mouth with his and kissed her. The kind of kiss that made her entire being melt. Deep and slow and sure, he showed her more than words ever could how much he wanted her.

When she finally broke away, they were both breathing heavily. "I was mistaken, wasn't I?" she asked.

"Yes." He nodded, a slight smile playing about his mouth. "I meant well, but completely botched things. What I need you to understand is that I don't want you to leave."

Since she didn't really want to, for a multitude of reasons, some of which she had no reason thinking, she bobbed her head. "I'm not going anywhere."

"Good." His smile made his blue eyes sparkle. "It's not safe."

It felt like he'd tacked that last statement on for good effect. Since it happened to be exactly what she'd needed to hear, she smiled back.

"Come here," she told him.

She didn't have to ask him twice.

Kissing, caressing, they helped each other shed their clothing as they made their way to her bed. Just like before, when they came together, the explosive passion made her forget everything but Parker.

Afterward, he continued to hold her close. She liked that he didn't immediately jump up, but treated her as if he thought her precious.

The realization stunned her. So much so, she pushed herself away from him and went to clean up. After that, she told him good-night, waiting while he headed into his own room to sleep. The moment he left, JB jumped up onto her bed to sleep. The little dog raised her head when Genna got in, her tail wagging.

The next morning, Genna got up and began a routine that had started to feel comfortable and familiar. She met Parker in the kitchen and nearly laughed out loud when he handed her a mug of coffee, already fixed the way she liked it.

"Thanks," she said, her heart light. Honestly, the roller coaster of emotions that had been buffeting her almost gave her whiplash.

"You're welcome," he replied, drinking from his own mug. Revis lay curled up at his feet. "Are you glad to return to work?"

"I am." She glanced at her bedroom door, wondering when JB would stir her little self. As if thinking about her had summoned her, the small dog came trotting out to the kitchen, tail wagging. She and Revis touched noses before Genna took JB outside for her morning constitutional.

When she returned, Parker had placed two toasted bagels and a tub of strawberry cream cheese on the table. "Breakfast," he said. He looked so pleased with himself that she wanted to kiss him.

Better if she didn't. Instead, she fed JB and, once her dog had eaten, sat down at the table to break her own fast. Funny how making love the night before could improve one's outlook on life.

They decided to ride into work together. Once both dogs were in his truck, Revis in the back and JB in Genna's lap, they headed to the office.

When they arrived, they walked in together, both dogs trotting along side-by-side.

"I have the first excursion of the morning," Parker said, his boyish smile tugging at her heart. "I'm taking a large group out fishing. That's perfect for an overcast sky like it is now."

He stretched, drawing her gaze. Then, realizing where her thoughts had inevitably gone, she shook her head at herself and blushed. "Well then, we'd better get busy," she said, making her voice brisk. "Let me get signed into my computer so I can get everyone checked in and you all can be on your way."

Not five minutes after that, a private bus pulled in and parked. At least fifteen people got out, all rushing for the front door. Though the sign clearly asked people to form a single line, several of new arrivals rushed the counter, all talking at once.

Though this sort of thing tried her patience, Genna

got everyone sorted out, politely insisting they all wait their turn.

It turned out most of folks were guests of one man named Miles Franklin, who owned a large vacation property in town. He'd booked the fishing trip as a treat, one last thing to do before his guests left. He insisted on being first, and since he'd paid, Genna figured that made sense. He had an exaggerated sense of self-importance, but aside from that, he seemed decent.

Either way, she treated each person the same way, with her usual mix of friendly efficiency. They all seemed excited about the possibility of catching fish and a few confessed they'd never been fishing before.

Once she'd checked everyone in, Parker took over, shepherding everyone outside and down the path that led to the boat docks.

Watching them go, Genna breathed a sigh of relief. This particular group seemed as if they might be a bit challenging and, honestly, if she'd been Parker, she would have enlisted Spence's help. But Parker hadn't appeared concerned and he'd been doing this long enough to know what he could and couldn't handle.

Spence arrived about an hour after Parker had left. "Good morning," he said, heading directly to the break room to grab a cup of coffee. When he returned, he settled in one of the office chairs and rolled up next to Genna.

"I checked the bookings today. Parker has a large group right now, doesn't he?" He grinned. "We switched. I get tired of taking people fishing. So he's doing that and I'm taking the next group on a nature hike."

Though she hadn't known that, she nodded. "Well, your group isn't too shabby, either. You leave in twenty minutes, right?"

"Yep." He glanced at the parking lot, which so far only contained the private bus from earlier. "If they show up, that is."

Almost as if his words had summoned them, several cars turned into the drive. As they parked, Genna opened the check-in software. "I'm ready," she told Spence. "I'll get them logged in and turned over to you in a hurry."

As people filed in through the front door and arranged themselves in a single line, she processed each one. Marveling at the difference between the two groups, she processed them quickly.

Once the last person had been logged, she gestured to Spence. With very little fanfare, he herded them outside and they started on the path that went up the mountain.

A short time later, Parker and his group returned. Just like before, they pushed through the front door, jockeying to be the first at the counter. Their mood seemed markedly different, and she caught herself glancing at Parker several times, just in case he wanted to give her a hint.

Instead, he crossed his arms and watched from the back of the room, his smile decidedly forced. Several of the customers grumbled loudly while waiting in line.

This time, Miles Franklin hung back, letting all his guests check out before him and sending them all out one by one to wait on the bus.

Finally, he was the only one of the group left inside. "I'd like a full refund," he demanded, glaring at Genna. "Not a single person in my party caught a fish."

Since this request had come up before, as unbelievable as it seemed, Genna had her answer prepared. "I'm so sorry, sir, but the agreement you signed clearly states that catching a fish is not guaranteed. We are not responsible for nature."

As she finished speaking, his expression darkened. "I don't care. I paid you people a lot of money to make sure my friends had a good time. We've already informed my cook that we are having a fish fry tonight. How can we do that if we don't have any fish?"

The anger simmering underneath his measured tone sent a chill through her. She glanced at Parker, very glad he was there. He watched silently, arms still crossed, but, judging by his intent expression, she could tell he'd jump into action if the situation got out of control and turned into something she couldn't handle.

She could only hope it didn't go that far.

Chapter 11

Watching while Genna tried to calm Miles Franklin down, it took every ounce of self-restraint Parker possessed to keep from intervening. This was definitely a case where the customer was not always right. Plus, the guy was needlessly being a total jerk.

But Genna's role as the office manager meant handling the customer interactions, both good and bad. Though this type of situation luckily had been rare, he needed to make sure she felt comfortable dealing with it. Unless she indicated the wanted him to step in, he'd let her handle things.

"Well?" Miles demanded, rapping his knuckles sharply on the counter. "Did you lose your voice?"

Revis, who'd been sleeping in his bed behind her, growled. Expression startled, Genna swung around to look. Not only had the big dog gotten to his feet, but her little JB had joined him. The two canines stared Miles down. The hackles on Revis's back were raised and they both looked decidedly unfriendly. Anyone who had any knowledge of dogs would take this as a clear warning.

Parker couldn't help but approve. It appeared he wasn't the only one watching over Genna.

After a brief irritated glance, Miles paid no attention

to the animals or to Parker. Instead, he continued to focus all his attention on Genna. "Well?" he demanded again.

Straightening, she took a deep breath. Parker guessed she was determined to keep her response cool and composed. "Since you are asking me how you're going to have a fish fry, I can suggest a couple of markets that stock an ample supply of fresh fish. Beyond that, there's really nothing else I can do for you."

At that, Parker had to stifle a laugh.

Miles bristled, likely about to hurl another set of insults or demands at Genna. Just then, the driver of the bus waiting out front honked the horn.

"You'd better get going," Parker drawled, unable to help himself. "It sounds like they might be getting ready to leave without you."

Face red, Miles looked from Genna to Parker. "You haven't heard the last of me," he declared. "I'll be posting a review online." He took two steps toward the door before whirling around. "And I will be contacting my bank to dispute the credit card charges."

With that, he bulldozed out the door and stomped off to the waiting bus.

Watching him go, Genna sagged against the counter in relief.

Parker sighed. "Please make a note in his file not to allow him to book with us again."

"Already done," Genna responded, shaking her head. "I can't imagine being so entitled that you think you shouldn't have to pay if you don't catch a fish."

"It happens. But luckily, not very often." He thought for a moment. "But it did remind me why I'd rather Spence take the fishing groups. At least when I stick to hiking or four-wheeling, people don't have unreasonable expectations."

As the bus drove off, Parker finally relaxed. Genna appeared to be trying, but she couldn't hide the way her hands trembled.

Just knowing how badly that customer had upset Genna made his entire body clench. "Are you all right?" he asked, his voice gruff.

Gaze locked on his, she slowly nodded. "It was all just so unexpected," she said. "I still don't understand why he got so angry."

"Some people are just like that. Like I said, it's rare."

"Is it? You're telling me that no one gets upset if they go out on a wildlife trip and don't see any? Or a whale-watching thing with no whales?" Genna asked, some of the color finally returning to her face.

"Oh, we have had some who might make a few snide comments here and there, but it's rare that someone demands their money back. And not just their own payment, but that of everyone in the group."

She glanced at her computer. "That would have been a significant amount of money. And he signed the disclaimer."

"Exactly." He moved around behind the counter and squeezed her shoulder, aching to do more. "Don't worry about it. He's gone. Hopefully, he'll move on with his life. And if he writes a bad review, once he explains his logic, no one will take him seriously."

"True." Finally, her tense expression relaxed and she smiled up at him. "I'm just glad you were here. You and the dogs."

They both turned to look. Revis and JB had returned to their beds and had curled up comfortably.

"Best decision I ever made," Genna said, her smile widening.

"Best decision *we* ever made," he corrected, barely able to keep from touching her again. "You did well handling all of that."

"Did I?" Apparently completely unaware of how she affected him, she got busy typing something into her computer. "I wondered if you would have preferred I offer him something. Like maybe a free pass to come fish again."

He snorted, about to comment, until he realized she wasn't serious. "Only if you guarantee he could catch a bunch of fish next time."

Brows raised, she met his gaze. "Thank you. Just being able to joke around about this has made me feel a lot better."

"I'm glad." He thought for a moment. "After Spence's group comes back, are there any more going out today?"

"Nope," she replied without even having to check the schedule on the computer. "It's a slow day."

"Which means maybe you can I could go to dinner after?"

She froze. "Maybe," she finally said. "Though, to be honest, I'd rather get takeout and go home and eat."

The way she referred to his place as home brought a lump to his throat. "That sounds good, too. Let me know what you want and we'll order ahead."

In the end, they decided on fried chicken. "I need comfort food," she told him, her expression serious. "Mashed potatoes and gravy, and those rolls with honey."

After Spence and his group returned, Genna put them through checkout, which went smoothly. Spence appeared distracted and left as soon as his tour did, which meant

Parker never had a chance to tell him about their irate customer.

"We can fill him in tomorrow," Genna said, correctly reading his mind.

"We'll definitely have to," he replied. He could only imagine Spence's response.

After Genna set her computer up for the morning, they turned out the lights and locked the door. They picked up the meal on the way home. Both dogs immediately perked up at the smell of fried chicken. Their intent fixation on the large paper sack made Genna laugh.

"None of this for you," she said. "But I promise I'll feed both of you your kibble as soon as we're home."

There it was again. *Home*. While he figured calling his place "home" wasn't a big deal to her, he couldn't help but like it. A lot.

He'd just pulled into the driveway and parked when she made an odd sound low in her throat.

"What's wrong?" he asked, killing the ignition and pocketing the key fob before turning to face her.

"Look at my car," she said, fumbling with the door handle so she could get out. "What the heck happened to it?" The urgency in her voice had him jumping out his side.

"Someone slashed my tires." Expression incredulous, she made a slow circle around her car. "All four of them."

Following her, Parker cursed. More than just jabbed, someone had repeatedly used a knife to create large gashes in each tire. Not only were they flat, they were in shreds. "Who would do such a thing?" he asked, unbelieving.

"I'm guessing my stalker figured out where I'm staying." A combination of fear and sadness colored her voice. "Until he's caught, no place is safe for me."

Pulling her into his arms, Parker kissed her forehead. "We don't know that this is the work of your stalker," he pointed out.

She lifted her head to look at him. "Oh, really? Who else could it be?"

"I'm thinking that irate customer from earlier today. It's a simple thing to find out where I'm living. Maybe he decided this would be a good way to act out his frustration."

Her eyes widened. "I didn't even think of that. I'd pretty much forgotten about him. But honestly, I'd rather it have been him than my stalker. I hate not feeling safe."

"I get that." What Parker didn't tell her was that he planned to pay Miles Franklin a call. No way could he let anyone get away with ruining the property of one of RTA's employees. She might work there, but she wasn't responsible for company policies.

"A new set of tires isn't cheap," Genna mused. "And as badly as these are slashed up, I'm thinking they're not repairable."

Right then and there, Parker determined if Miles Franklin had done this, he'd either be replacing all four of Genna's tires or they'd be pressing charges.

"Let's go inside, feed the dogs and have our meal," he said, arm still around her shoulders. "After that, let me see what I can find out."

She didn't comment.

They fed the dogs and then spread out all their fast food on the table. He'd gotten several sides, all comfort food. In addition to the mashed potatoes, he'd ordered macaroni and cheese, baked beans and small salads. Plus, he'd ordered extra rolls, butter and honey.

Despite expressing her eagerness for the food earlier,

Genna barely picked at it now. "Having my tires slashed messed with my appetite," she said. "But, hey, at least we have lots of leftovers. Maybe I'll feel like eating later."

He understood. While she packed everything up to put in the refrigerator, he left the room and stepped outside to the back patio. If he intended to pay Miles Franklin a visit, he would need company.

He'd just taken out his phone to dial Spence when Eli called. "I did some digging into Genna's ex and his new wife, Ann," Eli began.

"Wife?" Startled, Parker scratched his head. "I thought she was his girlfriend."

"Well, they got married," Eli replied. "I'm not sure when. Anyways, Ann is a piece of work. She's had a few assault complaints against her, but they were all dropped. I suspect her wealthy family had something to do with that."

"Assault charges?" Parker asked. "For other people? Not just Genna?"

"Yes. And some of the notes indicate Ann is a bit unstable, to put it mildly."

Parker scratched his head, digesting this. "Do you have any reports that she might have left Anchorage and traveled to Shelby?"

"None whatsoever. But that's not unusual. Unless she did social media posts or made a point out of telling a lot of people, there isn't any reason anyone would know or think anything of it. She's not breaking any laws by traveling."

Parker told Eli what had happened with Genna's tires, though he also made sure to mention the irate customer.

"Miles Frankin?" Eli asked, his voice thoughtful. "He has that huge summer house in town."

"That's him. I'm thinking about going over there and

confronting him. If he slashed Genna's tires, he needs to pay for her new ones."

"Are you sure that's a good idea?" Eli sounded concerned. "Someone that gets that irate about not catching fish might not appreciate you coming on to his property."

He had a point.

"Maybe I should go pay him an official visit," Eli suggested. "Just to hear what he has to say."

Though Parker itched to confront Miles himself, sending someone who worked in law enforcement packed a much more powerful punch.

"Would you mind doing that?" Parker asked.

"Not at all. I'll be sure to keep you posted as to what I find out."

Having her tires ruined felt like that last straw. In the time since her marriage to Chad had ended, Genna had endured countless harassment. She'd finally been able to get some peace after fleeing Anchorage and coming home to Shelby.

And that's actually what made all this worse. Enjoying a normal life for a few weeks before the tormenting had started up again.

The respite had given her a false sense of security. She'd finally believed she had been able to move on, to rebuild her life, with hopes she could make it a good one.

When Parker came back inside, she walked right over, wrapped her arms around him and held on tightly.

"It's going to be all right," he said, his deep voice rumbling through his chest as he hugged her back. "Eli is going to pay Miles Franklin a visit. If it appears for even an instant that Miles is the one who did this, I've told Eli that you're pressing charges."

"Thanks." Stepping away, she thought for a moment. "It has to have been him. I'd rather that than have it be my stalker. I don't like to think of the possibility that he might have found me."

"I don't like that, either." Parker admitted. "But I really think it was Miles. It's too much of a coincidence that it happened right after his blowup at you at RTA."

"Either way, it looks like I'm on the hook for new tires. I don't want to file a claim with my insurance company because, when Ann and Chad were harassing me, I had to file a couple. I don't want to get canceled."

"I see your point."

She considered a moment. "There's a possibility this is work-related. And maybe not Miles, though I can't for the life of me think of anyone else that go super angry at me."

"What do you mean?" he asked, glancing back at her over his shoulder.

"There have been quite a few hang-up phone calls lately," she replied, trying not to sound as nervous as she felt.

Her attempt mustn't have worked because Parker swung around to eye her. "When you say a few, how many do you mean?"

She shrugged, still attempting to be casual. "More than ten a day. At first, I thought it was someone dialing the wrong number. But now it seems deliberate. I've even started making a note of the time they come in. There's definitely a schedule."

"Like every hour?" He moved closer.

Grabbing her notebook, she slid it over toward him. "Take a look. As far as I can tell, they happen every forty-five minutes."

Frowning, he studied her notations. "That's really weird."

"I know." She shrugged. "It might be nothing. I don't

know. I've been meaning to check with some of the others to see if it's also happening to them."

"Good idea."

She checked the time. "By the way, I have a hair appointment after work. I don't know how I'll get there, but if I figure it out, would you mind taking JB home with you so I can go directly there?"

"I don't mind at all." He smiled. "In fact, you can borrow my truck. Indulge in a little bit of pampering. You deserve it."

"Oh, it's just a haircut. No pampering. But I'm going to enjoy it nonetheless."

When it came time for her to leave, she felt surprisingly torn about leaving her little dog. "I'll see you when I get home," she said, crouching down and kissing JB's adorable little nose. "I promise."

She looked up to find Parker watching her, smiling. "She's a lucky girl."

Touched, she thanked him before getting up. "You take good of her for me. I'll see you later."

"Sounds good." Handing her his keys, he hesitated a moment. "Keep your eyes open, okay?"

"Always." With a wave, she hurried outside to his truck.

As she drove away, even though she had to constantly check her rearview mirror to make sure she wasn't being followed, she turned up the radio and began singing along. Her mood light, she decided that after her haircut, she'd do a little retail therapy in one of the boutiques that lined the street next to her salon. A new outfit would do wonders for her self-confidence.

She found a parking spot right near the salon entrance. Smiling at her good luck, she got out, locked the truck, and headed for the door.

Inside, the cool air smelled slightly of lavender. Classic rock played softly in the background. The receptionist, a young woman with purple hair and a nose ring, smiled as Genna approached. Her nametag read Willow. "May I help you?"

"I have a four-thirty appointment with Shannon," Genna said and gave her name.

Willow's smile faltered. "I'm sorry, but I show that appointment was canceled."

It took a moment for the words to register. "Canceled? By who?"

"I don't know. Whoever took the call likely assumed it was you."

"When was it canceled?" Genna pressed. "I made this appointment several weeks ago."

"That, I couldn't tell you." Chewing the end of a pen, Willow met Genna's gaze. "Since you seem surprised, I'm guessing you didn't cancel. Is it possible a family member might have?"

"No. I don't suppose there's any chance that I can still have that spot?"

Slowly, Willow shook her head. "I'm so sorry. Shannon already took another client. What we can do is make a new appointment."

"Today?" Genna asked hopefully, even though she knew that possibility was highly unlikely.

"No, I'm sorry. Shannon has an opening in two weeks. Same time. Would that work for you?"

"Since I don't seem to have a choice, yes. I'll take it. And please make a note not to cancel it under any circumstances."

"Will do." Willow's smile had returned, full-force. "I'm so sorry about the misunderstanding."

"It wasn't your fault." Still perturbed, Genna turned to go. Out in front of the salon, she realized shopping no longer held its earlier appeal. Instead, all she wanted to do was go home, cuddle her dog, and fill Parker in on what had happened.

Whoever had been stalking her clearly had moved on to other ways to make her life miserable. At least she could take the truck back to RTA and pick up Parker and the dogs.

Though she wanted to head straight to RTA, her recent concern over being followed had her driving past her parents' place instead. She slowed, but didn't stop since her heart started pounding the closer she got.

This was her parents' home. The place where she'd grown up. This house had always felt like a safe haven. She'd retreated here immediately after her nasty divorce and again when she'd decided to relocate to Shelby.

And now she couldn't even bring herself to sleep in the place. This made her heart hurt.

Continuing past, she took a roundabout route to work. While driving, she constantly checked her rearview mirror to make sure she wasn't being followed. As far as she could tell, she wasn't.

What should have been a fifteen-minute drive turned into thirty. Finally turning into the parking area, she pulled up, hoping he was still there. Even though, technically, she could consider herself safe, she still sat in her car for a moment longer, the doors locked and the engine running.

She didn't like who she'd become. Paranoid, stressed, too worried about the possibility of something else happening to enjoy the moment.

Parker must have noticed her arrive because the front

door opened and he hurried out. Only then did she finally turn off her motor and get out of the truck.

"Everything okay?" he asked, the concern in his eyes warming her heart. "Why are you back so soon?"

Instead of replying, she swiftly crossed the distance that separated them into his arms. Holding her, he made soothing noises while she told him what had happened. "This is exactly the kind of thing that was happening to me back in Anchorage."

Steering her toward the building, he waited until they were inside with the door locked behind them before speaking. "I think it's time you have to consider that your ex and his wife might have something to do with this."

"Wife?" she blinked. Then, without waiting for his response, she grimaced. "That makes sense. Ann and Chad are exactly the same. Of course they got married as soon as our divorce was final."

He studied her. "Does that bother you?"

"No." She didn't even have to think about it. "I just hate having to consider the idea that they might be the ones tormenting me here. They're the main reason I moved. I'm far enough away from Anchorage that they'd really have to make an effort. And neither of them are the type to want to exert themselves. That's why I don't think this is them."

Considering her words, he nodded. "Maybe they have friends or family here in Shelby who are doing things for them."

The idea didn't make sense. "Who would want to get involved with something like that?"

He started to say something but she reached out and touched his arm to stop him. "I don't want to talk about this anymore," she said. "Would you mind taking me home? Also, giving me a ride to work tomorrow?"

His gaze locked on hers, making her knees go weak. "Yes, I will," he replied. "Let's lock up and we can go. And I'll call my buddy Mike at the tire shop to see if he can get someone to come here and change out all four of your tires."

Relieved, she gave in to impulse and hugged him. When he tipped her face up to kiss her, she met him halfway.

When they broke apart, they were both breathing heavily.

"We'd better get going," he said, his voice husky.

She nodded, waiting while he gathered his things. They called the dogs and once they were safely in the backseat of the truck, drove home.

When they go there, he kissed her again. This time, they didn't even make it to the bedroom.

The next morning, she woke up in her own bed, pleasantly sore. Smiling, she began the now-familiar routine of shower, coffee and breakfast. Parker grinned and winked at her when she strolled into the kitchen. Happy, she found herself grinning back.

As they rode into the office together, she caught herself wondering if life could get any better. Instantly, she chided herself for letting her clearly foolish heart get ahead of her common sense. This—whatever it was—would be fun while it lasted, but it was only temporary. Not the kind of thing she needed to be building hopes and dreams on. She'd already learned her lesson about things like that.

They arrived at RTA early. True to his word, Parker had called his friend in tire repair, ordered the set of tires and arranged for them to be installed on her car as soon as they came in. She'd handed over her credit card, trying not to wince at the amount.

They'd barely finished that transaction when vehicles started pulling into the parking lot. She'd powered up her computer and checked the schedule first thing. Today promised to be a busy day with back-to-back tours this morning and again after lunch.

A steady stream of guests kept her too busy to think.

After logging in each of Parker's, Spence's and Hetty's groups, Genna went around and tidied up the office. Since they had a weekly cleaning service, most of the difficult work had been done, but she liked to keep busy.

As there were no new groups scheduled to go out for at least a few hours, Genna immediately tensed up when she saw a car pull up and park out front. Though her first impulse had her wanting to run to the front door and lock it, she remained behind the counter. Grabbing her phone, she was ready to dial 9-1-1 if she had to.

When she saw Lakin step out of the car, she nearly sagged against the counter with relief. Instead, she waited, wondering what had brought Parker's sister here. Lakin hadn't visited since Genna had started working at RTA.

When Lakin sauntered inside, the two women hugged. She followed Genna back to the breakroom. She grabbed a bottle of water from the fridge and took a seat at the table.

For a few minutes, they chatted about inconsequential things. Finally, Lakin pinned Genna with her gaze and got to the point.

"I understand you're staying with Parker." Though Lakin asked her question in a casual voice, Genna stressed inside.

"I am, for now. It's only temporary. I just haven't felt like it's safe to go home."

"I hear you. But I heard you put in an alarm system and new front and back doors. How much safer could your house be?"

Ah, now Genna understood. Though she and Lakin had always gotten along, Lakin asked the hard questions because she was looking out for her brother. Instead of upsetting her, this made Genna like the other woman even better.

Genna decided there wasn't any point in beating around the bush. "I'm not taking advantage of Parker, if that's what you're thinking," she said.

Though Lakin's surprised expression felt gratifying, Lakin didn't back down. "I think he has feelings for you."

"If he does, that's his business," Genna shot back. "And mine. Both Parker and I are adults."

Lakin could have bristled, or come back with some kind of sharp retort. Instead, she did none of those things. She stared at Genna for a moment before her mouth curled up and she laughed. "Dang, you're every bit as prickly as he is."

"Maybe," Genna allowed. "But Parker warned me that his family would be talking about this. I suggest, if you want any more detailed information, that you should speak to him."

Admiration shone in Lakin's eyes. "I always liked you," she said. "So, relax. As long as you don't hurt my brother, I think you and I will get along just fine."

"You know how Parker is. He does what he wants. Once he makes up his mind to do something, I don't think anyone can change his mind."

Lakin nodded. Expression delighted, she clapped. "Oh, wow! You have feelings for him, too."

Again, Genna didn't want to start any more gossip. "We're friends, okay? Don't make this something it's not."

After a brief pause, Lakin sighed. "Fine. It's just that Parker has been alone for so long, I've just been hoping he'd find love."

"Then take that up with him," Genna quipped. Then, after a deep breath, she got serious. "Lakin, I've always liked you, too. But I need you to understand what's happening here. I have a stalker. Someone who has broken into my house twice. And slashed all the tires on my car."

She took a deep breath and then continued. "Someone is calling the office and hanging up numerous times during the day. I went to get my hair cut and someone had canceled my appointment. Eli looked into it, but so far we don't have any idea who might be doing this. Honestly, I don't feel safe. That's the only reason Parker offered to let me stay with him, in his guest bedroom, I might add. That's all there is. Nothing more."

Though Lakin grimaced in disappointment, she finally nodded. "Fine. I get it. That said, is there anything I can do to help?"

"I appreciate that." Genna squeezed Lakin's arm. "But I think I'm good right now."

"Were you able to get another hair appointment?" Lakin asked. "If not, I can call my hairdresser and see if she can fit you in."

"That's kind, but I was able to rebook. I did tell the salon not to cancel it under any circumstances."

Finally, Lakin got up to leave. She hugged Genna again, holding on a bit tighter this time. "You take care of yourself, okay?"

Genna promised she would.

"And while you're at it, take care of my brother, too." With a broad smile and a wave, Lakin went out the door, leaving Genna staring after her.

Chapter 12

Parker couldn't shake the feeling that he'd overlooked something. The entire time he led his group up the steep trails, he tried to figure out what.

Hell, he wasn't even sure what his feeling related to. What had happened at Genna's house? Or to her car? Or the multiple hangs-ups as she answered the phone at RTA.

All around him, the sights and sounds of nature. This trail had long been one of his favorites. This group, which consisted of avid birdwatchers hoping to check a few more species off their list, made appreciative noises at all the usual places. They paused at the halfway point, overlooking a small waterfall.

As the guests milled around, talking quietly among themselves, Parker gazed out over the familiar landscape and all he could see was Genna's beautiful face. He didn't notice one of the women moving closer until she bumped elbows with him.

"Penny for your thoughts," she said, smiling.

Blinking, he stared. It took a moment for her words to register. "Can I help you with something?" he asked in his best professional voice.

"Not really." Tone breezy, she casually touched his arm. "You just seemed really deep inside your head."

Somehow, he managed not to jerk his arm away. Realizing she was flirting, which had happened more than once over the years, he managed to murmur some banal nonsense about just taking in the scenery. Then he moved away, cleared his throat, and informed the group they were moving on.

This trip, the wildlife sightings were abundant, which meant no one should have a reason to complain. Not that anyone ever did. With one notable, recent exception. Miles Franklin. He wondered if Eli had talked with him yet.

They saw a black bear, from a respectable distance, across the water. Several bald eagles put in an appearance, as well as two river otters. A number of guests voiced their hope of seeing a wolf, but none was visible this day. Even so, between the gorgeous scenery and the wildlife, everyone seemed happy.

The woman who'd come up to him earlier stayed close, made sure she was first to comment when he addressed the group, and slipped him her phone number. He almost made her take it back, but didn't want to humiliate her in front of the others, so he pocketed it. He'd toss it later.

When headquarters came into sight through the trees, the overwhelming sense of relief made him shake his head at himself.

It wasn't that he didn't appreciate the flirting, though he—and RTA—had an ironclad rule of not dating guests. Even if the company didn't, he just couldn't imagine himself with anyone else besides Genna.

His feelings for her no longer surprised him. The more time they spent together, the more he realized how well they meshed. Not only the sex, though that alone was amazing, but everything else. He'd come to love her. Even though he didn't believe she felt the same way about him, he'd do just about anything to make sure she was happy and secure.

Once everyone had filed inside, he left them with Genna for checkout and took himself off to the break room. Once there, he grabbed a cold can of cola from the fridge and sat down to drink it.

From the other room, he could hear Genna talking sweetly to all the guests. He took the folded piece of paper from his pocket, tore it in pieces and dropped it into the trash.

Just that simple act made him feel better.

Before he had time to think better of it, he called Eli. When Eli answered, he sounded tense. "What's up, Parker?"

"Is this a bad time?" Parker asked, already regretting making the call.

"No. Well, maybe a little."

Parker could envision the other man checking his watch. "If you're calling about the cookout, I already told Lakin I'd attend."

"Cookout?" Since Eli sounded busy, Parker decided to let it go. "No, I wanted to see if you'd ever had a chance to talk to Miles Franklin about Genna's slashed tires."

"I did. He vehemently denies having anything to do with that." Eli sighed. "Oddly enough, I believe him. He said he got his revenge by posting bad reviews online."

Parker made a mental note to check. "Okay. Then I guess we'll have to keep trying to figure out who did it then."

"You know, it might have just been vandals. I'm sorry I can't be of more help. This Fiancée Killer case is taking all of my energy and time."

"How's that going?" Parker asked, genuinely curious.

"Not good. The killer is becoming more dangerous.

There have been five bodies discovered so far and I keep expecting every day for there to be another." He exhaled. "I've just learned one of the victims is the sister of a friend."

"Who?"

"Noelle Harris."

Parker winced. Eli had been in love with Noelle back in college. "Damn, I'm sorry."

"Me, too. I'll always regret losing her."

Though Eli had never said this before, most of the family had long suspected. "That's why you've always said we should always go after someone if we truly want them."

"Exactly." The sadness in Eli's voice made Parker think. "And that's why I'm going to say it again. Go after what you want, Parker. Don't hesitate or wait too long. If you do, it might slip from your grasp."

"I have no idea what you're talking about," Parker lied.

"Yes, you do. We're not blind. Everyone knows how you feel about Genna. But I suspect she has no idea. If you truly want a chance with her, you've got to make a move."

"Sometimes, Genna reminds me of a wild doe," Parker said, surprising himself for speaking his thoughts out loud. "She's beautiful but easily spooked. I don't want to do anything that might make her run."

"Then take things slow. But at least let her know you care about her."

Since his brother had his well-being at heart, Parker mumbled something noncommittal and attempted to end the call.

"Wait," Eli ordered. "I thought you were calling about the cookout. Did you know that Lakin is organizing a cookout. Sunday afternoon, at RTA headquarters? She made sure there aren't any tours on the books. If you haven't heard, I'm sure you'll be hearing from her soon. She expects everyone to be there."

Parker wasn't sure how to react to that. "Even you?" he asked, aware of Eli's busy schedule and how seriously he took this investigation.

"Yes, even me. She thinks it's time everyone in the family got reacquainted with Genna. I've got to run. Talk to you later." And Eli ended the call.

No one ignored a direct order from Lakin, but since she hadn't spoken to him yet, Parker briefly considered trying to avoid her. But that would be pointless. When Genna had first come to work at RTA, Parker had tried to organize a get-together at a restaurant. The weather had thwarted that effort and then he'd never attempted to reschedule anything.

A cookout would be fine, he thought. Casual, in a familiar setting, which would set Genna at ease. Truthfully, he wanted his entire family to meet her. Even if she didn't know it yet, he hoped someday she'd be part of them.

Right now though, he needed to figure out who was stalking her and why. Eli had to focus on the Fiancée Killer, which in the grand scheme of things had a much greater urgency. But Parker wanted to find out who was tormenting Genna. As soon as possible, he planned to put a stop to it once and for all.

When another vehicle pulled into RTA's lot and parked, again Genna found herself stiffening. She had to get past this fear, she knew. She didn't intend to live the rest of her life terrified.

When the tall, graceful woman wearing an Alaska State Trooper uniform emerged and headed toward the front door, Genna allowed herself to relax.

It must have been Colton female visit time. First Lakin and now Kansas Colton. Maybe, just maybe, Kansas had come here on official business.

"Welcome," Genna said, smiling as Kansas strode up to the front counter. Like all of the Coltons except Lakin, who'd been adopted, Kansas had vibrant blue eyes. With her long dark hair pulled back, she looked both competent and professional.

Though Kansas and Lakin had both been several years behind Genna in school, when Genna had worked at RTA during high school, she'd gotten to know them since all of the Colton siblings had either worked there in some capacity or made a habit of stopping by.

Like Eli, Kansas had gone into law enforcement. From what Genna heard, she was damn good at her job.

"Any news?" Genna asked, not even trying to contain her hopeful eagerness.

"On the Fiancée Killer case?" Kansas shook her head. "Eli is taking the lead on that one." She came back around the counter. "I just came by to see if you have a minute to talk."

"I do," Genna replied. "Let's go back to the break room. I just made a fresh pot of coffee, but we have soft drinks and bottled water in the fridge." She glanced around. "Parker's group just left. He's around here somewhere, if that's who you came to see."

"Nope. I wanted to talk to you," Kansas answered. "Though I can say hi to Parker, too, if he puts in an appearance."

"I'm sure he will."

Kansas grabbed a water and took a seat at the table. Genna, who'd just finished her coffee, poured herself another cup and joined her.

"I heard about what's going on with you," Kansas said, covering Genna's hand with hers. "About your stalker and everything. Lakin told me and then Eli. I'm really sorry you're having to go through all that."

"Thanks." Figuring the next comment would be about her living situation, Genna decided she might as well mention it first. "I'm sure you've heard that Parker was generous enough to let me stay in his guest bedroom."

Kansas nodded. "I did. That's really kind of him." A quick smile flashed across her pretty face. "And I'm sure he has no ulterior motive whatsoever."

Startled, Genna reluctantly laughed. "He's a good guy. I really appreciate the way he's helping me."

"You know my entire family is talking about it." Kansas thought for a moment. "As they should. Do you have any idea how long it's been since Parker brought anyone to a family function?"

Before Genna could respond, Kansas answered the question herself. "High school. Since he's a year older than me, and the last girl he brought home was at senior prom, that's almost ten years."

Not sure why Kansas had brought this up now, Genna shrugged. "That's a long time. But Parker isn't bringing me home to meet the family. I'd think I would know if he was."

Kansas stared. "He didn't tell you about the cookout we're having here on Sunday? RTA is closed for the afternoon and the entire family is coming, along with their significant others."

"No." Perplexed, Genna swallowed. "Is Parker the one organizing it?"

For some reason, Kansas found her question amusing.

"Parker? No. Have you ever seen a man organize a family get-together?"

Genna couldn't help but smile. "I guess not."

"Lakin decided to do this, kind of on the spur of the moment. She's pretty much ordered everyone to attend. In fact, she started a group chat and is assigning each of us dishes to bring."

"Weird that she hasn't mentioned it to me," Genna said. Then she pushed to her feet and went to look for her phone. She'd left it on the shelf under her computer. The screen showed there was one missed call, a voicemail and several text messages. She'd heard none of the notifications. Checking, she realized that somehow she'd managed to accidently put her phone in silent mode.

"Lakin has been trying to reach me," she said, feeling sheepish. "No doubt to invite me to the cookout."

"I told you." Kansas kicked back in her chair and took a long drink of water. "I have to say, I've never seen Lakin happier. It's funny how all of this kind of flipped a switch with her."

Curious, Genna eyed her. "What do you mean?"

"Turned out, she's always wanted to renovate a hotel. Or so she claims. Either way, she's in her element. And I think the place will be fabulous when it's all finished."

"I've been meaning to stop by and take a look at it," Genna said. "I told Lakin I would."

"I kind of envy her, just a little," Kansas admitted. "Relationships are hard."

Genna nodded. "That, they are. Does that mean you're seeing someone?"

"Not really. I'm getting pressure from a guy named Scott at work, though he's in the Wasilla office. But he doesn't really do anything for me. Not like—" She seemed to catch herself, abruptly going quiet.

Since Genna didn't want to pry, she simply waited to see if Kansas would continue. When she didn't, Genna smiled. "I take it you are interested in someone else."

Kansas's casual shrug fooled no one. "Not really. I just want to be prepared for when the right person does come along." She took a deep breath. "How about you?"

"What about me?" Genna asked, making a face. "My divorce was brutal. And he and my ex best friend harassed me so badly that I had to leave Anchorage and come back home to Shelby." She shuddered. "I'm in no hurry to go through anything like that again."

"I don't blame you," Kansas said. "And that's why I won't bug you to try and find out if you have any feelings for Parker. But I can't speak for the rest of my family. Once we're all together at that cookout…"

Genna sighed. "Point taken. All I can do is tell them the truth."

"And what would the truth be?" Kansas leaned forward, her gaze intent. Despite claiming she wouldn't ask, Genna could tell the other woman really wanted to know. She didn't mind. In fact, she found the Colton family's dedication to Parker admirable.

When Genna didn't immediately answer, Kansas shook her head. "Sorry. I'm not trying to pry, honestly. I'm just curious to hear what you plan to say to the rest of my family."

"What am I going to tell them?" Genna lifted her chin. "That's it's none of their business."

Both women laughed.

"I like you, Genna MacDougal," Kansas said. "RTA is lucky to have you."

"Thanks." It had been so long since Genna had an actual friend that she wasn't quite sure how to react. Early in their relationship, Chad had gradually isolated her from all of her friends except one. Ann. Now she knew why. By the time they'd dissolved the marriage, Genna hadn't been able to lean on a single friend, because she'd had none left.

To be honest, since she'd returned to Shelby, she hadn't made any effort to befriend anyone. At first, she'd been too busy wallowing in self-pity. Then she'd gotten this job, realized she had a stalker, and somehow she and Parker had become friends. *With benefits*, she thought, glad Kansas couldn't read her mind.

When she looked up, she realized Kansas was studying her.

"Are you okay?" Kansas asked quietly.

The sound of the front door opening saved Genna from answering. She pushed to her feet. "It sounds like Parker is back."

Kansas stood also. "I'll say hi to him, but then I've got to run. It was great chatting with you. I'll see you on Sunday."

"Sunday?" Parker came around the corner. "Hey, Kansas. Did you stop by to tell Genna about the big cookout?"

"I did." Kansas smiled. "And I'd heard about everything that's been happening to her, so I wanted to check on her, too."

He met Genna's gaze, his expression serious, before looking back at Kansas. "Be honest. You also heard she is staying with me, and you wanted to check out the situation yourself."

Though Kansas had the grace to look sheepish, she simply shrugged. "Genna was kind enough to humor me."

"Did she set you straight on the situation?" he asked.

"She did." Kansas moved toward the break room door. "And now I have to run. I'll see you both at the cookout."

They followed Kansas into the front office. Side by side, they watched her drive off.

"How's it been going today?" Parker asked. "Any more hang-up calls?"

"All morning," she replied. "I'm even thinking about calling the phone company and having them check to make sure something isn't wrong with our line."

"That's a great idea." He put his arm around her shoulder and pulled her close. She allowed herself to lean into him, enjoying the comfort of his muscular body. But then she remembered Spence and his group were due to return soon and stepped away. The last thing she needed was to give the Colton family anything else to talk about.

She made a call to the phone company. After they promised to check the company phone lines, she hung up. Turning around, she saw Parker had taken the chair in front of the other computer and appeared to be checking the schedule.

"Are you okay?" he asked, glancing at her.

"Yes," she replied. "Why does everyone keep asking me that?"

"Maybe because you seem a little bit jumpy?"

"Do I?" Then, without waiting for an answer, she continued. "You can't blame me, though. I think anyone would be unsettled with all that I've got going on."

"Agreed." His smile crinkled the corners of his eyes. "I have an idea. How would you like to get away for a couple of days? After the cookout, of course."

Intrigued, she nodded. "Tell me more."

"We could take one of my favorite hikes," he said, his smile widening. "Starting on one of the trails I take clients on, but branching off to another where they don't go. It's pretty remote. Perfect for camping out. We could spend a couple days out in the wilderness, just the two of us."

"Isn't that where the Fiancée Killer is finding his victims?" she asked. "On remote hiking trails?"

"On public land," he countered. "This is Colton land. And, also, those women were all hiking alone. You'll be with me. I promise, I'll protect you."

Though she'd never been the hiking or camping type, she really liked the idea. Except for one thing. The gossip their going away together would cause.

"You're worried about my family, aren't you?"

"Honestly, yes. They're already talking about us," she said. "The cookout has the potential to be brutal."

This comment made him laugh out loud. "Not my family. They're nosy. They'll ask a lot of intrusive questions, but all of it will be out of love. Do you really feel you have to worry about what they think?"

"Don't I?" she asked. "I do work for them, after all."

"Come on, just think about it." He got up and stretched, the movement drawing her gaze to the way his shirt stretched across his muscular biceps. "No pressure, but I really think it might do you good to get out of here for a while."

"You might be right about that," she admitted. "But we both have to work. I can't just ask for additional time off when I haven't been working here that long."

"You have two days off already scheduled," he said. "And I've moved mine so we're both off the same time."

Which explained what he'd been doing on the computer.

"I've never been camping," she admitted, bracing herself for his reaction. This was Alaska, after all.

"Never?" he asked, clearly not sure if she was joking.

"I tried once, when I was in high school and a bunch of us partied a bit too hearty up in Crowder's Meadow. They pitched a couple of tents, one for the boys, another for the girls. But Linda Sudan's dad showed up and insisted we all load up in the back of his truck." She shook her head, remembering.

"Several people got sick on the drive down to town. He woke up everyone's parents and told them what we'd been up to."

"Ouch." Parker covered his mouth with one hand, clearly trying not to laugh. "How old were you?"

"Seventeen. I was a senior. I'd lied and told my parents I was staying at my friend's house. They were not happy with me."

"I bet." His shoulders shook but somehow he managed to keep his face expressionless. "Well, at least you no longer have to worry about someone's dad. Or a bunch of drunk teenagers. It'll just be the two of us. We'll unplug and unwind. It'll be fun, I promise."

Seeing the eagerness in his handsome face, her heart squeezed. Though camping had never, not even once, appealed to her, she realized she liked the idea now. With him.

And not just because they were friends, either.

"I'll go," she finally said. "As long as you give me a detailed list of what to bring."

His answering smile felt like the sun coming out at the end of several dull, dreary days. "I'll take care of everything we need. You just pack a change of clothing and whatever toiletries you need. We'll plan on leaving right after the cookout."

And just like that, she realized she was going to go camping.

Chapter 13

Watching Genna struggle to decide whether or not she wanted to go camping, Parker tried to contain his own eagerness. As soon as he'd come up with the idea, he'd realized how much this outing meant to him.

He'd watched Genna's tension and stress spiral, helpless to do anything to make it go away. When the idea of taking her away from it all had first occurred to him, he'd felt a sense of relief.

Except he remembered her saying that hiking wasn't her thing. She'd said something along the lines of never going hiking, so he wasn't sure she'd even go for the idea.

"It's fine if you're not into it," he said. "We can figure out something else we can do."

She locked gazes with him and then slowly nodded. "You know what? I do need to get away. And maybe it's time for me to try something new. So, yes, I'd very much like to go camping with you."

He couldn't help but grin. "Hiking, too?"

"Hiking, too." She smiled back.

"How do you feel about fishing?" he asked. "I know where the best spots are."

Lifting her chin, her smile widened. "I used to be pretty

good at fishing. My dad took me a lot growing up. But it's been a long time."

And then, before he could express his happiness about that revelation, she grabbed him and pulled him to her.

"Kiss me," she ordered.

Needing no second urging, he did exactly that.

They managed to peel themselves off each other and head home. As soon as they took care of feeding the dogs, they kissed again.

They ended up in his bed, their lovemaking as wild and passionate as ever. Later, as she dozed in his arms amid the tangled sheets, he found himself hoping that she might stay the entire night. But sometime later, while he slept, she got up and went to her own room. He'd only realized that when he'd reached for her and come up empty. He managed to fall back asleep, knowing he'd see her again once he woke.

Sunday morning dawned sunny and bright. Humming under his breath, he got up and showered before making coffee. When Genna came out to the kitchen for her own coffee, her lack of a smile and tight expression revealed her nervousness. She made her coffee and carried it over to the table. He'd already taken both dogs out and fed them their breakfast.

Sensing Genna's nervousness, June Bug immediately went to her and demanded petting. Genna's expression softened as she gathered her dog close.

"Are you all right?" he asked.

"I'm not sure about this," she admitted. "I'm all for socializing with my coworkers, it's the rest of your family that worries me. Everyone seems determined to make something out of nothing."

Her words hurt him, though he took care not to show it. "Define 'nothing,'" he said.

She gave him a sheepish look. "You know what I mean."

Since now was not the time to ask her to put labels on their relationship, he let her off the hook. "Just have fun with it. You already know most of them anyway. I've got your back, Spence and Hetty do, too. And you've already talked to Lakin and Kansas and Eli. That leaves my brother Mitchell, if he even shows up."

"And your parents and aunt and uncle," she said. "I guess I'm a little worried about seeing them again, that's all. Do you think they've heard the gossip about me staying with you?"

He couldn't help but chuckle. "Since Aunt Abby is a reporter for the newspaper, I'm sure she has. And since she and Uncle Ryan are super close with my mom and dad, it's likely they've heard the speculation."

"I see." She took another large gulp of her coffee.

"Do you mind if I ask why this bothers you so much?" he asked, even though he wasn't sure he wanted to hear her answer.

When she lifted her gaze to his, the anguish he saw in her eyes made his chest ache.

"I don't want them to think I'm taking advantage of you," she said. "You've been kind enough to let me stay here until I'm ready to go home. If I've overstayed my welcome, I need you to say so. Because I'm still not comfortable with being alone in my parents' house. I won't until whoever has been breaking in is caught."

Reaching across the table, he covered her hand with his. "No one will think that," he said. "They know me. I asked you to stay. I'm enjoying having you here."

A ghost of a smile flitted across her face. "It's the sex, isn't it?"

"That, too," he agreed, smiling just a little. "But it's been awesome getting to know you. I like you, Genna."

Some of the tension seemed to leave her. "I like you, too, Parker. I'm really looking forward to going camping with you." She took a long drink of her coffee. "But first, we've got to get through the cookout. Speaking of that, I'm going to go make sure I look presentable."

After she went back to her bedroom and closed the door, he decided he'd better do the same. A quick shower and a change of clothes later, he figured he was as ready as he was going to be.

When he came out to the living room, he found Genna already there, dressed and pacing.

"There you are!" she exclaimed, coming to a stop. "Are you ready to go?"

Surprised, he checked his fitness watch. "Sure, but we'd be way too early. It doesn't even start for another hour."

"True." She resumed taking laps around the room. "I definitely don't want to be the first ones there. But I don't want to be late, either. That will draw too much attention."

"Genna."

Stopping a few feet away, she looked at him. "What?"

"Come here." He held out his arms.

She walked right into them without hesitation. Wrapping her up and holding her close, he kissed the top of her head. "It's only a cookout. Don't make too much of it."

Face pressed against his chest, she sighed. "I know. I'm not generally so high-strung. Usually, a social get-together like this would be something I'd enjoy. But with the feeling that someone is always watching me and might jump out from the shadows at any moment, it's hard to feel even remotely normal. It feels like anxiety simmers just under the surface in everything I do."

"I get it. If you'd rather we cancel, we don't have to go." He kissed her again, loving the way she clung to him, and aware in that moment he'd do anything to make her happy.

She shook her head. "No. A cookout will be fun. I'll be fine. I want to see everyone."

Though everything she said sounded like well-rehearsed reasons she'd used to convince herself, he simply nodded. "Up to you," he said. "But I think if we get there a few minutes after the start time, that'll be when everyone else is arriving. Except maybe Lakin. She's been known to be fashionably late."

This made Genna laugh. She moved away from him and went into the kitchen to grab a bottled water. "Thank you," she told him when she returned. "I'm all packed for the camping trip, too."

"Great. After the cookout, we'll come back here, collect the dogs and our stuff, and head out."

She nodded and then frowned thoughtfully. "Are you sure Revis is up for a hike?"

"He'll love it," he assured her. "I've taken him out a couple times and he truly enjoys it. We're not doing anything too strenuous, so he'll be fine."

"Good." Clearly relieved, she picked up her little JB, who'd come running over the moment Genna said Revis's name. "I'll be carrying her. I want to keep her close because I don't want to risk her getting eaten by something."

When the time came to leave for RTA, Genna appeared much calmer, even though she'd changed.

"You look great," he said, admiring her yellow sundress.

"Thanks. I changed four times." Her self-depreciating smile made him want to kiss her.

"I even put on makeup," she continued. "Which means no kisses, or you'll be wearing my red lipstick."

He held out his hand and she took it. They walked out to his truck together. Genna had been instructed to bring chips, so she carried a cloth tote with four bags of them. "They didn't want me cooking," she said. "Which is fine, since they don't know me yet. There'll surely come a time when they'll be begging me to make my signature cheesecake."

Since the drive to headquarters wasn't long, he took his time. Unusually quiet, Genna kept her head turned so she could watch the landscape out the passenger's-side window.

When they turned onto RTA's long driveway, they could see the parking area already had numerous vehicles. A large sign had been hung from the covered porch: Closed to the Public. Private Party in Progress.

"Just in case," Parker said, finding a spot and pulling into it. "You never know when some customer is going to take it upon themselves to just show up and expect to be included in the festivities."

"Seriously?" She shook her head. "Has that actually happened?"

"More than once," he replied. "We treat our customers like family, so sometimes they actually think they *are*. That's why we've learned to put up a sign to discourage them."

Once he'd killed the engine, he went around to her side to help her out. The sun blazed up above from a blue sky, with little wisps of perfect white clouds dotting it like fat, woolly sheep in a field.

"Do you want to go in together?" he asked, guessing she wouldn't want to hold hands as that would be making too much of a statement. The scent of meat on the grill filled the air.

Glancing sideways at him, she nodded. "Of course."

Relieved, he took her arm. "Then let's do this."

"Okay," she replied.

Though they kept moving forward, he squeezed her arm. "Nervous?"

"Surprisingly, not really."

"Good," he said.

Inside the small office, two older women stood behind the counter, chatting. They fell silent as Parker and Genna moved toward them, though they both smiled. Genna recognized them from when she'd worked at RTA as a teen. The taller, curvy woman with the short brown hair was Abby Colton, Ryan's wife. Though he hadn't been by since she'd started working there, in the past he'd stopped by frequently because he loved to fish.

And the petite woman with the beautiful silver hair in the messy bun was Sasha Colton, Will's wife and Parker, Eli, Mitchell and Lakin's mother.

"Hi, Mom," Parker said, smiling back.

"Come here, you," she said fondly, holding out her arms.

The two hugged and then, to Genna's surprise, Sasha pulled Genna in for a hug, too. Then Abby hugged them both, before dragging them out back to see the rest of the noisy family.

Almost immediately, Parker and Genna got separated. Lakin, Kansas, and Hetty dragged her over to a buffet table where they were setting up a huge charcuterie board. Since Genna appeared to be having a great time, Parker decided not to worry about her and went over to help his dad, uncle and cousin Spence man the grill and smoker.

The next couple of hours flew past, with lots of laughter, good food and great company. Despite Eli's usual focus on work, he didn't once mention the Fiancée Killer. No one did. It was as if everyone needed a respite from the ominous shadow that hung over their town.

As things started to wind down, Spence and Hetty, holding hands, slipped away. Next, Mitchell and Dove said goodbye. Lakin and Troy claimed they needed to check on something they were doing in their hotel renovations. Parker and Genna glanced at each other. With a slight smile, she gave a tiny nod and they, too, made their excuses and left.

"That was fun," Genna enthused, practically bouncing in her seat. "You're lucky to have such a large family. They're a lot of fun. Growing up, I always wished I had a brother or a sister or both."

"Thanks. I guess your family cookouts are a lot quieter."

"When we had them, yes. Since I'm an only child, I'd often invite one of my friends. But that was a long time ago. Both my parents embraced a vegan lifestyle after they retired, so there hasn't been a lot of grilling out." She shrugged. "When I stayed with them after my divorce, they didn't even allow meat inside the house. If I wanted a burger, I had to eat out."

They turned onto his street. She sat up straight, her expression eager. "I can't wait to see my little June Bug. I almost took her to the cookout today, but wasn't sure how that would go over."

"Same with Revis," he admitted. "Hopefully, they'll both enjoy camping."

As he pulled into his driveway, Genna gasped. "The front door is wide open."

Since he'd locked it, that meant someone had broken in.

Parking, he ran for the house, Genna right on his heels.

"June Bug," she called. "Revis. Where are you?"

Heart sinking, he realized there were no signs of the dogs anywhere. Either whoever had broken in had taken them or they'd escaped out the open door.

"No." Genna stood frozen for a moment. "They have to be here somewhere. Help me search the house."

Quickly and methodically, they conducted a thorough search of every inch of the place. They opened closet doors, checked under beds, and even looked in the fenced backyard in case they'd been locked out. The entire time, Parker found himself praying nothing cruel had been done to the dogs.

"Time to search the neighborhood," he finally announced. "Depending on how long they've been gone, we can only hope they didn't get far."

"Or that someone took them," she responded, her tone as bleak as her expression. "I swear no one had better have harmed a single hair on those dogs."

"I don't think they did," he reassured her, even though he wasn't positive. He kept his worry and anger banked low inside, wanting to offer Genna nothing but hope. "If it's your stalker, their main objective seems to be to make you aware they have access to your life. Harming an innocent pet wouldn't serve any purpose."

"I hope you're right."

Outside, after closing the front door, they faced the street. "You go west, I'll take east," he said. "Call me if you see them."

Speed walking, while searching for any sign of either of the two dogs, Genna felt as if her heart had been pulverized inside her chest. Not only was she terrified, worried about her beloved little dog and Parker's big one, but for the first time since all of this stalking had begun, rage simmered inside her. How dare they—whoever they were—come anywhere near JB and Revis?

She could only hope the two had simply wandered off. Because if someone had picked them up and taken them somewhere, the chance of getting the dogs back would be slim to none.

If they were out here, she'd find them. She had to. Swallowing hard, she kept looking, refusing to cry.

Her phone rang. Parker. "Did you see them?" she asked, breathless with hope.

"Not yet. If I remember right, the shelter microchipped them before we adopted. That's a good thing."

Rubbing her aching temple, she agreed. "Only if they're found."

"They will be." He sounded confident. Clearly, he didn't share her secret fear that whoever had taken them would harm the dogs.

"I've checked all the way to the end of your street," she said. "I'm thinking maybe we should call animal control, but they're probably not open on Sunday."

"I'll call and leave a message. Since they're part of the police department, they'll know Eli. Let me do that now."

After Parker had ended the call, Genna turned north and continued searching. She continually called June Bug's and Revis's names, even though she wasn't confident either dog knew their new names yet. She had no idea what they'd been called before ending up in the shelter.

Each step she took without spotting them felt like another nail driven into her heart.

Finally, she turned around and headed back to the

house. If she wanted to cover a greater distance, it would be better to use a vehicle.

She and Parker got there at the same time. "I think we need to drive around and keep looking," he said. "I also left a voicemail for my friend who works for animal control."

Trying not to panic, she agreed. They got into his truck and drove slowly, with the windows down, calling their dogs' names over and over.

"Still no sign of them," she said. "They've got to be around here somewhere. Unless whoever broke in took them."

"I refuse to consider that possibility," Parker responded. "Whoever broke in, deliberately left the door open, knowing the dogs would run off."

A flash of black in the trees caught her eyes. "Stop," she said. "I think I might have seen Revis." Either that, or some other kind of wildlife. The kind that would make a meal of JB in two bites.

Immediately, he pulled over. "Let's be careful. Just in case."

"Agreed." Cupping her hands to her mouth, she called out June Bug's name. A second later, Parker called for Revis.

If she'd hoped for one or both of the dogs to come running out of the woods, she was sorely disappointed.

Side by side, she and Parker pushed through the tangled undergrowth into the forest. Up above, birdsong continued, but they saw no footprints, no trampled plants, no sign the dogs had been there.

"Maybe you saw a deer," Parker said. He called for Revis once more. Genna joined him, her voice breaking as she said June Bug's name.

"Let's go back." Parker took her arm.

"I'm not giving up."

"We're not," he told her. "Let's keep driving around the neighborhood and hope we spot them."

"Maybe we should make signs and stick them up at every intersection," she said, climbing back up into the truck.

"If we don't have any luck this time, we'll do that," he replied.

Heart in her throat, she nodded.

His phone rang. "It's Spence," he said. "Let me fill him in on what's going on. I'll put the call on speaker."

"Hey, Spence, what's up?"

Spence laughed. "Did you lose something?"

Genna sat up straight, exchanging a look with Parker.

"What do you mean?" Parker asked.

"I had to go back to headquarters to help my mom find something, and those two dogs you and Genna got just showed up."

"What?" Genna squealed. "I can't believe it. We've been searching all over for them."

"We brought them inside and gave them water," Spence said. "They seemed a little thirsty."

"We're on our way," Parker said, starting the truck. "See you in a few."

After ending the call, he leaned over and gave her a jubilant kiss. Unable to contain her relief, she kissed him back. Then he put the truck in gear and they went to collect their dogs.

As they pulled into RTA's lot, Spence came out to meet them. He waited on the covered porch as they hurried over.

"Mind telling me what happened?" he asked, looking from one to the other. "How the heck did your dogs wind up here?"

"Long story," Parker drawled. "Which we'll be happy to tell you after we see Revis and JB."

"Go for it." Spence stepped aside.

Genna rushed past him, pushing open the door. Once inside, she spotted her little dog all curled up in her dog bed. "June Bug," she said, dropping to her knees and holding out her arms. "Baby girl, come here."

JB lifted her head. Then, tail wagging, she trotted over to Genna.

Focused on reuniting with JB, Genna heard Parker calling Revis. A second later, Revis blew past her, barreling toward his owner. He barked twice, ran a quick circle around the room, and then settled on his belly in front of Parker.

"I can't express how glad I am that they're okay," Genna said, looking up at Spence. "Thank you for holding them until we could get here. I had all kinds of awful scenarios going through my head."

Spence nodded. "I still want to know how they got loose."

Fingers still tangled in Revis's fur, Parker told him. As he listened, Spence's expression darkened.

"Did you make a police report?" Spence asked.

"Not yet. We didn't have time to look around and see if anything is missing," Parker replied.

"I bet nothing is." Genna spoke up. She scooped up her dog and got to her feet. "I think this was another attempt by my stalker to mess with me."

Parker nodded. "I agree."

Spence looked from one to the other. "This needs to stop," he said. "Have you talked to Eli?"

"Yes. And to Kansas," Genna said. "But this time, whoever is harassing me went too far. You don't mess with my dogs. I'm pulling out all the stops. I intend to do whatever it takes to catch this person and put a stop to all of this."

"What are you going to do?" Spence asked, crossing his arms.

"I don't know yet," Genna admitted. "But we'll figure something out."

"Let me know if I can help." Spence squeezed Genna's shoulder before clapping Parker on the back. "I've got to run. Will you two lock up?"

"Of course." Parker walked his cousin out, Revis trotting along at his side.

When he returned, Revis rushed over to check on JB. Genna set her down and the two dogs walked off together, curing up with each other in the larger dog bed.

Parker watched them for a moment and then heaved a sigh.

"Do you still want to go camping?" he asked.

"I don't know. We haven't even had time to see if anything is missing from your place."

"Checking that will only take a few minutes," he said, his unruffled tone matching his expression. "And I vote we go. Now we need to get away even more."

She couldn't help but agree with him. "We're all packed. Let's do it. I'll actually feel safer getting out of town."

"And you could use some time to decompress," he said.

After loading up the dogs, they drove to Parker's place. After he backed his truck up to the garage, she cuddled JB close and sat for a moment before getting out.

Parker and Revis stayed close and they all went inside

together. As far as Genna could tell, nothing appeared to have been disturbed.

"I don't think they took anything," Parker said, turning a slow circle so he could view the entire room. "Let me check my bedroom really quickly. You check yours."

Though she already knew she wouldn't find anything missing, she nodded. Still carrying JB, since she didn't want to let her out of her sight, she took a quick look. As far as she could tell, nothing had been disturbed. Still neatly made, her bed hadn't been touched. She opened a few dresser drawers just in case, but everything remained exactly the way she'd left it.

When she returned to the living room, she found Parker waiting for her. "I'm beginning to think I've lost my mind," he said. "Maybe I didn't close the front door all the way and it blew open. Not only has nothing been disturbed, but I can't even find a point of entry. No broken windows and the back door is still locked with the dead bolt, so I'm beginning to think no one has been in here."

Except Genna felt positive that someone had. The same person who'd broken into her house twice. The one who'd slashed all four of her tires. She just needed to find proof.

But how?

Setting JB down, she went over to the front door and inspected it. As Parker had said, she saw no sign of forced entry.

"I'll be right back," she said and stepped outside. Walking the perimeter of the house, she wasn't entirely sure what she was looking for. She only felt she'd know when she saw it.

Opening the fence gate, she made a mental note to tell Parker it needed to be locked. She stepped into the backyard. On the backside of the house, she finally noticed something. A small bush under one of the windows appeared crushed.

It could have been anything. It could have been nothing. Or it might be the clue she'd been looking for.

She moved closer. There. That impression in the dirt next to the bush could be a footprint.

Curious, she stepped closer and tried to lift the window. To her astonishment, it easily opened.

"The point of entry," she said out loud. She spun around so quickly, she almost lost her footing. To her shock, she realized Parker had followed her and was standing a few feet behind her.

"See?" she asked, gesturing toward the still-open window.

"I do." His furious expression at odds with his calm tone, he moved past her and shoved the window the rest of the way up.

"Should we notify the police?" she asked.

"And tell them what? That nothing was taken? No, if someone broke into my home, didn't touch anything, and left the front door open so the dogs could get out, they only had one intention. To harass us."

She nodded.

"I agree with you a hundred percent," he continued. "Mess with our dogs and you've gone too far. This means war. We're going to find out who is doing this. They need to be stopped."

"And pay for what they've done," she finished. "Now we just need to figure out how."

He touched her shoulder. "Let's get out of here. Camping will help clear our heads. Surely, we can come up with a plan."

Chapter 14

After making sure all the windows in the house were now locked, Parker and Genna loaded up his truck. They'd packed the dogs' blankets to sleep on, as well as their food and bowls. As usual, he'd been able to fit everything in his oversized backpack.

"What about the tent?" she asked, looking around. "Honestly, I don't know how we're going to carry all the stuff we need."

"I've packed it." He patted his gear. "Over the years, I've mastered the art of filling this. I think we've got everything we need."

Her eyes widened but she nodded. "No ice chest?"

"Nope. There's a stream with fresh running water near the campsite," he replied.

"I guess that's good." She didn't sound too certain.

Eyeing his pack, she looked at her significantly smaller one. "How heavy is that?"

"A little heavy," he said. "But not too much for me to carry."

Once they were settled in the truck and had driven off, the righteous indignation that had fueled Genna earlier appeared to dissipate. She put JB in the backseat so the two dogs could sleep and then heaved a sigh. "I need this more than I realized."

"I know you do," he said, aching to touch her but keeping his hands on the steering wheel. "I do, too."

Her answering smile stole his breath. For a heartbeat, he considered telling her how he felt, but decided not to. Not yet. In case she didn't feel the same way, he didn't want to make things awkward on the camping trip.

"You were pretty impressive back there, figuring out how they got into the house," he said instead.

Just like that, the smile vanished from her face. "If you don't mind, can we not talk about that for a little bit? I'd like to forget, even if just for a few hours."

"You got it," he replied, mentally kicking himself. Fiddling with the radio, he asked her what kind of music she wanted to listen to.

"Hip-hop or rock," she said, surprising him. "Though I usually tend to listen to country music, I need something fierce and loud to go with my mood right now."

This made him laugh. "I do something similar. I don't know why, but it helps."

"It does," she agreed. "Once I get this out of my system, I'll be fine." She glanced back at the dogs, now sleeping. "Unfortunately, we can't blare it. I don't want to hurt their ears."

He found the only station that played what they called "Hit Music and Classic Rock."

"KVAK, 93.3," he said. "Hopefully there's something on their playlist that will hit the spot."

A country song was playing. They exchanged looks. "Hit music," she said. "It's fine. Any music is good."

They drove past RTA headquarters, continuing on for a few miles. The elevation increased as they headed up the side of the mountain. "This is where we take the hiking expeditions," he said as they pulled into the small parking lot with a sign that marked it as the trailhead.

"Are there going to be other people here?" she asked, not even trying to mask her disappointment. "I'm not sure I'm up for a big crowd."

Unable to resist, he squeezed her arm, battling the urge to let his hand linger. "No. There's a point midway up where the trail splits off. I take the tourists up on the south side. We're heading up the north."

They shouldered their backpacks and set off. He let Revis range ahead of them, but Genna insisted on carrying JB. "She's so small, I'm afraid something will eat her," she explained.

Which made perfect sense.

As they headed up the trail, Genna kept a good pace. Since he didn't want to make her overdo it, he watched her carefully in case she needed to rest.

"I'm not going to topple over," she said dryly, catching him as he sneaked a sideways glance at her. "Despite me telling you that I don't go hiking, I'm still in pretty decent shape physically."

"I'll say," he drawled, earning her laughter.

When they reached the halfway point, marked by a bench and several signs, Parker removed his backpack and plopped down. "Let's take a quick break," he said, whistling for Revis. The dog immediately returned, sitting down at Parker's feet.

With a grateful smile, Genna took off her own pack and sat next to him. "Thanks," she said, grabbing her water bottle from the side of her backpack and drinking deep.

Parker opened a collapsible dog bowl and poured water into it for the dogs. They both drank eagerly.

"Now the fun begins," he said. "The trail is going to get markedly steeper once we make that turn. If you need to stop and rest, just say so, okay?"

"Okay." She grimaced. "So far, this hasn't been too bad. And it's beautiful here."

"Just wait until we get to the meadow where I usually camp," he told her. "And at night, the skies are amazing."

"How often do you camp up here?" she asked, genuinely curious.

He shrugged. "Whenever I feel the need to get away. Most times, I come by myself. But Spence has been here with me a few times. Eli, too. Mitchell has even been a couple of times." He flashed a sheepish grin. "It's a great place to get your mind aligned with your soul."

His poetic choice of phrase made her melt. To be honest, not only did he continually surprise her, but the more she got to know him, the more she realized how unique he was. Looking at him, with his muscular, toned body and outdoorsy appearance, the depths of his personality added to his already compelling sex appeal.

Renewed, they carried on. The exertion felt good, as if the hike brought a rush of endorphins. She felt strong and capable and unbelievably alive. Happy.

"Are you doing okay?" he asked. Then, without waiting for an answer, he asked her if she wanted him to carry JB for a bit.

"Thank you, but I've got her," she replied. "I'm fine and she's not heavy at all."

The trail grew progressively steeper and narrower as it curved up the side of the mountain. Since they could no longer hike side by side, Parker trekked ahead. She found she enjoyed having his backside to look at, especially since the height made her feel a little dizzy.

The drop-off to her right looked treacherous, even though there seemed to be plenty of trees to help break the fall. Luckily, the path they were on seemed solid. Despite that, she kept to her left, just in case her clumsy self were to take an accidental misstep. She wasn't too worried about hurting herself. But she couldn't risk anything happening to JB.

Apparently unconcerned, Parker walked a few feet ahead of her, though he kept close. She realized he'd purposely made his own pace slower to match hers, which she appreciated.

"Where's Revis?" she asked, looking around for the large dog.

Hearing his name, Revis came trotting back to them, panting happily. He made a few loops around both Parker and Genna before settling in to walk in between them.

"He's really enjoying himself," Parker said. "I'm so glad I was able to get him out of the shelter."

"Me, too."

"What about you?" he asked, glancing over his shoulder. "Are you having fun?"

She thought for a moment. "Actually, I am. More than I expected. It's not as physically taxing as I thought it would be."

His grin made her breath catch. "I can think of some other activities we can do later that will definitely be exhausting."

Grinning back, she wondered if he knew her entire body flushed. "You know, I might be able to be convinced to do this again," she mused. "With the right incentive, of course."

His laughter echoed off the rocks. "Look." He pointed. Above them, an eagle wheeled, beautiful against the bright blue sky. She'd grown up seeing the majestic birds, but for some reason out here, the sight hit differently. To her surprise, tears stung her eyes.

Keeping her hold on JB, she quickly wiped them away. Though she'd felt raw ever since realizing she'd simply traded one stalker for another after moving here, the emotion felt like a different kind of vulnerability. Was she ready to take the kind of risk she'd sworn she'd never take again? Did she dare to trust Parker with her heart?

Completely unaware of her thoughts, Parker stopped and turned to face her. "Up ahead, the path looks like it ends at some boulders," he warned. "It's a good place to stop and rest, as long as you watch out for snakes."

She started. He'd said that so casually. "I think I'll pass," she said. "Since I'm not a fan of snakes, I'd rather just get to our camping area."

"I get it." He smiled at her before moving forward. Though he loved his large family, both immediate and extended, being out here with Genna and the dogs felt like another kind of family togetherness. Both wholesome and intimate. He could definitely get used to this. He wondered what Genna thought, but decided it would be better not to ask.

Finally, the incline started to level out. "We're almost there," he told her, glancing over his shoulder.

"Good," she replied, huffing and puffing just a little. She wiped at her forehead with the back of her hand. "I'm getting to the point where I'd been thinking about telling you I need to rest."

"Not too much longer, I promise." Though he wanted to pick up the pace, he stayed steady. "We keep a little storage building up here with supplies like a cook stove and folding chairs. And if whoever camps up here last has firewood left over, it's stored in there, too."

"Interesting." She seemed to be struggling to catch her breath. "But why not store your tent there, too? Seems like it would be less to carry."

"There's a spare tent in case it's needed. But we all have our own tents, and I prefer to bring mine. You'll like it, I promise."

"I'll like it when we can stop hiking," she grumbled, shifting JB in her arms. "My little dog has gotten heavier."

This made him chuckle. "A few more yards." Unable to contain his eagerness, he moved ahead.

Her pace slightly slower, she followed.

Genna didn't want to be a party pooper, but she clearly wasn't as fit as Parker. He hiked for a living, while her exercise routine consisted of riding her Peloton bike. She'd always considered herself in pretty good shape, but this uphill hiking took things to another level.

"Here we are," he announced, turning a slow circle with his arms outstretched. "My favorite meadow."

More of a clearing than a meadow, the grassy area sat nestled in between a rock wall on one side, forest on two others, and the sloping hill that led to the cliffs on the fourth. There was more than enough area to pitch a tent, build a fire pit and set up some chairs. A small, weathered wooden building had been built near a grove of trees. Close to the place they'd stopped, someone had already made a stone fire pit, the circle large enough for a decent fire.

"I should've brought marshmallows," she impulsively said.

Glancing at her, he grinned. "I did."

Unable to keep from smiling back, she sighed. "What about bears?" she asked, slightly nervous.

He looked up. "As long as we don't keep food out, they tend to leave us alone. The shed comes in handy for that, too."

"Food." She swallowed. "I didn't even think to pack any of that. What did we bring to eat? And please don't say we're going to forage for berries and mushrooms and edible plants."

"You stole my line," he teased. She loved the way the sun made his blue eyes sparkle. "I thought we'd fish for our dinner and eat from the endless bounty that nature provides."

Dismayed, she stared at him. "You're kidding, right?"

He held her gaze, expression serious. "It's fun and easy, I promise."

Though she had a feeling she'd be going hungry tonight, she reluctantly nodded. "I guess I'll just have to trust you."

"If you weren't carrying JB, I'd hug you right now," he said. Which made her want to set her little dog down, which she wouldn't just yet. She wanted to thoroughly check out the area for snakes and any other kind of menace, before letting JB set her little paws on the ground. On a leash, of course.

"Maybe later," she said. Then, as he tilted his head and drank her in with his eyes, she amended her statement. "Definitely later."

"I'll say." Setting his pack on the ground, he began removing what she guessed must be the tent. "Do you want me to help you set up?" she asked.

"Sure." He continued unpacking. "By the way, I was kidding about foraging for our meals. I brought food.

Most of it's in cans, which the bears can't smell. Nothing fancy, but enough to fill our bellies. And if we catch any fish, I can clean them and fry them up."

Thinking of a fish fry, her stomach growled. She'd picked at the spread at the cookout, too nervous to sit down and do justice to the repast.

"You didn't eat earlier?" he asked, his brows raised.

"I tried." She shrugged. "I actually got kind of busy socializing. I did grab a pulled pork sandwich and some pasta salad, but that was early on. All this exercise has made me work up an appetite."

His smile widened. "Me, too," he said, the husky thrum in his voice making her think he wasn't talking about food. Flushing, she ducked her head, which made him chuckle again.

After getting everything laid out in the spot he'd chosen, Parker showed her what he needed her to do to help.

The tent, once spread out, looked a lot bigger than she'd expected. "This is really nice," she said, finally clipping June Bug's leash on and setting her on the ground. Immediately, Revis ran over and sniffed his friend before bounding off, eager to show her around.

Aware of the leash, JB glanced up at Genna, as if pleading to be set free. Since Genna wasn't willing to do that, she decided she'd take her little dog to follow Revis once they were done.

Her assistance mostly consisted of her standing around and holding poles up while Parker hammered pegs into the ground. June Bug, clearly bored with the entire situation, laid in the grass and watched them. Revis returned and sat down next to his little friend.

Once the tent had been set up, Parker thanked her for helping and immediately got busy doing other things.

"I'm going to take June Bug to go potty," she told him.

"Okay," he replied, looking up from where he'd begun stacking firewood for them to use later. "Don't go too far. And stay close to the path. There are quite a few cliffs up here and if you wander off the trail, you could easily take a tumble before you realize the danger. Over the years, we've had more than a few hikers take nasty falls."

She nodded, eyeing his growing woodpile. "I'll keep that in mind. Do you want me to bring back any branches or anything if I find some?"

"If you see any good ones in your path, sure. Otherwise, I'll just keep foraging. There seems to be no shortage of them right around us, in the woods close to the camp, so there's no need to go out of your way."

After double checking the leash onto JB's collar, Genna waved at Parker and walked away. Luckily, even out here in the flatter area, the trail looked well defined and she stuck to it. Revis ranged ahead, but little JB trotted a few paces away.

Glad she'd had time to rest from the hike, Genna glanced around. It might only be her imagination, but the air felt clearer, the sky seemed bluer and the sun warmer. She felt...lighter, somehow.

As Parker had promised, out here in the wilderness she felt like she could look at things differently. As if her burdens had fallen away when they'd left civilization behind. When she got back to camp, she'd thank him. Imagining his reaction made her smile.

Despite the beauty and the sense of peace, she stayed alert and continually scanned the woods around them. She kept her bear spray handy, tucked into her pocket. Hopefully, she wouldn't have to use it.

June Bug seemed eager to explore. Genna smiled as she

watched the little dog trot ahead of her, pulling slightly on the leash. Revis made joyous circles around them before bounding ahead and disappearing momentarily from view.

As they so often seemed to do these days, her thoughts circled back around to Parker. She'd never felt closer to another human being. Her feelings had slowly blossomed over time. Now she couldn't imagine life without him.

Love. A word that, until recently, had only meant anguish, pain and bitterness. She'd thought she'd never trust her heart again. But Parker, sexy, kind Parker, had showed her there was another way.

Damn it, this had become more than next-level physical attraction. The sparks that blazed between them at even the slightest touch, the way his kiss rocked her all the way to her core. And the lovemaking. Oh, hell. She'd never had lovemaking so intense, so...perfect.

She loved the man. She just hadn't said it out loud. Because she wasn't sure he felt the same way. And if she scared him off...well, she thought losing him might just destroy her.

JB wandered off the trail and Genna followed her, careful to only let her go a few feet as she remembered what Parker had said about the cliffs. Above, in the tree canopy, birds sang and flitted from tree to tree. She'd hoped to see some smaller wildlife, a rabbit or a deer, but figured Revis crashing through the underbrush probably scared them off.

Again, she wondered how Parker would react if she told him how she felt. Just trying to imagine made her stomach ache.

Maybe it would just be better to keep going the way they'd been. Day by day. Hoping that once her stalker was caught and she returned home, she and Parker would continue to see each other.

Behind her, a sound. A twig snapping. Heart skipping a beat, she spun, canvassing the woods for signs of wildlife. JB whined. Quickly, Genna scooped her up, holding her close, ready to run if she needed to.

Revis returned immediately, panting. He came to Genna for a pet, sniffed JB, and then continued his exploration. Since he didn't seem alarmed, she relaxed slightly. But decided it was time to return to camp.

Turning, she and her two canine companions went back the way they'd came.

At camp, she saw that Parker had up two chairs around the stone fire pit and had piled a neat stack of wood inside for later. The door to the storage building sat open, and he'd pulled out what looked like a small grill or cook stove.

Spotting Parker, Revis gave a happy woof and ran over to him, plumed tail wagging. Parker dropped down to his haunches and gathered his dog close to him. "He's a good boy," he crooned, which made Revis wiggle his entire body with joy.

JB watched all this, tilting her little head. Genna realized, to her little dog, Revis was family. The notion made her chest tight.

Something of her thoughts must have showed on her face.

"What's wrong?" Parker asked, looking up from his dog.

"Nothing," she answered quickly. "I just enjoy how much you love Revis."

Getting to his feet, he shrugged. "About the same as you love your June Bug."

She decided to tell him the truth. “Honestly, I’m having a hard time letting go of what happened earlier. Breaking into my house is one thing, but breaking into yours is another. And messing with our dogs…” Swallowing hard, she tried to tamp down her still-simmering rage.

“I’m going to level with you. I’ve had enough of this stalking nonsense,” she told Parker. “Whoever is trying to terrorize me has finally gone too far. I want them caught.”

Watching her, he slowly nodded. “I agree. What are you thinking?”

“Simple. We set a trap. Pretend to be gone but one of us—likely me—stays hidden in the house. If we can catch them in the act, it’ll all be over.”

“Maybe so, but that could be incredibly dangerous,” he cautioned. “I don’t think it’d be safe at all.”

“Maybe not, but the thought of losing our dogs made me physically ill. This has gone on far too long. I’m going forward with my plan, with or without your help.”

He studied her for a moment. “Then I insist that I be the one who stays behind. Not you.”

Instead of arguing, she shrugged.

“Tell me this first…” He asked, “What’s the plan once we catch them?”

“Turn them over to the authorities,” she answered promptly. “I will definitely be pressing charges.”

“Can we let this go for now? It bothers me, too, but the entire reason we came up here was to escape from all the stress of what was going on back in town.”

He had a point. “I’ll try,” she promised. “I actually feel better now that I’ve let you know how I feel.”

“Good.” Crossing over to her, he kissed her. Not on the mouth but on the cheek.

Bemused, she considered asking for more, but decided

there'd be time enough for that later. After all, they were sharing a tent.

Now that her heartbeat had slowed, she once again looked around them. Surrounded by nature, the sheer beauty of this Alaskan wilderness would be enough to calm even the most stressed-out psyche.

"I'm letting it go," she promised.

"I'll hold you to that." Moving away, he grabbed a battered, plastic tackle box, opened it and looked through it. Then, apparently satisfied with what he'd found, he closed it up and stood.

"This looks great," she said, gesturing at their campsite. "Like something out of a camping magazine. One of the ones we keep in the waiting room at headquarters."

Her comment made him beam. "Thanks. I really think you're going to enjoy this experience."

She almost told him she knew she would. She had everything that she could ever want and need right here.

"What's on the agenda for the rest of today?" she asked, dropping into one of the chairs, still holding JB on her lap.

"There is no agenda," he answered. "That's the entire point in coming up here. Just relax and do whatever feels right." He blinked then grinned at her. "It's all very Zen."

Startled into laughter, she leaned back and closed her eyes. "Maybe I'll just sit here and rest," she said, covering a yawn with one hand. "I also brought along a book I've been dying to read. I can do one or the other."

"Enjoy," Parker said. "Revis and I are going fishing. You're welcome to come if you want."

Shaking her head, she waved him away. "I'm good. I hope you catch something. I'm looking forward to that fish fry you promised earlier."

His short bark of laughter made her smile.

"I'll be back," he said. "The river isn't too far away, but I probably won't hear you if you holler for me. Please call or text if you need anything. But only if it's urgent."

She loved that he tacked that last sentence on. "What could be urgent out here?" she said and then thought of bears and wolves and even an angry moose. Pushing those images out of her head, she watched until he and his dog disappeared from sight.

"You never know," Parker replied. "Just be careful. Cell service is iffy at best."

Once Parker and Revis had left, she glanced all around the campsite one more time, just in case. All quiet, all calm. And still rustic. One deep breath and then another. She leaned back, exhaled and closed her eyes again. Slowly, she felt all the tension leaving her body.

JB felt it, too. Still curled in Genna's lap, the little dog began to quietly snore.

In the peace and quiet, she must have dozed off. A loud crash from somewhere in the woods startled her awake. JB jumped down and, completely disregarding the leash trailing after her, took off in the direction of the sound, barking urgently.

"June Bug!" Genna jumped to her feet, grabbing for the leash. She missed. Calling for JB, which the dog ignored, she ran after her. Heart pounding, she hoped and prayed the little minx wasn't pursuing something dangerous.

Leaves and twigs cracked under her feet as she ran. JB had crossed the hiking path and run down the first of several inclines. Aware she had to be careful—but also knowing she needed to catch JB before something awful happened—Genna kept going. Holding on to saplings, skidding down the slope and praying she didn't fall as she followed the sound of June Bug's frantic barking.

Whatever this was couldn't be good.

Finally, she caught sight of her dog. JB had stopped in one spot, though she continued barking at something hiding in the brush. As Genna drew closer, a chill raced up her spine. The spot where JB stood appeared to be mere feet away from the edge of a particularly steep drop-off.

"Baby girl, come here," Genna begged. She wished she had some dog treats or something she could use to lure JB to her. Still barking and intent on whatever she'd found, the little dog ignored Genna.

Moving slowly so she didn't startle her pup, Genna crept closer. All she could do was hope whatever JB had cornered wasn't something big and vicious.

A shape stepped out from behind the tree. Genna gasped. "You!" That was all she got out before they grabbed her and shoved her off the cliff.

Chapter 15

Reeling in a good-sized salmon, the sound of shrill barking broke the quiet of the late afternoon. In the act of tying the fish on a line and placing it into the water, Parker froze and listened. Frantic barking, again and again. Since they were alone in the woods, he could vividly imagine what kind of creature the dog might have discovered. It might be something small. But then again, it might not be.

Revis had also been listening, head cocked. He glanced at Parker, almost as if asking for permission.

"Go," Parker ordered. "Find JB."

The dog took off. Parker briefly debated gathering up his gear, but in the end just left it and ran. Revis had already disappeared from his sight.

And then he heard Genna scream. The shrill sound was abruptly cut off, which seemed even worse. JB however, continued barking.

Heart pounding, Parker increased his speed. He knew this area like the back of his hand. Judging from where the barking seemed to be coming from, he thought he had a good idea of the location. It was where the hiking trail made a sharp turn before continuing to make a zigzag path up the steep face of a rock cliff. The terrain there grew tricky, the path even narrower. Most hikers turned around at that point, unless they were into rock climbing. Parker had only gone up there once and that had been enough. He sure as hell hoped Genna hadn't tried making it up with her dog in tow.

JB's continued frenetic barking meant at least she was alive.

Still running, Parker reached camp and found it empty. JB continued barking from somewhere in the distance. He realized he couldn't hear Genna calling for help, though he was aware that could be a bad thing, too.

If June Bug had gotten into some sort of trouble, he knew Genna would be there trying to rescue her. "Genna!" he called, stopping to try to catch his breath. "Where are you?"

She didn't respond. But a moment later, Revis reappeared, running a quick circle around Parker before heading back the way he'd come. The big dog slowed and looked over his shoulder, almost as if watching to make sure Parker followed.

"Genna!" Parker called again. "June Bug!"

The little dog had stopped barking. Parker's heart sank, hoping that didn't mean something awful.

Revis appeared, standing on the trail ahead. He woofed once, likely urging Parker to hurry.

Once he'd caught up with his dog, the two of them continued together. The plateau sat ahead, the trail's sharp turn to the left, a staggering cliff face to the right. And no sign of Genna.

Then JB appeared, squeezing out from under a bush. Though she whimpered, she looked unharmed. "Where's Genna?" Parker asked then mentally scolded himself since he knew the dog couldn't answer. "Genna!" he called again.

This time, Genna responded. "Down here. Help me. I hit my head."

Parker started forward.

A figure stepped in front of him, blocking his path. Tall and almost painfully thin, the woman had long blond hair tied up in a high ponytail. She wore black leggings and expensive hiking boots that looked brand-new.

"Back away," she said, raising a pistol. "Or I'll shoot you." Revis growled and she glanced at him. "Maybe I'll shoot your dog, too. Call him off me."

Her wild eyes warred with her serious expression. Not wanting to risk Revis or JB getting hurt, he called them both. Revis came immediately, taking a seat by his side. JB barked once before disappearing into the brush. No doubt going back to Genna.

"Who are you and what do you want?" Parker asked, wondering if she was skilled with the weapon. He judged the distance, figuring if he played his cards right, he might be able to jump the woman and disarm her.

Instead of answering, she continued to stare, her grip on the pistol steady. "You have one option," she said. "Take your dogs and leave. Genna is mine to deal with. You won't be seeing her again."

"Not a chance," he replied, keeping his hands hanging loosely by his sides. "What have you done with her?"

She laughed. "She's hurt. But not hurt enough. Yet. I'm thinking she'll bleed to death. If not, the wolves will get her."

A chill snaked up his spine. "Who *are* you? And why do you want Genna dead?"

"Move," she ordered. "Go back the way you came. Now."

"No."

At his response, she slowly swung the gun away from him, pointing it at Revis. "Then I guess I'll have to shoot your dog."

Now! Parker leapt forward, sweeping his arm up and kicking the pistol from her hand. She let out an unearthly squeal of rage, snarling at him as she staggered backward.

They both dove for the gun at the same time. Since he was bigger and heavier, when they collided, Parker's momentum sent her flying. As he grabbed the pistol, she scrabbled to maintain her balance. Instead, she toppled over the edge of the embankment, screaming as she went.

Revis tried to go after her. Worried his dog would fall, Parker called the Lab to him. Carefully, the two of them walked to the edge of the incline. The woman had grabbed a large branch as she'd fallen and was hanging on for dear life. Since her feet were planted on another branch below her, Parker judged she wasn't in immediate danger of plunging any further down.

"Help me!" she called.

"After I help Genna," he shouted back.

JB barked again then popped up from the underbrush. She eyed Parker and Revis before barking a few more times, clearly trying to direct him toward Genna.

Moving carefully, Parker made his way down the slope after the dog. With all the trees and plant growth, he couldn't see Genna. Using trees and branches and roots as handholds, Parker continued making his way.

Revis remained at the top, watching him, aware this time he couldn't follow.

Finally, Parker spotted Genna. She lay on a ledge. When she saw him, she lifted her head and then winced in pain.

"I'm coming," he promised. "I need to call for help. Don't move just yet."

"Move?" Her voice sounded strangled. "I can't. My arm is broken. Maybe my leg, too. I don't know how I'm going to get out of here."

Hearing Genna's voice, little JB whimpered. She ran back and forth, a few feet from where the ground dramatically dropped off.

"Don't let her fall," Genna cried. "I couldn't live with myself if anything happened to her."

He couldn't get a cell signal, which didn't surprise him. It was one of the reasons he and his family like to unwind up here. No interruptions.

"I'm going to need to climb up higher and see if I can get a signal," he said. "First, I need to check on the woman who attacked you."

Genna didn't answer. When he looked, he realized she'd lost consciousness. Which might mean she'd been badly hurt.

Just the thought made him fight back panic. Forcing himself to move, he went to the place where Genna's assailant had fallen. No longer hanging on to a branch, she'd managed to pull herself up enough to be able to straddle it, using the limb as a kind of a seat.

"Help me," she ordered when she noticed Parker looking down at her. "Throw me a rope or something and pull me out."

"In good time," he told her. Then he turned and walked away without another word. Calling both dogs, he headed for the path that ascended the rock face, hoping once he reached the summit, he could manage to get enough of a cell signal to call for help. Revis walked with him, but JB only lay down and refused to leave Genna. Aware the smaller dog might need protection, Parker made Revis go back to stay with his little friend.

The old dog cocked his head and then trotted over to sit next to JB. "Good boy," Parker called and then continued on.

At the base of the cliff, he stopped and took a deep breath. It had been years since he'd attempted a climb like this. He couldn't fail. If he did, no one would be able to come help him or Genna, not to mention the unnamed woman who'd pushed Genna.

Forcing himself to move slowly and deliberately, he began the climb. Since there was a trail of sorts, it wasn't as if he were trying to pull himself up the rock. While the path turned incredibly narrow and he had to hug the side, technically it was still a hike, though an incredibly arduous and dangerous one.

By the time he made it halfway, Parker had to stop and wipe away perspiration. Though he'd never been afraid of heights, he knew better than to look down.

Once he'd caught his breath, he carried on. He kept seeing Genna lying on that ledge, broken and helpless. Pushing past frustration and rage, he only knew one thing. He had to help her. He couldn't lose her, not now. Not ever. And he hadn't even told her he loved her.

He clenched his jaw. Almost there. One foot over the other, keeping as close as he could to the rock, Parker kept going.

Finally, he reached the summit. Here, he could see the valley below and the other mountains. Carefully digging his phone out from his pocket, he held it up.

Still no bars.

Cursing, he turned in a slow circle and tried again. Even in remote areas, he knew he could call or text 9-1-1. The call would be picked up by the closest cell tower.

He tried dialing first. The call immediately dropped. Since he had nothing to lose, he sent a quick text.

Help. We are camping up on the trail near Crowder's Meadow and need help. Someone has fallen and is injured.

Once he'd sent it, he waited. And waited. Usually, the screen said "Delivered" once a text had been received. It did not this time.

A moment later, he got a red error message, letting him know his phone had been unable to send his text.

Damn it.

He tried several times to make the call. It wouldn't go through.

On the western side of the cleared area, there were several huge boulders, larger than his truck. He'd never tried to climb them and, truthfully, didn't have the equipment. Even if he managed to make it up onto one, he didn't know if doing so would even give him a signal.

Still, he had to try.

Making a quick circle around the nearest rock, he saw no way to scale it. The second one looked better. There were several trees close to it. Some of the branches even brushed against to the stone. Since time was of the essence, he didn't waste it. He climbed up one of the trees; high enough and close enough to the top of the rock. From there, he could see several flat surfaces that he could stand on, if he could just manage to get there.

Now or never.

Hoping that the branch didn't break, he grasped it and swung out over the boulder. As soon as his feet touched stone, he let go.

For a second, he remained crouched, stunned that he'd made it. Then he stood and took out his phone.

This had to work. It had to. Otherwise, he'd have to hike back to his truck at the trailhead parking area. He'd definitely have a signal there.

Lifting his phone, his heart stuttered when he saw two bars. Not a strong signal, but should be enough to call 9-1-1.

Just then, his phone rang. Eli.

Parker answered, talking without giving his brother a chance to speak. "We're at the remote campsite, Genna's badly hurt. I need you to get some help up here. We'll need a medevac copter to get her down. And her stalker's here also."

"Parker?" Eli asked, his voice fading in and out. "You're breaking up. Did you say Genna's hurt?"

Repeating what he'd just said, Parker asked Eli if he understood. But Eli didn't answer. That's when Parker realized he'd lost the signal.

He tried again and again, but couldn't get his phone to work. Texts weren't delivered and no calls, even to 9-1-1, would go through. He had to hope Eli had understood. But in case he hadn't, Parker knew he'd need to come up with an alternative plan.

When Genna came to for the second time, it took a moment for her to realize what had happened. She managed to sit up, ignoring the searing pain in her arm and leg. If she could get to her feet, she honestly thought she might be able to climb back up to level ground. But when she tried, she realized her leg wouldn't support her weight. Definitely broken. Between that and her arm, going anywhere would be impossible. At least Parker had found her.

She had to hope he'd been able to get a cell phone signal and call for help.

If he couldn't, she knew the only other choice would be for him to hike down to his truck and either try to call from there, or drive to town. By then, darkness would have fallen. While her location would likely protect her from predators, she hated the thought of spending an entire night trapped on this ledge and in pain.

But she also knew she'd do whatever she had to, to stay alive. At least she knew Parker would make sure June Bug and Revis were safe.

At that moment she realized she had no idea what had happened to Ann. Seeing her ex-best friend and ex-husband's new wife way out here, she'd finally understood that it had been Ann—and likely with Chad's help—stalking her all along. Why and how, she didn't know, since Shelby was so far away from Anchorage.

Clearly, Ann had decided that simple harassment was no longer enough. She'd decided to push Genna off a cliff and end her life. Even worse, since Ann hadn't succeeded, if she were still out there in the woods somewhere, she might decide to come back and finish the job.

Not knowing made Genna's entire situation worse. Except, as she looked up the steep slope, she knew Ann couldn't get down to her ledge without risking serious injury. For now, she'd be safe. From both Ann and any other predators.

Genna dozed, drifting in and out of consciousness. Her head hurt, which meant she'd likely hit it when she'd fallen. Likely a concussion, she thought.

JB's insistent barking made her open her eyes. She had no idea how much time had passed, if it had been minutes or hours.

"Genna," Parker called. "How are you doing?"

"I'm okay," she managed to respond, though her voice sounded weaker than she would have liked. Clearing her throat, she tried again. "Please make sure my dog doesn't fall down the cliff."

"She won't," he promised. "She and Revis are sticking pretty close to my side. I think I got through to Eli. The call kept breaking up, but I'm hoping he understood enough to realize he needs to send help."

"What about Ann?" she asked. "The woman who pushed me."

"She's still trapped," he replied. "She fell, too, but landed on top of a large tree. She's straddling the branch and as long as she doesn't move, she'll be safe there until we can pull her out and arrest her."

"Okay." Again she struggled to sit up, wincing at the pain. Not only her arm, leg and head, but her entire body felt bruised and battered. "But what if Eli didn't hear you? How will you know?"

"I thought about that," he said. "That's why I'm hiking down to the parking lot now. I should have signal there and I can find out if help is on the way."

"Sounds good," she rasped. She really wanted to beg him to promise not to leave her alone in the dark. Instead, she swallowed hard and told him to be careful.

Once he'd gone, Genna slowly slid back down to lie flat on her back and close her eyes. She had to believe this would all work out. Luckily, the temperature had stayed mild, even at night. And despite some cuts and scrapes, she wasn't bleeding a lot. She didn't think her other injuries were life threatening, and she would likely survive even an overnight stay.

She just wanted to be somewhere else—anywhere

else—other than stuck on a rock on a cliff in the Alaskan wilderness.

Time passed. How long, she had no idea. She slept some, woke in fitful starts, and drifted back off again.

When she finally heard Parker calling her name, for a dazed moment she thought she must be dreaming. But then JB barked and so did Revis.

"A chopper is on the way," Parker told her. "They're sending a team to rescue you. Is there enough room for a stretcher to fit on that ledge?"

Blinking, she looked around her. The stone outcropping that had broken her fall was large. "Easily," she replied. She'd seen enough television shows to realize they'd lower a couple of EMTs and a stretcher to her and then lift her out via helicopter. While she wasn't really fond of that plan, she also understood she had no choice.

More time passed and she struggled to stay awake. Parker kept up a steady stream of conversation, no doubt trying to cheer her up. She tried to make occasional responses, but the drowsiness dragged her back under.

The whomp-whomp sound of a helicopter roused her. Instinctively she sat up, way too fast, which brought blinding pain. She groaned. Above her, JB started barking again. Parker tried to shush her.

"Help is on the way," he said. "Just stay still and let them rescue you."

"I will," she promised. "But please keep the dogs safe."

"They're with me. And they'll stay with me until the police arrive and take Ann into custody."

Then it would finally be over. Tears stung her eyes. She wiped them away before stealing herself for the ordeal yet to come.

In retrospect, her rescue from the side of the mountain seemed like something out of a movie or a television drama. The chopper, the EMTs landing on the ledge, carefully checking her out—it all seemed to be happening to another person. Later, there were a few times she wondered if she'd dreamt it.

But there were a couple of things she remembered quite well.

The paramedic, or doctor, speaking quietly to her, with a patient smile. She'd found his positivity encouraging, which was exactly what she'd needed. She regretted that she'd never gotten his name. Even as she'd struggled to remain awake, she had felt herself slipping away.

"She's in shock," he'd said, speaking to someone else before lightly touching her arm. "Genna, I need you to try and focus, just for a little bit longer. We're going to need your help if we're going to get you out of here, okay?"

She'd nodded, immediately wincing at the pain. A stretcher had somehow materialized, no doubt let down by the hovering chopper. Carefully, she'd tried to lift herself up so her rescuer could slide it underneath her. The entire time, she'd had to bite her lip to avoid crying out, mainly because she'd known Parker would hear and she hadn't wanted him to worry.

The EMT had strapped her in. Heart pounding, she'd stared at him with wide eyes, dreading the moment when the chopper lifted her into the air.

"Don't worry, we've got you," her rescuer had told her and then given the signal.

Her stretcher had lifted, sending her airborne. Though she'd known the straps holding her in were secured, she'd gripped the sides so tightly her hands had ached. She'd wished fervently that she could black out, because knowing she was suspended by a rope several hundred feet in the air had terrified her.

At some point, she must have lost consciousness, because the next time she'd opened her eyes, she was in the back of an ambulance and on her way to the ER.

Once there, she'd been poked and prodded. X-rays had been taken, her injuries deemed not life-threatening, and she'd been given a small room. A kind nurse had placed her on an IV. "The fluids will make you feel better," she'd said. "A doctor will be in to see you shortly."

Genna waited, but no one came. She figured all the ER doctors were busy with genuine emergencies and would get to her when they could. Since she no longer had her phone and had no idea what had happened to it, she closed her eyes and tried to rest.

But with all the sounds and the machines and the way-too-bright lights, she couldn't.

When Parker walked into the room, she let out a glad cry. "You made it back," she said, unable to hide her relief.

"Yes." His smile warmed her to the core. He lifted up a cloth grocery bag. "I brought you some clothes since yours were likely cut off of you. And before you ask, Revis and JB are fine. I took them home and fed them."

She couldn't look away. "What about Ann?"

"They lowered a rope and helped her get up. Once she was out, she was arrested. I told them that you definitely wanted to press charges."

"I do." Swallowing, she reached for her water and took a sip. "And did they also arrest Chad? I'm reasonably sure she didn't travel all this way alone."

"Your ex?" Parker frowned. "I think Eli contacted him to let him know about his wife, but I'll find out."

"Thanks."

He came closer and sat down in a metal chair next to her bed. "What about you? Are they getting you all fixed up so we can get you out of here and back home?"

Home. For no good reason, she once again found herself blinking back tears. "They said I'll get a cast for my arm, a splint or boot for my leg, and they're referring me to an orthopedic specialist. I'm not sure when all that is supposed to happen, but hopefully soon. And they think I have a concussion. They gave me something for my headache and said to follow up with my regular doctor within seventy-two hours."

Taking her hand, he leaned over and kissed her cheek. "I'm glad you're all right. I have to tell you, there was a moment when I really thought we'd lost you."

Openly crying, she reached for the tissue box with her free hand and blotted at her eyes. "I never even saw her. One minute, I'm walking June Bug, and then Ann came out of nowhere and shoved me off the side of the mountain."

"Your little dog's barking is what alerted me," Parker said. "After this, I'm guessing you'll never want to go hiking or camping again."

Almost against her will, she laughed, even though it made her head hurt. "Not for a long time, that's for sure." She thought about it for a second and then amended her statement. "If ever, that is."

The doctor and a nurse came in then.

Letting go of her hand, Parker got up from the chair and moved out of their way.

Before long, she had a cast on her arm and a clunky walking boot on her leg.

"It looks like just your ankle is broken," the doctor said cheerfully, pushing her glasses up on her nose. "Hopefully, the boot will take care of it and you won't need to have surgery. I'll have my nurse discharge you. Once that's done, someone will bring a wheelchair around to get you out to your car. Then you can go home and get some rest."

Genna thanked her.

Once the doctor left, the nurse went over the discharge instructions. Basically, Genna needed to keep the cast dry. They'd send a referral and an orthopedic specialist's office would be contacting her.

"Here are your discharge papers," the nurse said. "I just need your signature in a few places, and then you'll be free to go."

Accepting the clipboard with her good arm, Genna signed where directed and then passed it back to the nurse.

"These are your copies," the smiling woman said. "You have a nice rest of your day."

After the nurse left, Genna looked up to find Parker watching her. He had a peculiar expression on is handsome face.

Alarmed, she touched his hand. "What is it? What's wrong?"

Leaning in, he brushed her mouth with his. "I'm just awfully glad you weren't seriously hurt," he murmured, lips against hers.

Her heart skipped a beat. Though he clearly was trying to be careful, she kissed him back with all of the pent-up passion she had inside.

For an instant, he allowed the familiar fire to ignite. But then he quickly pulled back. Breathing heavily, he got to his feet and dragged his hand through his hair. "You need to rest and heal," he said, his voice raspy. "We shouldn't be doing that."

"I want to do all that and more," she murmured, watching his gaze darken. Then, just as she opened her mouth to tell Parker how much she loved him, her ex-husband walked into the room.

Chapter 16

When Genna paled, as if all the blood had drained from her face, Parker turned to call for the nurse. Instead, when he saw the tall, broad-shouldered man standing just inside the doorway, he realized that was the cause for Genna's distress.

Short dark hair in a military cut, hard brown eyes and an aggressive stance, the stranger glared at Parker before directing his gaze to Genna.

Acting on instinct, Parker moved to place himself between the intruder and Genna.

"Who are you and what do you want?" Parker demanded.

Jaw tight, the stranger took another step into the room. "I might ask you the same question. Please leave. I need to talk to my wife alone."

"Ex-wife, Chad," Genna corrected. "Parker, please stay. I don't want to be alone with him." She took a deep breath. "In fact, call security."

"No need," Chad quickly responded. "Ann called me and asked me to bail her out. She told me everything she's done, including trying to kill you. I just wanted to let you know that I had nothing to do with her actions. Ever since

I left her for Claudia, Ann has been unhinged. Claudia even had to take out a restraining order on her."

"So did I," Genna reminded him, her voice and expression tired. "You've said your piece. Now please leave."

Jaw working, Chad simply stared, unmoving. "You look terrible," he mused. "Small-town life obviously hasn't been good for you."

"She asked you to go," Parker said, keeping his tone level. "It's time for you to do that."

For one split second, he thought the other man would refuse. But then Chad shook his head, muttered something unintelligible under his breath and stalked off.

"Whew," Genna exhaled. "I'm just glad he didn't start any trouble."

"Me, too." Dropping back into the chair next to her bed, Parker glanced at the doorway. "Do you believe him when he says he had nothing to do with Ann harassing you?"

"I'm not sure. I know right after they got together, he was pretty invested in tormenting me. But it's been a year. I had no idea it was her." Genna shifted restlessly. "She traveled all the way to Shelby just to continue hounding me."

"I'm surprised she didn't move on to the new woman," Parker said.

"Me, too. That would make a lot more sense than her continuing to stalk me. I've moved on. I would have thought Ann would, too." She sighed again. "Well, now that I've been discharged, I'd like to get dressed and get out of here."

Parker handed her the bag of her clothes that he'd grabbed at the house. After pulling the curtain around the bed, he stood guard while she dressed.

"All done," she said.

He pulled open the curtain. "Still no wheelchair. Let me go see if I can find one for you."

"I don't really need it," she protested. "A pair of crutches would help just fine."

Just then an orderly arrived, pushing a shiny-black wheelchair. "Are you ready to go home?" he asked, his cheerful voice matching his smile. He helped Genna into the chair before turning to Parker. "Go ahead and pull your vehicle around to the side entrance and I'll bring her out."

Finally, with Genna buckled carefully into the passenger side, Parker headed home. Since he didn't have a wheelchair, he stopped at a drugstore on the way and purchased an inexpensive portable one. After he'd loaded it into the rear of his truck and got back in, Genna shook her head.

"I plan on using crutches," she said. "I have some in the garage at my parents' house. I think you can return thc chair. I don't need it."

"Crutches will be impossible to handle with a broken arm," he pointed out. "You can't hold on."

She stared at him for a few seconds. "I didn't even think about that. I guess I don't have a choice but to use the chair."

Since he was driving, he couldn't give in to impulse and kiss her. He promised himself he'd make up for that once they got home.

After pulling up in front of the house, he asked Genna to wait in the truck while he got her chair. Though she nodded, her grimace told him she was unhappy with the situation. Opening her door, he bowed low.

"Your throne awaits, my lady," he said in his best British accent.

Though she shook her head, her frown turned into a smile. When he gently lifted her out of the truck and into the wheelchair, she clung to him a millisecond too long. Which he didn't mind at all.

Then he pushed her through the garage and into the house.

Once inside, both Revis and JB greeted her, tails wagging. She spent time with them both, crooning endearments. JB appeared beside herself and, after Genna invited her, the tiny dog jumped into her lap and snuggled into Genna. "She thought I was going to die," Genna said, her eyes shiny. "She didn't leave my side."

"She's a good girl," Parker replied. "Her barking is what alerted me to the possibility that there was some kind of trouble."

She nodded. "I'm just glad all that's over and Ann is in police custody."

"Me, too." He pushed her over toward the couch. "Do you want to lie here or should I take you into your bedroom?"

"Neither." She hesitated. "I have another favor to ask. I really need to take a shower. I don't feel clean. Will you help me?"

Due to her condition, he tried like hell not to imagine her naked, water sluicing down her body. But the sensual images wouldn't stop and his body immediately reacted.

"I'll help you," he offered. "I know you have to keep that cast dry."

"And my foot, too," she said. "They wrapped my ankle inside this boot. I'll need you to help me wrap both of those in plastic."

"Are you hurting at all?" he asked.

"No." She didn't even have to think about it. "I'm

guessing whatever pain medication they gave me at the hospital is still working, because I feel fine."

Luckily, the main shower had a place where she could sit. He pushed her wheelchair inside and carefully helped her to undress.

Then he wrapped her arm, using several plastic bags and a rubber band, hoping like hell he didn't inadvertently hurt her. Moving on to the foot, he knelt in front of her wheelchair and carefully undid the Velcro straps.

After he wrapped her foot so the bandage wouldn't get wet, he helped her from the chair to the shower ledge. He then turned on the water, waiting until the temperature seemed perfect before turning the showerhead on her. He placed a couple of towels nearby, within easy reach, and then beat a fast exit.

"Call me if you need anything or when you're done," he said, closing the door behind him.

Though he suspected there was no way she could have missed his arousal, he hoped she understood that he'd never do anything that could hurt her. She'd been through a lot. And he'd do whatever it took to make sure she healed. Including resisting his ever-present desire for her.

Waiting for her to finish her shower, he finally admitted how terrified he'd been at the prospect of losing her. Seeing her lying on that ledge on the side of the mountain, unable to discern the extent of her injuries, the thought of losing her had nearly brought him to his knees.

Even now, with her hurt and needing to heal, he couldn't bear the concept of inadvertently doing something wrong.

He heard the water turn off. Though he tried not to, he pictured her toweling herself off. He kind of wished she'd asked him to help her, even though he knew doing so would only make him rock-hard again.

"Parker?"

Blinking, he shook off his thoughts and went to help her get dressed. She'd asked for a soft T-shirt and a pair of terry-cloth shorts, telling him they were her version of pajamas.

A short time later, Eli arrived at the house, bearing gifts. "A pizza from Pizza World," he said, handing the box to Parker. "And a decent bottle of red wine to go with it."

"Thanks." Ushering his brother in, Parker led the way to the living room, where Genna, JB and Revis were all snuggled on the couch. Though both dogs looked up at the intruder, they must have decided Eli was safe because they laid their heads back down on Genna.

"I brought you food," Eli announced, gesturing toward the pizza box in Parker's arms. "Hopefully, it'll make up for whatever crap they fed you in the hospital."

"Thank you." Genna smiled. "Any news? Did Ann bond out?"

"Not yet. She kept saying her husband would be coming to rescue her, but the dude never showed. Now she's demanding to talk to you."

"Me?" Recoiling, Genna looked at Parker. He shrugged.

"I'm sorry," Eli said. "I have no idea what she wants to say, but apparently there's something she needs to get off of her chest."

"I don't think I care to hear it."

"I don't blame you." Eli looked at Parker. "She tried to kill you after all."

"She probably wants to try and talk you into dropping charges," Parker interjected.

"That's not going to happen." Eyeing the pizza box, which Parker still held, she gestured. "I'd really like to have some of that. Would you mind grabbing some paper plates so we can eat?"

Both dogs perked up at her words.

"Not for you," she scolded, half laughing.

"I brought wine, too," Eli pointed out.

"Thanks, but I'm not sure I can drink with all these pain meds."

Eli shook his head. "Sorry, I didn't think. Well, just save the bottle for later."

Parker went into the kitchen and returned with plates and napkins. Eli set the pizza box down in the middle of the coffee table and opened it. "I just got basic pepperoni," he said. "And a large, in case you both are hungry. I hope that's okay."

Parker's stomach rumbled, reminding him he hadn't eaten in a long while. "That's perfect," he said.

"That smells so good!" Sitting up, Genna shooed the dogs away. Making an appreciative sound, she grabbed a couple of slices, looking up at both men. "Don't be shy. Help yourself," she said, licking her fingers. "Thanks for getting this, Eli."

Parker grabbed a few slices and Eli did the same. They all ate, sitting around the living room, with the two dogs watching intently. Both men took seconds, though Genna declined.

"That was wonderful," Genna said, covering her mouth as she yawned. "And now I'm going to close my eyes for a bit. Please don't mind me. I just really need to rest."

"I'd better be going." Eli stood. He grabbed the empty pizza box while Parker gathered up their plates. Together, they carried everything into the kitchen.

"I'll walk you out." Moving quietly so not to disturb Genna, Parker led the way to the front door.

Outside, Eli stopped on the front porch. "How's she doing mentally?" he asked, his gaze searching Parker's face. "This is a lot for anyone to deal with."

"She still seems to be processing it all," Parker replied. "I've been awfully worried about her." He shook his head. "To think it was Ann all along. Genna really thought moving five hours away had put an end to the harassment."

"Normally, it would, at least under normal circumstances. However, that woman has been talking up a storm." Eli grimaced. "We're going to have to ask for a psych evaluation."

"I imagine. Her ex, Chad, stopped by at the hospital."

Eli went very still. "How did he know he'd find her there?"

"Good question. I have no idea." Parker thought for a moment. "Are you thinking he was with Ann when all this went down?"

"Now I am. Because otherwise, wouldn't he be back in Anchorage?"

"True. But when he visited Genna, he told her that he'd left Ann for another woman." Parker shook his head. "Which seems about right, considering what Genna has said about him."

"Did he now?" Eli asked. "Because Ann is somehow convinced that Chad and Genna got back together. She claims he told her so. When he left her, she decided to make Genna's life a living hell. In the end, she decided to kill Genna. In Ann's mind, that would make Chad go back to her."

"Wow." Unsure how to react to this, Parker finally

shook his head. "Are you going to bring him in for questioning?"

"If we can find him, yes. I've had people looking for him since Ann was arrested."

"He told Genna his new girlfriend's name is Claudia," Parker said. "He claims this Claudia had to take out a restraining order on Ann. Maybe that will help you find him."

"If it's the truth and not some BS he made up, it definitely will help. I'll have Kansas look into it. Since she was very upset when she heard about Genna being attacked, she asked to be assigned to this case in addition to her Search and Rescue work"

"Once again, you two have proved it's good to have family in law enforcement," Parker said, his voice breaking. "I appreciate all your help with all of this."

Eli eyed him, expression concerned. "Are you okay?"

"I am," Parker replied. "It's just been a long day. Genna and I went camping to get away from all the stress, and drama still found us. I don't know that she'll ever want to hike or camp again. Which really would be a shame, considering how much I love both of those things."

"And her?" Eli asked quietly. "Do you love her?"

Parker almost didn't answer. How could he confess his feelings to his brother before he'd even discussed them with Genna? But he knew Eli cared, and since Parker planned to talk to Genna as soon as possible, he didn't see any harm.

"I do love her," he admitted. "I have since the moment we first reconnected a year ago."

Eli's eyes widened. "That long?"

"That long."

"Does Genna know?" Eli asked.

"Not yet." Parker took a deep breath, about to admit his greatest fear. "I'm not sure she's ready for any kind of committed relationship, to be honest. I really don't want to screw things up."

"I get that." Eli nodded. "But I think she's more into you than you realize. Haven't you noticed the way she looks at you?"

With that, his brother walked away, climbed into his vehicle and drove off.

Parker stared after him, a hope so strong it hurt blooming inside his chest.

After eating the pizza and deciding to take a short nap, Genna slept so deeply that when she woke up in bed, she had no recollection of how she'd gotten there. She still wore the same T-shirt and shorts that doubled as pajamas. Her new boot had even been removed, though placed within easy reach.

Since her wheelchair had been pushed next to her, turned just the right way to make getting into it easier, she realized Parker had either carried her to her bed or put her in the wheelchair to get her there. What she didn't understand was how he'd done all this without waking her up.

Her ankle throbbed, letting her know she'd need to take something to help with that.

"Are you ready for some coffee?" Parker appeared in her doorway, steaming mug in hand. He set it down on her nightstand and smiled at her. "I hope you feel well rested. You must have really needed your sleep."

"I do." Sitting up, she stretched, wincing slightly. "Let me get this boot back on and then, if you don't mind, I could use some help getting back into my chair."

After she swung her legs over the side of the bed,

Parker knelt and helped her guide her foot into the clunky boot. She tried to close it up herself, but like just about everything else, it proved impossible to do with only one hand.

Once Parker had helped her with that, he carefully assisted her shift from the bed into the wheelchair. Handing her the coffee he'd brought, he pushed her into the living room. On the way there, she told him she wanted to use the bathroom, and also wash up and brush her teeth. Despite knowing she'd probably need it, she declined his help and insisted she could do it all herself.

And she did, though none of it was easy. Finally back in her chair, she called for him to open the door.

"You're doing great," he said, pushing her into the living room. "When do you see the specialist?"

"I think they're supposed to call me today."

"As soon as you have an appointment, let me know. I'll get you there. And if I happen to be working, someone else in the family will drive you."

She smiled. "Thanks. I hate to be a bother, but I really appreciate all the help."

Parker got her all set up on the couch with her coffee. He brought her breakfast, sat with her while she ate, and then took the plate away. He made sure she had snacks, some bottled water, the remote, a book, and anything else she could possibly need, before telling her he had to head to work.

"I'd rather go in with you," Genna protested. "I can do my job sitting down."

"Not until you see the specialist and you're cleared," he said, lightly kissing her cheek. There'd been a lot of that cheek kissing lately and she wasn't sure why. She considered turning her head so his mouth connected with hers, but didn't. If he didn't want to give her a real kiss, she wasn't going to force him.

"Hetty is going to fill in for a couple of days," Parker continued. "I've got a couple of tours today, but if you need anything, just call the office. If I'm not in, someone else will make sure to get you taken care of."

With that, he smiled, waved and disappeared out the door. As she listened to the sound of his truck starting and driving away, she tried not to feel depressed. It wasn't easy.

For most of her life, Genna had never been one to sit around and do nothing. But having her ankle in the boot with orders to keep all weight off of it, and her arm in a cast, had severely limited her mobility. She knew she should count her blessings and be glad she had Parker and wasn't dealing with this on her own, but she couldn't seem to get there yet. Maybe she just needed to indulge herself and have a little pity party before she could get back to feeling semi normal.

It didn't help that she kept obsessing about revealing her feelings for Parker to him. She wasn't sure of the timing, or even if she should. Sometimes she thought maybe it was the kind of secret she should keep inside and take with her to her grave.

To occupy and distract herself, she tried watching TV, but found every show she tried annoying. Sitcom, drama, news or documentary—it didn't matter. Finally, she turned it off and decided to try her book.

A few weeks ago, she'd purchased a popular new thriller with every intention of reading it. As of yet, she hadn't even cracked open the cover. Parker had seen it on her nightstand and placed it near her on the coffee table just in case.

She read a few chapters, got sleepy and took another short nap. Her new capacity for sleep amazed her, but she also knew a lot of rest would help her body to heal.

Lakin stopped by shortly before noon. She's knocked a couple times before letting herself in with a key. "Parker gave me his key and asked me to check on you," she said, smiling. "He said you might have difficulty navigating the wheelchair around the kitchen, so I brought you something to eat."

She held up a white paper bag. "Burger and fries," she said. "Not the healthiest thing, I know. I actually almost got you a salad, but then I thought about how much it would suck to have a broken ankle and arm, so I went with this instead."

Accepting the bag gratefully, Genna laughed. "Thank you. I really appreciate this." She peered inside, saw only one wrapped burger and container of fries, and frowned. "Are you not eating?"

"Not that!" Lakin rolled her eyes. "I just had a protein smoothie, so I'm not hungry. But I can keep you company while you eat, if that's okay?"

"I'd like that." She thought for a moment. "Would you also mind letting June Bug out? Parker took Revis to RTA with him, so I just have her."

"I can definitely do that," Lakin said. "I imagine it's a bit difficult navigating things in that wheelchair with only one usable arm." She called the little dog. JB appeared uncertain, but when Genna assured her it was all right, she trotted out after Lakin.

Once she was alone, Genna sagged in her chair, a wave of exhaustion washing over her. Her stomach growled, reminding her she needed to eat to keep her strength up. And the burger smelled mouthwatering. She unwrapped it and took a tiny bite, and then another. She didn't want to eat the entire thing while Lakin was out back.

A moment later, both Lakin and June Bug returned. "She was a good girl," Lakin said, smiling. "What a special little dog you've got there."

This compliment made Genna grin. "Thanks. I love her."

"She loves you, too, I can tell." She gestured at the unwrapped burger. "Does it taste all right? It doesn't look like you've eaten much of it."

"It's delicious," Genna replied. "I've been trying to wait until you came back."

"No need. Go for it."

Lakin chatted about her hotel renovations while Genna practically inhaled her burger. "This is so good," she said, trying not to talk with her mouth full. "Thank you for bringing it. First, Eli got us pizza, and now you…"

"I talked to Eli this morning," Lakin said. "It seems they brought your ex-husband in for questioning. Kansas is handling the case."

Genna went still. "Chad? They think Chad had something to do with this." Then, without waiting for a response, she shook her head. "I knew it. When he showed up at my hospital room, I wondered how he'd gotten there so quickly. And how he'd known that I'd been injured. He must have been there with Ann in the woods, waiting for me."

Patting Genna's hand, Lakin grimaced. "I'm sorry all that happened to you. What an awful lot to have to go through."

"Thanks. I don't know how I would have made it without Parker's help. He's been amazing."

Lakin's gaze sharpened. "He might be my brother, but

I agree. He's pretty special." She gave Genna a thoughtful look. "I take it you two are getting along pretty well?"

"We are." Genna could have elaborated but didn't want to open the door to questions about the two of them and their relationship. Not yet. Especially since Parker had no idea how she felt about him.

Luckily, Lakin didn't press. "I should be going," she said. "But I wanted to make sure you were doing okay. Please, and I mean this, call me if you need anything. Anything at all."

"Thanks." Genna smiled. One thing about the Coltons, once they decided they liked you, they had your back. No matter what.

After Lakin left, Genna stretched out on the couch to nap again. She couldn't seem to get enough sleep. Why not embrace it?

Some time later, her phone rang. Sitting up, she rubbed her eyes and squinted at the screen. Caller ID showed it was Kansas.

"I have news," Kansas declared. "And I wanted you to be the first to know. We've arrested Chad, too. He's being charged as an accessory to murder. Ann admitted he was there with her. She seemed rather proud of that, claiming it proved he loved her the most since he wanted you dead."

Genna shuddered. "But why? That's what I don't understand. I moved away. Got out of their lives. What did I ever do to make them hate me so much?"

"We're trying to get to the bottom of that now and establish motive. Ann claims that Chad never stopped talking about you and comparing Ann to you. Apparently, that was one of the numerous things that sent her over the edge, though between you and me, she was already there."

"I'll say," Genna replied. "Chad was a serial philanderer. He left me for Ann, someone I thought was my best friend. And then he claimed he left her for another woman."

"Claudia. That's the name he keeps saying, but he can't provide any specifics. I'm beginning to wonder if he made her up." Kansas paused. "We'll get this all sorted out. But I thought you'd want to know that they're both in custody."

"For how long?"

"Well, once the judge sets bail, they'll have to stay here until they can make it. Attempted murder usually carries a pretty high dollar amount. And then they need to find someone to pay their bond. Do they have family around here?"

"Ann's family is pretty wealthy," Genna said. "They've been really good about getting her out of trouble in the past. Who knows though? They might have finally reached their limit."

"You never know." After asking Genna if she needed anything, Kansas said she had to go.

Parker swept in around five, bringing takeout. Apparently, the Coltons believed a good meal went a long way to fixing what ailed a person.

"Chinese," he said, holding up a large paper bag. "I got us a little of everything."

Revis pranced over to JB and sniffed her before coming to greet Genna. Parker took the food into the kitchen. When he returned, he leaned against the wall. "How was your day?" he asked. "Kansas told me both Ann and Chad have been charged."

"Yes and they're in custody. So at least I don't have to worry about them for a while."

"I know." His smile widened. "Kansas thinks their bond will be set really high. At least there's that."

Watching him, for the first time she realized how powerful he appeared. Despite his broad shoulders and muscular arms, he never made a show of his physical strength. This, combined with his chiseled features and bright blue eyes, made him one of the most appealing men she'd ever met.

But she found the tender gentleness with which he treated her sexier.

Before she let desire take hold of her again, she wanted to get everything straight. "We need to talk," she declared. Parker stared at her, the expression on his handsome face going from relaxed to wary.

"I'm not sure I like the sound of that," he said. Then, before she could say another word, he continued. "Listen, I understand how you might feel it's safe for you to go back home now that your stalkers are locked up. I get it and I agree. Except I really think you ought to consider staying here just a little bit longer."

Stung, she swallowed. "Why?"

"Because you need to heal." He came closer. "Let me help you with that. I'd like to take care of you."

She pretended to consider. "But you have to work. What's the difference if I'm alone over here or alone at my parents' house?"

"You don't want to stay?"

Since she couldn't tell if he minded or not, she countered with her own question. "Do you really want me to?"

"Of course," he answered without the slightest hesitation.

"But only because you think I need to be here until I get better?"

"Do you want the truth?" he asked, dropping down on the couch next to her wheelchair.

Though she suspected it might hurt, she turned her chair around to face him and answered in the affirmative.

"I know you've been through a lot," he said. "And I'm aware you're not looking for anything serious. But I kind of like having you around."

She suppressed a smile. "Kind of? I'm touched."

Clearly frustrated, he dragged his hand through his hair. "Damn it, Genna. I don't want to scare you away."

Not sure how to respond to that, she simply waited.

"Do you think you might want to extend this living together thing?" he asked, his casual voice at odds with the intensity in his gaze. "No pressure. Just hanging out with each other and seeing where this might go?"

Looking up at him from her wheelchair, she wasn't sure whether she wanted to laugh or to cry. While she'd been fully prepared to tell him how she felt about him, now she'd begun to realize she might have been premature. Her heart ached and she could barely swallow past the lump in her throat, but she had to know the truth. If he only wanted to continue the "friends with benefits" situation they had going, this would crush her. Because she wanted more.

And if he didn't, it was definitely time to move on.

"Why?" she asked. "I need you to be honest with me."

Instead of answering, he leaned over and kissed her. Not on the cheek this time, but full on the lips. As always, his kiss made her melt.

When he finally stopped, she could easily have dissolved into a puddle.

"Is that enough of a reason?" he asked, smiling slightly.

"No. We have great chemistry together, as you're fully aware." She smiled back, hating that she already felt as if her heart were breaking. Bracing herself, she continued. "But what if I want more?"

"Do you?" His expression sharpened, a warm glow making his eyes appear even more blue. "Want more? Because I do, too. I've been afraid to ask you, thinking I might scare you away."

She lifted her chin. "I'm not afraid. Not of you. Never of you."

Taking a deep breath, she decided the time had come to tell him the truth. "I think I'm falling in love with you, Parker Colton. Actually, I know I am. I love you."

Keeping her gaze locked on his, she wished she could have taken a step forward. "There, I've said it. I love you."

Heart pounding, she waited for him to respond.

He could have done several things. Walked away. Kissed her again. Or returned her declaration of love.

Instead, he only bowed his head and took several deep, shuddering breaths.

She sat frozen, unsure of what to say or what to do next. The urge to flee was strong, but since she couldn't, she stiffened her spine and tried to brace herself for whatever Parker would say. No matter how much it might hurt, she refused to regret giving him her truth.

Finally, he raised his head. Were those *tears* she saw shining in his amazing blue eyes? But then he smiled, his face so full of joy that her heart began to sing.

"I've loved you from the first moment I saw you," he said. "That night a year or so ago when we met in that bar. I kicked myself for losing your number. And then you moved back."

Moving closer, he knelt down beside her chair and cupped her face with his hands. "And in the time since, working with you, living with you, I've gotten to know you. My feelings have only deepened."

He kissed her, a slow and sensual movement of his lips over hers. Blissful, she let herself lean into the sensations—warmth, desire and love.

When they finally broke apart, he rested his forehead against hers. "I've been wanting to tell you how I felt for a long time. But I wasn't sure you were ready to hear me, especially considering everything you were going through."

"I might not have been," she admitted. "It took me a while to see that you're the best thing that's ever happened to me."

"The best thing?" he asked, one brow arched. "What about June Bug?"

As if on cue, the little dog barked in agreement.

They both laughed.

"We're quite the little family now," Genna mused.

"Yes we are," he agreed.

And then he kissed her again.

* * * * *